BASTARD BACHELOR SOCIETY

SARA NEY

1

BROOKS

"Eeny, meeny, miney, mo…" I knock one of the tiny model cardboard houses off the development community layout I've been working on. Flick it with my forefinger until it flies off the board and onto the floor, landing in a corner with the rest of them.

"Catch a tiger." Flick goes another one. "By." Flick. "The." Flick. "Toe."

Flick, flick.

Five more fly off the flat board. It's large, square, an exact replica of a subdivision the architectural firm I work for is developing. Or…proposing. Or…was going to?

I'm not on the project anymore, thank God. I've been promoted—fucking *promoted!*—and moved to the project I've been salivating over since I started here. Literal drool comes out the side of my mouth when I talk about it.

I've only been at this company for one year; I rose up the ladder quicker than I'd planned, not because of nepotism or favoritism or sleeping my way to the top, but because I'm a great fucking architect.

I'm not just good at my job.

I'm great at it.

I love it.

Dream about it.

Architecture isn't only what I do for a living. It's my *passion*.

I'm not sad to see this development project leave my hands and my office. Now, if the intern, Taylor, would get his ass in here to remove this goddamn model, that would be swell. It's cluttering up all the space—I may have been promoted, but my office is still small as fuck.

Leaning forward, I hit the button on my phone's intercom and buzz the front desk. "Hey Taylor, can you come to my office to grab this community model?"

He clicks his tongue. "Will do."

"Thanks."

I swivel in my desk chair, plucking a sheet of loose paper from the printer. Fold a piece in half once, twice. Fold down each corner into a triangle, smoothing it down with my nail.

The paper airplane I've folded is a crisp, dynamic flying machine. I press it between my thumb and forefinger. Squeeze my left eye shut like I'm a four-year-old, aiming for a spot on the window in my corner office. The spot where I have the small, orange and white basketball hoop suction-cupped. My mom gave it to me as a gift, hoping it would distract me from work during the day, saying I'm too keyed up, but I don't know what good she thought a toy fucking basketball hoop was going to do for my stress level.

Whatever.

She shouldn't be spending money she doesn't have on junk.

Still. I plastered it on my office window anyway—as she intended—when I should have thrown the dumb thing in the garbage.

Waste not, want not...

I squint again, aiming the airplane toward the target, pull it back before launching, and let it fly in a smooth arc.

Instead of hitting the backboard of the hoop, it ricochets off the glass, bounces, and falls to the ground amongst the tiny white houses.

I leave it, a heap in the graveyard of my shitty ideas.

Fuck.

I need inspiration for this new project I've been assigned to before my promotion turns into a demotion. Need to prove to my bosses that they didn't make a mistake when they trusted me with this assignment. It's a lot of pressure.

I need a fucking drink.

I need to take a piss.

Standing, I grab my cell before exiting my office to hit the restroom at the end of the hall, pushing through the door and unsnapping my jeans. There's one urinal and one toilet, and the latter is occupied—dammit. The toilet has a stall and is the perfect place to text, unlike my office, which is a veritable fishbowl of repression with its massive glass walls.

After I pee, re-zip my pants, and wash my hands, I pull out my cell, slanting against the cool tile wall for support. Tap out a message to my idiot best friends as I walk back to my office: *What time can you meet at The Basement?*

Phillip: *Yeah*

Yeah? What kind of answer is that? I'm looking for a time the bastard can meet for drinks tonight, not whether he can commit or not.

Me: *What time, dude?*

Blaine isn't responding, but if Phillip and I are going for drinks, he's going to have the fear of missing out. No way will he not show.

Phillip: *Six.*

Fine, six o'clock it is. I'll be fucking starving by then, but The Basement is the closest pub to my apartment, located in the middle of my neighborhood. It's convenient, old, filled with tons of character, and in the basement of an ancient building that used to be a national bank, which is pretty fucking cool.

The Basement has appetizers and I can eat more when I get home if I'm still desperate, but actual food would be great. Either I eat or I get drunk on two.

I might have been a member of a fraternity in college, but I'm still a lightweight. Cannot handle my liquor. Have always been that way, always will be.

I return to my office, and just as I'm about to construct another paper airplane, a jaunty little knock sounds at the door; Taylor is rapping his knuckles on the glass wall, eyes trailing to the pile of houses and planes littering my carpet.

"Stressed?" He pushes a pair of black frames up the bridge of his nose.

"Very." Why lie to the kid? If he wants to be an architect once he graduates, he oughta know it's not always ribbon cutting ceremonies, fundraisers, networking, and champagne lunches.

It takes actual work.

It takes engineering, long hours, lack of a social life, and countless sleepless nights to meet deadlines.

Taylor? He still has years of hopes and happy hours and bullshit dreams ahead of him.

"I don't mean to sound bitter, I'm just having a day."

The smile he gives me is sympathetic. "We all have them."

I look over at him. "When do you have shitty days?" The guy radiates unicorns and rainbows and happiness.

He considers my question. "I have shitty days when, like, Starbucks gets my order wrong."

"Get the fuck out of here. That's not an actual problem." I laugh, bending to help him retrieve all the pieces of paper discarded on the ground.

"Where should I take this model?"

I blow a strand of dark, hair out of my eyes, mentally noting the need for a haircut, or a trim at the very least. "Conference room B, maybe? I don't think anyone is using it. Then Daniels can decide what he wants to do with this." I hand Taylor a stack of teeny houses with three-car garages. "This development is his brainchild, but I don't think he has space in his office for one more model mockup."

"Got it, boss."

I snort. "I'm not your boss." *Not even close.*

"But you could be, someday," Taylor points out, bending down to grab a paper airplane and extending as if he's going to send it sailing across the room.

I pause. He's right; I could become his boss someday if I keep working my ass off. They make associates partners around here. Technically, if I stay and work hard, there's a chance I could become one, too.

"How old are you?" Taylor asks hesitantly, scooping up a paper house.

I glance at the model of the community resting on a drafting table in the corner of my office. There must have been two hundred little houses on that giant platform, half of which are now scattered on my floor.

"Twenty-six."

"See? And you're already on a major project. It only took you a year."

Shit, is he keeping track of my career? That's...weird.

I eye Taylor suspiciously. "Are you stalking me?"

He laughs, blushing. "No!" Adjusts the bowtie around his neck. "But I'm following your career because I'm trying to learn how to become successful."

Holy shit. Wow.

I clear my throat, choking up a bit. "I'm just a guy from a crappy neighborhood, Taylor. I paid my way through college, busted my ass, took a lot of drugs to stay awake late so I could study—sometimes it's worth it, sometimes it's not."

I doubt I should be giving this kid advice. He probably came from the suburbs—not unlike the communities this architecture firm designs and develops, with two married parents, a picket fence, and a dog.

"I know what you're thinking," he finally says. "But you're wrong."

My brows go up. "Oh yeah? What am I thinking?"

"That I had it easy and was popular, got good grades *and* all the ladies."

Um—that's not what I was thinking. Close enough, though.

"Fine—my parents paid for everything and my dad got me this job, but that doesn't mean I don't want to be an architect, or that I can't be a good one. I just want someone to mentor me, someone I can relate to."

"Aren't you gay?"

"I mean at work. I don't want to follow you around *after*ward. I have a feeling your personal life is a shitshow—no offense."

"None taken." Because it is.

He nods, the thick, navy, tweed vest he has buttoned over a white dress shirt far too dressy for a Thursday, but who am I to judge? I'm wearing denim jeans for fuck's sake.

Wrinkly ones.

"So will you? Mentor me?"

"I don't know what the hell that even means."

"I'll write you a proposal."

Jesus Christ. "Proposal as in job description?"

"Exactly."

"Fine."

His excitement is evident, especially when he stands. I swear to God, the dweeb has pep in his step even as he dumps all the little houses onto the board and scoops it up from the bottom, teetering.

"Don't get your hopes up—you probably won't learn anything from me."

"That's alright. We all start somewhere."

Such optimism.

I wish I felt it too.

2

BROOKS

We're seated in a semicircle, lounging in big, comfortable chairs, straight from work and ready to triumph and brag about what cool shit we did at our jobs today, discuss our weekends, and toss back a few.

Truthfully, though? They're not bragging; *I* am.

Seems I'm the only lucky bastard who's in the mood to boast about his job. Not only have I been granted a promotion, a bit of recognition, I somehow seem to have landed one of the interns as a quasi-assistant.

Fine. Technically, Taylor isn't *my* assistant, but I'm able to use him as a resource, and therefore, my friends are jealous.

Goddamn, I really am one spoiled son of a bitch.

We order a round of shots.

Then another.

Then another.

"You know what I can't stand? Listening to you gloat about your great new job for an entire hour straight. It's annoying," says Phillip, one of my best friends, as he splits a roasted pecan in half.

Blaine, my other sidekick, nods. "Yeah, quit the bragging

and tell us something about you that isn't amazing for once in your damn life. No one wants to sit and listen to how happy you are."

"Something nice and shitty to make us feel better about ourselves."

"You know what I can't stand?" I begin rather abruptly, already a bit drunk.

Blaine rubs his hands together with glee. "What?"

"*Couples.*"

Blaine chuckles, motioning for the server. "Couples of what?"

"Couples—people." I wave my hand around in the air, pantomiming my irritation. "On the street, in restaurants. Getting freaking coffee in the morning. Hogging all the space and stealing my air."

When both my friends laugh as if I'm hilarious, I go on.

"I'm seriously sick of watching them. Jesus, I practically smashed into three of them—six people—on my way in here, all holding hands and shit."

"Three of *them*." Blaine uses air quotes to mock me. "They're not zombies who are part of the apocalypse."

They might as well be.

"They're in my way." I pout into my half-empty glass.

My friends stop to stare at me, confused by my harsh tone. I'm not normally like this—honest.

"This is shitty? Couples annoy you? Life sucks because there are too many people in love crashing into you on the sidewalk?" Phillip wants to know, pounding the rest of his cocktail, tipping his glass to get a few ice cubes out then chewing them loudly. "Sounds to me like someone is still butthurt they were dumped a few weeks ago."

Try six months.

And now that I'm single, I notice blissfully happy couples everywhere, and what do I have to show for it? Nothing but my amazing job.

Adding to my melancholy? The fact that now that I'm earning a decent wage, I've started semi-supporting my mother, sending her cash and checks when I can since she's broke and it's all I can do to help her out.

I go to work in the morning.

I go home to an empty apartment at night.

I see these two clowns a few times a month, and they're the closest thing I have to an actual relationship since my girlfriend dumped me. Fuck, maybe I miss being in a relationship more than I thought.

This must be the alcohol talking. Those three shots and that cocktail have gone straight to my head and are messing with my good nature.

I can see by the looks on Blaine and Phillip's faces that they're not impressed with my sudden change of attitude, but I don't give a shit. I'm feeling a certain kind of way and this is how I'm dealing with it.

"Sounds to me like someone is a wee bit jealous." Phillip tries at light banter, affecting an Irish accent—he knows I fucking love it when he sounds like the Lucky Charms cereal leprechaun, damn him.

"Jealous? Me? Of *what*?"

"Couples?" Phillip hesitantly ventures to point out, giving a sidelong glance at Blaine, the only one of us dating a woman at the moment.

"Should we be adding that to the list we made last week of things that drive you nuts? I took notes." Blaine whips out his cell, pulling up the notes app. "Let's see," he reads out loud. "Puppies. Dogs peeing on the sidewalk. Dogs in the city. Women wearing sneakers with skirts on their lunch breaks."

Phillip chimes in. "You forgot men who wear ties that are too short for their torsos."

Blaine grunts, typing on his phone. "Ah, good one. Totes forgot about that one." He studies the list we compiled after I began complaining about streetsweepers—I was in a foul mood then, too.

Seems to be a common theme, but then again, my personal life is crap, so that's not such a huge surprise.

Blaine clears his throat so he can continue reading from the list. "Meal prep posts on Instagram. Bloggers who smile with their mouths open in every photograph." He rolls his eyes after reading that one. "People who wake up before five to work out."

Phillip grins. "Is he missing anything?"

I grunt. "Whatever, you can't deny those things are fucking nauseating."

"Yeah, but not enough to bitch about them."

"All I'm saying is that shit cannot be sustainable." I'm in a mood, and nothing they say will break it.

"Sure it can. I wake up at four forty-five to jog." Blaine likes to constantly rub in our faces how fit he is. How well he eats at every meal. How disciplined he is about going to bed at a reasonable time. How great the chick he's been dating is.

The fucker *meal* preps.

"No one wants to hear about how amazing your life is, either," Phillip tells him.

Wow. Aren't we a barrel of laughs?

"You're such an ungrateful bastard." Blaine laughs, picking at the olive in his empty highball glass before leaning back in the big, overstuffed leather chair.

"Bastard. God I love that word." I smirk, doing more than just chugging rest of my cocktail. It's cold—full of ice—and sour, just how I like it. It slides down smooth…a bit too smoothly, because the alcohol keeps going straight to my head.

Damn. I should probably eat something besides condiments and cocktail snacks.

"Yeah, you do love throwing that word around for no apparent reason," Phillip declares, telling us all what we already know.

"You also love *being* a bastard," Blaine adds unnecessarily, reaching for a handful of the mixed nuts set on the decorative table in front of us. It's no bigger than a footstool, just large enough for all our drinks and the tiny bowl of free snacks The Basement provides.

And yeah—yes. *I love being a bastard.*

"Bastards are the new nice guys."

Phillip rolls his eyes harder than a twelve-year-old teenage girl arguing with her mother. "They are not."

Snapping my fingers, I point toward my friends. "That gives me a fantastic fucking idea."

"You swear way too much," Phillip points out, ignoring me, determined to snub the light-bulb moment I'm having.

Blaine has no such reservations about my foul mouth or my ideas, instantly curious for more details. He's always been a bit of a follower. "What's your great idea?"

"The Bastard...b, b b," I repeat the first letter of the word for encouragement. "What's another word that goes great with the word bastard, begins with the letter b?"

"Bagel."

I roll my eyes. "How the hell does bagel make any sense?"

"Considering I have no idea what the hell you're even talking about, I'd say it makes total sense."

"Bandits," Phillip tosses in, chewing on nuts.

Bastard Bandits? The fuck? "No."

"*Baggage*," says Blaine.

"Boomerang?" says Phillip. "B words are hard."

"No!" I exclaim, excited. "Think bigger. Like—what could we call a club?"

"What club?"

I sit forward, balancing my elbows on my knees, looking both of them dead in the eye. "Back in the day, they used to have secret societies and they would get together and smoke cigars and talk women and gamble."

Phillip scratches his balls through his polyester slacks. "I still don't get it."

"We should do that."

Phillip glances at me, then at Blaine, then back at me. "So you want to have a secret club?"

"No?" Actually, yes. Yes! It's a great fucking idea! Maybe it's what I need to get out of the funk I've been stuck in at home and at work. Maybe it's what I need to feel some creativity—the creativity that dimmed when Kayla left me. "Yes. A secret club sounds so badass."

"You want us to have a secret club and act like bastards?"

"I personally don't want to act like a bastard." Blaine pouts. "You've got the market cornered on that lately. I want to be one of the good guys."

My head shakes. "That's not what I meant. You don't have to act like a bastard. We could meet every week and smoke cigars and shit."

"Stogies—me likey." Phillip nods, warming to the idea like I knew my friends would. "And we can drink scotch on the rocks."

"Let's order another round right now!" Blaine enthuses, getting into the moment. He raises his hand for a second time, like a grade-schooler to get the server's attention, and when she comes over, he orders us a round.

B, b, b…

Bastard drinking club.

Nah, doesn't have the nice ring to it I'm going for.

Bastard brigade. Bastard…

"Bootleggers."

"Oh Jesus." Phillip sits back, crossing his legs.

"What does bootlegger even mean?"

The server sets the drinks in front of us, interrupting the flow of our conversation and doing her best to keep a straight face. "Bottoms up, gentlemen."

Blaine tips his head to the side, a sour expression crossing his features; he's downed the most alcohol of the three of us. This place might be in the basement of an old building, but it's bougie as fuck and serves the best of everything, the best liquor in the best atmosphere. We're seated beside a brick wall covered with plaques from members who were part of an era gone by, from when The Basement was in its heyday.

In its prime, back when you had to pay to take a seat at the table and share a drink.

Now, anyone can frequent The Basement to imbibe, but that wasn't always the case.

"Maybe we should get drinking jackets if we want to act like gentlemen," Phillip suggests. "Like Hugh Hefner used to wear before the old goat kicked the bucket."

Blaine pats his rosy cheeks. "Yeah, but navy blue instead of red. Red isn't a complimentary color for my complexion."

We stare. Did he just argue a case for a jacket to flatter his skin tone?

He shrugs at us, no shame. "What? It's not."

"Try not to push down so hard on your razor when you're shaving," Phillip tells him. "You're giving yourself razor burn, you douche." Reaches forward to give our friend's cheek a light smack with his palm. "And use an aloe-based moisturizer."

Blaine swats Phillip's grabby hands out of his personal space.

I ignore them both and power ahead with my idea.

"The club is still in need of a proper name, but we've already got a dress code?" I laugh, excitement building. "Where the hell do we get our hands on three velvet smoking jackets?"

Blaine is rubbing his ruddy face.

"Lisbeth." Phillip swirls his glass. "I'll have my sister look into it—she can find anything."

Phillip's sister Lisbeth is hot, smart, and a stage manager for a Broadway production company in New York City. If anyone can get us jackets to wear on a lark, it'll be her. And did I mention she *hates my guts?* Granted, she seems to hate everyone's guts, but particularly mine. Pretty certain it has something to do with the fact that when we were in our teens, I accidentally walked in on her while she was in the bathroom. Saw Lisbeth naked before she had tits and told the guys at school how flat-chested she was, before I learned about respecting boundaries, and privacy, and because I didn't know she would carry a goddamn grudge the rest of our entire lives.

She's treated me like shit ever since—not that I blame her in the least.

"Hot Lisbeth?" I love calling her that because it pisses him off so bad.

"Don't call my sister hot. She hates your fucking guts."

Even better—her anger makes her that much hotter. I love a good loathing, and a hard hate fuck does every body good.

"She can hate me all she wants because she's hot." I'd have hate sex with her any day. "Besides, it's not like I said I want to bone her."

His laugh is less than amused. "I'm not telling her this involves you. She'd burn your jacket and the building it was manufactured in to the ground before she'd give it over to you."

Sometimes it makes me jealous that he has a great relationship with his sister; I barely see mine. We've never had a great relationship, not since we were young and in grade school. Val was a mama's girl, I was a daddy's boy, and our piss-ass broke parents did nothing but fight. Home life sucked; Dad could never hold down a job, and I spent half my life defending that piece of shit to my sister when he didn't deserve it because I was too ignorant to know better.

My sister and I played outside a lot back in those younger years, but not together. Sometimes in the road, we'd kick the can around until the streetlights came on at dusk.

I had neighbor boys to hang with, a small gang of hoodlums with no curfew and fewer rules. We'd play Bloody Murder and

Ghosts in the Graveyard and ride our bikes around the block until the rubber wore off.

Val had *one* little girl across the street named Jessie, whose mother didn't want them playing together after "The Incident." It's not like Val was a sassy brat—I remember her being pretty chill for a kid.

Except for that one time.

One afternoon, Val gave Jessie's long hair a cut without permission. Granted, they were six years old and barely out of kindergarten at the time, so someone should have been watching them.

No one was. No one was ever watching us—our parents couldn't afford babysitters or childcare. Valerie and I survived on common sense and by the grace of God.

After the horrifying haircut, the two weren't allowed to play together; us guys didn't want my little sister tagging along after us, either. It wasn't the cool thing to do.

So Val had no one. And now? We don't speak and rarely see each other.

I frown down into my glass.

Shit. I should call my little sister.

Or text. See how she's doing and what she's been up to lately.

"B, b, b..." Phillip's fumbling interrupts my drunken, morose internal monologue. Somehow I missed the fact that my buddies are sitting here, repeating the same letter and B words over and over. "Basket, blanket, blaze."

"Blowhard, bedazzle, booze."

Christ, where are they coming up with these so fast? It's like they're playing a name game and trying to win a competition.

No. None of those pair well with the word bastard.

"Business, ballbusters, blasted."

"Break, breaking, *breakup*."

Breakup? Hmm, that gives me pause. "Bastard breakup. Bastard...batches."

We all keep talking at the same time.

"Bastard Bachelor's Club," Phillip suggests. It's a stroke of genius.

Shit, I actually like the sound of that. "Fucking love it."

Blaine's nose wrinkles. "Meh. Not loving the word club. That belongs on a treehouse, and we're not five."

Has he conveniently forgotten that he was in a fraternity in college, which is a glorified club? One you pay to be a member of?

Still, I humor him. "Fine, come up with a better word than club and that's what we'll call it."

He stares at me like I'm an idiot, raises his glass in the air as if he's a victorious gladiator. "Society. Boom shakalaka, nailed iiit."

And the Bastard Bachelor Society is born.

"What's the club for?" Phillip is palming a handful of nuts, shoving them in his mouth. "Like, why are we doing this when it's just the three of us?"

"We're socializing. Relishing the fact that we're single and ready to mingle. Doing manly things, like smoking cigars and drinking scotch."

"We're not all single." Phillip looks pointedly at Blaine. "And we do those things literally a few times a month."

No, we're not all single—but we should be.

Who needs a relationship? Who needs to be *coupled*?

Not Phillip.

Certainly not *me*.

We look at Blaine.

"Can we talk about Bambi for a quick second?"

Blaine pauses, glass of liquid halfway to his lips. "What about her?"

Bambi is the girl he's been seeing. It's not serious, but I think this one might eventually stick, though she's a complete Yoko Ono intent on breaking up the band.

"I mean…dude. Bro." I soften my tone as I break it to him gently. "You can't really see her anymore."

"You want me to break up with her?" His voice rises a few octaves.

"Bastard Bachelor Society—the word bachelor is in the *name*. It won't work if we're exclusively dating people."

"Then why can't we just change the name?"

"Because." I sigh, frustrated by his lack of enthusiasm. "It won't have the same ring to it. Your options are: to not be a member of the society, or to become single."

Phillip clinks his glass with the fork from the olive bowl. "Guys, we've been in business for a whole two seconds—why are you being pricks?"

"We're bastards, not pricks." I'm being stubbornly literal, fanning the flames of Blaine's pity party. I'm kind of drunk and in the mood to be an ass.

My friend's features contort, mouth a serious line of annoyance. "I like this girl. What the hell would I break up with her for?"

I pick an imaginary piece of lint off the front of my button-down dress shirt. "You won't win any bets if you're not single. That makes you ineligible." My knowledge sounds superior.

"What bets?" he inquires, unsure.

"Back in the day, they had betting books in these gentlemen's clubs—we can use the notepad in Blaine's' phone for keeping track of our bets—and noble blue-blooded dudes would keep track of who was doing what, with who, how much money they lost at the gaming tables. We could do the same thing."

"Can we not keep comparing ourselves to those guys? They lived two hundred years ago—they didn't have Hulu or *Game of Thrones*. They were bored and didn't have phones and only banged their wives to get them knocked up. *We* have phones. *We* are not bored—you are. *We* can bang whoever we want, whenever we want."

I think he's completely missing the point. "The point is, let's have a little fun. Let's put a few wagers down on paper like they did in the old days."

Blaine has been quiet for a few moments, finally breaking his silence to say, "I have fun with Bambi."

Bambi isn't fun—she's someone who monopolizes my best friend's time to the point where he rarely sees us anymore. She tells him when to jump and how high. Some might call her insufferable—I mean, honestly, the woman insists on being named after a fictional cartoon deer.

We'd be doing him a favor if we got him to break up with her.

I study the ice in my glass. "Really? You have fun with Bambi?" I squint in his general direction, clearly skeptical. "Do you though? You can still have sex with someone, but does it have to be the *same* person?" Does it have to be *her*?

"Uh—*yeah*. I like having sex with the same person, you asshole. I'd rather not get a sexually transmitted disease by sleeping around."

"You're missing the point."

"No, I think *you* are." Blaine's dark brown eyes get darker the more pissed off he gets. "You sound sexist and like a woman-hater."

"Me, sexist? I love women!"

"You haven't loved anyone since Kayla dumped you six months ago. You're bitter and nasty."

So what? Am I not entitled to be hurt?

Kayla was my first true love, the first woman I let myself fall in love with, the first woman I've felt anything for. I let myself be vulnerable, let myself get lost in her, let myself depend on her for my happiness.

Then she dumped me without warning.

Ghosted me, really. No texts, no voicemails. Blocked me from her pages and from her life, offering me no closure.

It was devastating.

I ignore Blaine completely. He's unbearably in like, and right this second, I don't want to hear about it. "Dude, write this down. Rule 1: *No member of the society shall date the same person exclusively while an active member of the society.*"

"What if we get invited to something, like a holiday work party?"

"That's fine, as long as you're not exclusively dating. That's what exclusive means, dipshit. Rule 2: *No seeing the same woman more than three nights a week. Mix it up.*"

Blaine nods. I can't tell if he's on board just yet or if he's just being agreeable, but at least he's entertaining the idea. "Right. Okay."

"Rule 3," Phillip adds. "*No giving gifts.*"

"That would be impossible since you have no money."

He clearly disagrees. "Just so we're clear, I have some money. I can pay my rent. Shut up."

Yeah, the rent on his shithole apartment, but who's judging? We've all been there, though I wasn't as old as he is while I was living in a dump. My first apartment was in an old building and I shared it with two other dudes; we were all in college and scraping by. None of us had jobs, let alone careers.

Benji and Miles were fucking fun roommates. I wonder what they're up to these days. Should definitely look them up when I get back to the office in the morning…

"Rule 4: *No marriage or babies.*" Phillip throws this down with a superior tone, crossing his arms and nodding.

Blaine scoffs, sipping his cocktail. "Who the hell is going to have a baby?"

"Uh, I don't know about you, but my boys are strong swimmers. There's a chance I'll get someone knocked up."

"You better start putting a lid on it then," Blaine tells Phillip. "No riding it raw."

Riding it raw. Who are these guys? Jesus.

Certainly no one wants any illegitimate babies running around.

"Rule 5: *We don't speak of the BBS.*"

"The what?"

I roll my eyes. "The Bastard Bachelor Society."

"Oh. Right, I forgot."

"Rule 6." Blaine still looks a bit like he's been whipped, but at least he's getting into creating the rules, contributing. "*Never let a girl wear your BBS smoking jacket*—that shit is sacred. Never, not even after sex, and not even if she's hot as fuck." He pauses. "Do you think we should have them monogrammed? I have an uncle who knows a guy who owns a place."

Monogramming the jackets is fucking brilliant. "Hell yeah!"

"Rule 7: *These rules are getting borderline ridiculous.*" Blaine crosses his arms, still griping like a little bitch.

"Do you want a rad navy velvet smoking jacket or not?" I threaten, because he hasn't lost his whiney tone since I brought up this idea.

I have a feeling he's going to be a pain in the ass about dumping his girlfriend, Bambi—though I hate even labeling her his girlfriend. Give me a break, they see each other and fuck—huge difference. I don't know what he's so irritated for. She's entirely replaceable; we just have to prove it to him.

"Yes." He scowls, lowering his head.

"Then put the kibosh on the pissing and moaning." I realize I sound like a bully, and I take a deep breath, wishing I had a cigar to puff on. "Rule 7: *If you want out of the BBS, it has to go to a vote. Same goes for adding new members.*"

Both my friends nod solemnly.

"Bros before hoes."

Blaine grunts. "Bambi isn't a ho." But even he doesn't sound convinced.

I personally prefer the statement *Bambi ain't no ho*, but potato, potahto.

"Sorry, but her name is Bambi. It even *sounds* promiscuous."

"Bambi is *history*," Phillip declares, chugging down the remainder of his drink, hand already in the air, signaling for another. He sets his glass down on the table with a resounding thud. "In fact, go ahead and text her now. Get it over with. Do it before we call our first official meeting to order."

"Now?" He visibly gulps.

"No time like the present."

Wow. Phillip has really taken a shining to this being single bastards concept; he's being a real douchebag right now. I mean, I agree that Blaine should break up with Bambi, but at least let the guy do it in private. It's bound to get ugly; she's kind of a control freak.

The last time he disagreed with her about something, she wouldn't have sex with him for two whole days! Then another time, she took his dog without telling him and didn't bring it home until the next afternoon.

"Wait—what happens if we break the rules?"

"Are you already planning to?"

"No." He doesn't sound convincing.

"How about this—if you break a rule, you don't win the wager."

Why am I using the word wager like it's 1824? Jesus Christ.

"What are we winning?"

Something that will make it worthwhile to stay single and not stick your wick in the same someone.

"How about my season tickets to the Jags?" The Chicago Jags are a professional baseball team who have won the Series dozens of times over, and my seats are fan-fucking-tastic: second row, between home plate and first base.

They're worth a *fortune*, and my friends damn well know it.

I inherited them from my grandfather when he died. Inheriting them is the only way to come by them these days; anyone on the waiting list waits years. Actually, the odds of winning the lottery are better than getting Jags season tickets, and they were the one and only thing of any monetary value I received when he died.

Four eyes damn near pop out of their sockets.

"Are you fucking with us right now?" Blaine can hardly believe his ears and whips out his phone.

I shake my head. "Serious as a heart attack. That's what I'll pony up if I lose. What about you?"

"Shit, I don't have anything nearly as valuable, but…" Phillip sits back in his chair, thinking hard, brows furrowed into a deep V between his eyes. "Fuck. What about my four-wheeler?"

That shitty thing? "Yeah, that works, I guess." Although we live in the city, so where the fuck would any of us put it? Phillip keeps it at his parents' place. They have a farm just outside the city, and every so often, we go out for a guys' weekend and ride the ATVs through the fields.

"Season tickets, a four-wheeler, and…" Phillip looks to Blaine. "What are you going to throw in?"

Blaine shrugs. "My timeshare?"

He has a timeshare? Random. "Where is it?"

"Myrtle Beach. It's no Hawaii, but it gets the job done."

Phillip pulls a face. "Winner takes all?"

I nod. "Yup. Winner takes all."

I glance from him to Blaine, who is furiously tapping out a message, fingers moving wildly over his cell phone screen at an alarmingly rapid pace.

"Dude, what are you doing?"

"Breaking up with Bambi." The tip of his tongue is actually sticking out of his mouth he's concentrating so hard.

"And I'm texting my sister about the smoking jackets. Navy." Phillip glances down at his phone then glances up. "What size suitcoat are you assholes?"

"Extra-large, duh." I box out, squaring my broad shoulders. I work out every goddamn day for this body—how is it not obvious I'm an XL? I sit up straighter. "Phillip here looks like a ladies' medium."

"Shut up, dickhead. I'm a large." He chews on a mouthful of

nuts, a grin slowly taking up real estate on his entire face. "I think we need a pledge."

"Fantastic idea."

Phillip stares at the ceiling, centuries old and covered in a rich cherry wood. Sits up and clears his throat. *"I, (state your name), do hereby agree never to break the rules set forth by the Bastard Bachelor Society, formed on this day, September fifteenth…"*

3

ABBOTT

"I, Abbott Margolis, do hereby promise to never again eat another donut with custard in the center, on this day, September fifteenth." I slouch my shoulders and groan. "I feel like I'm going to vomit all over my new sweater."

"There you go, being all sexy again." My best friend Sophia laughs, swiveling on the stool in the coffee shop to face me. It's the middle of the afternoon, but I haven't seen her in days, and we both stole an hour from our work day to meet. "Here, wipe the drool off your face—you have schmear in the corner of your mouth."

Yeah, I'm a real prize, snacking on a donut I promised myself I wasn't going to eat. But it's round, filled with goo, and has white frosting and pink sprinkles…so cute and yummy it was practically calling my name from the bakery case, and I've been eating so healthy lately I felt I deserved a treat.

Water and fruit? Meh.

Donuts and coffee? Yes, please.

"I can't help it—the sex appeal oozes out of me like this cream filling. It's going to *ooze* right out of me later when I get home and can finally unbutton these pants."

Sophia laughs again. "How are you single? You're a prime

catch."

I can't tell if she's being serious or sarcastic, but yeah—damn right I'm a prime catch! Too bad I live in a city where prime catches lurk around every corner. Some with bigger boobs, some with better hair. Bigger personalities, fewer evil cats.

I shrug. "Because I only hang out with you? And other women. Come on—what guy wants to approach a gaggle of girlfriends out in public?"

We're an intimidating bunch when we're at a bar for drinks: loud, obnoxious, and out for a good time—not to pick up men. Well, they're not. I occasionally am, but I'm the only one who's single (and ready to mingle), despite the bloat in my stomach and the oozing goop coming from the corner of my mouth.

It's a lovely mouth, I've been told. Pink and perfectly shaped. Full bottom pout and bow-formed upper. Bow-formed upper? If that's not a romantic description, I don't know what is…

"That's not the reason you're single," Sophia dryly points out, rearranging the napkin dispenser on the table in front of us. "It's the fact that you use words like gaggle in conversation. That word is two hundred years old."

"I like using relics in everyday jargon—you know this!" I'm always affronted when she points this out. She knows I love Britain, knows I love all things vintage.

I'm a romantic, okay? Old buildings, architecture, and English estates warm my heart like butter and make my knees weak. Is it a crime for me to love a generation that defined us as a people? Is it wrong for me to use slang from 1876? Pfft. Whatever.

"Don't act so insulted. I'm trying to spare you."

"How about next time I order a donut, you break my kneecaps instead of letting me order one?" I pat my waist and hips. "These don't need any more carbs."

Sophia ignores me, taking a bite of her Long John donut—the deliciously, cakey confection. "Yeah but it's so carbalicious. The only thing that would make this better is butter."

"That's disgusting."

"What can I say? I'm from the South."

"You're from *Missouri*."

"Which is south of here. Duh."

"Alright." I roll my eyes and stand, brushing the crumbs off my pant legs. "As much as I'd love to sit here and shoot the shit all day, I should get back to work before someone notices I'm not in an actual meeting. Between the two of us, we have accomplished zero things today."

Sophia makes a show of checking the time. "Yikes. Yeah, I have a few reports to print out and run over to human resources, so give me a smooch and get the hell out of here."

I laugh at her good-natured dismissal, knowing we both have work to do, and plant a kiss on her upturned cheek then give her a quick hug for good measure.

I love Sophia—she's the sister I never had. We didn't grow up together but became fast friends after once waiting in line next to each other at the cell phone store near my apartment.

She gives me another wave as I push through the coffee shop door. "I'll see you later, weirdo. Text me."

"See ya, sexy pants."

I give my tail end a shake. "*Byeee.*"

It's a short walk to the office, and I weave my way through the pedestrians on the sidewalk to save time. Punch the up button once I reach the elevator banks and wait patiently for the car to reach my floor once I'm standing inside.

My office—yeah, I'm a lady boss with her own office—is located at the far end of the hall (door closed because I shut it before evacuating for carbs and sugar), and I palm the doorknob with wet, sticky fingers I haven't bothered to wash or lick clean.

It's sunny, light blasting me from every direction. I take a seat and regroup, cracking my knuckles before powering up the desktop situated in the center of my desk. Unkink my neck. Wiggle my fingers as if I'm about to perform a magic trick.

The monitor comes on and I tilt my head to study the screen

in front of me, frowning at the glowing image.

It's from the creative department, and nothing about it is right, though I've given them directions twice already—very specific directions, down to the numbers on the color wheel so the shade is perfect. Down to the size I want the font.

I steeple my fingers, cheeks getting warm.

Take a few deep breaths and click open my email, find the last email exchanged with the art department, and click compose. Now, I'm not saying their refusal to take my suggestions is intentional, but it's becoming habitual, and I have to wonder if it's because of my age.

I'm young—one of the youngest ad executives in the company—but I earned this position the same way they did: hard work and the occasional long night.

Before graduating at the top of my class, I'd been taking college courses since my thirteenth birthday. By the time I graduated from high school, I was already a sophomore in college, and by the time I graduated from college, I had two degrees.

I'm a giant nerd.

The fact that my grandfather's name is on the outside of the high-rise is neither here nor there. The fact that my last name is on billboards and in magazines shouldn't be an issue.

Initially, no one was supposed to know. Technically, when I was hired, I used my mother's maiden name à la Tori Spelling when she was trying out for that television show in the 90s a billion years ago. Not wanting to be hired because of nepotism, she used a stage name so producers wouldn't know her father created the show.

Got the part.

Obviously.

I'm not lazy, and I'm not a snob. I earn my salary and bonuses like everyone else in this building. So what if my family owns it?

"Easy for you to say, asshole," I grumble as I pound out a

curt reply to the art department's latest mockup of a billboard that will be plastered in Times Square. "You're the one who was born with a silver spoon in her mouth, and they hate you because of it."

Don't choke on it.

I have no desire to kiss anyone's ass because I was born into a family who owns a business, but I am wary of their reaction to it. That, plus my age.

I'm twenty-four. Most of them think I'm way too young to be in this position, and sometimes, they might be correct. But I stay off social media, I don't post anything on Instagram, and I don't twitter. Or tweet. Or whatever you want to call it.

The last thing I need is someone from work following me and seeing the stupid shit I get up to on the weekends. Well, me and Duchess Desdemona, my amazing cat.

Grabbing my phone, I thumb through my music and open a moody playlist. I must be hormonal. There is no rational reason this mockup should make me emotional. It's just a stupid graphic sent up by an artist who thinks she's right.

Bambi Warner always thinks she's right.

Unfortunately, the Times Square account is mine, and the graphics that go up there are my responsibility—so if she wants her work represented, she better tweak the shit she keeps sending me until she nails it.

Or I'll…

I'll…

Well, I'll probably do nothing but send her email reminders, too passive-aggressive to confront her in person—which is something I'm working on.

But, baby steps. First, I'm going to conquer middle management, then I'm going to grow a spine.

Goals!

There is a banana on my desk and I grab it, peel it, and stuff one end in my mouth. Chew while the entire thing hangs. A knock at my door jars me from my troubles with Bambi and I jolt in my desk chair, banana still dangling from my lips—a move that would leave my mother needing her smelling salts.

Dale, my counterpart, stands in the doorway, watching me.

I avert my eyes, because *never make eye contact while deep-throating a banana.*

I risk a glance up—his brow is furrowed, mouth downturned into a frown.

Shit.

Frickety frack.

Also something to work toward: *cursing like an adult and not a teenager.*

I pull the fruit from my mouth, chew, and shoot Dale a wobbly smile. "Hey. What's up?"

"Has the art department sent you the specs for the TS ad?"

He has the verbiage all wrong; I send the art department specs, not the other way around.

"Um…if you're asking about a mockup, yes, they just sent it through. I was just emailing Bambi my feedback." Without a napkin, I'm forced to wipe banana on the leg of my slacks. "I noticed she didn't copy you on it. Want to have a look?"

"Sure."

Dale enters my office, hands jammed in the pockets of his pressed navy pants. His shirt is a hot pink, gingham check. Fun and not at all stuffy, unlike a lot of the other guys walking around this office.

Dale is younger, too, and creative. He makes his way around my desk as I swivel my computer monitor.

The ad is center screen, bright and punchy.

Dale leans in. Hesitates before pulling back. "It's missing something."

It is.

I nod.

"The color isn't right."

"I know." I push the monitor back into place. "I gave them the exact pink I wanted, but she has yet to use it."

"How many times have you told her?" He knows who's working on the draft, knows what Bambi can be like.

"Twice."

"Fuck." He glances down at me. "Shit, sorry."

"Don't apologize. I just… How much fuss do I make over a simple color?"

He walks back around my desk and rests his hand on the back of a chair. "May I?"

I hold a hand out. "Please do."

Dale plops down across from me, the tension leaving his body. "Can I be honest?"

Well this is something new—someone on the staff about to confide in me. I lean forward, tamping down my excitement. "Yes, absolutely."

"That whole department pisses me off. Why hasn't Linda done anything about it?"

Linda is their direct supervisor, though I am technically Bambi's boss.

Linda is rarely around, spending tons of her time networking at lunches with magazine editors and salespeople to get the accounts we need that generate our revenue.

"Linda is clueless." I slap a hand over my mouth. "Oh my God, don't repeat that to anyone."

I'm going to hell for talking shit behind her back. Either that, or Dale is going to repeat it and I'm going to get my ass chewed out.

This is what I get for being socially awkward and only hanging out with my cat during the week. I need to branch out and hit up happy hour.

Dale crosses his arms and grunts. "I need a stiff drink."

I'm more of a wine girl, but I agree. "Same."

My co-worker leans forward and fiddles with the silver spheres on my desk, plucking one so it swings on the pendulum it's suspended from. "So other than that, what's going on with you? What else are you working on?"

"Times Square, a new development on Bell Air Avenue, and something for the NBA." No small potatoes.

Dale whistles. "Nice."

"What about you?"

He pauses. "Arena, a series of bus ads for this author with a huge book coming out, and one cool spread in *Men's Health* for a fitness line. Pretty pumped about that one."

Dale sits up straighter in his chair, and it seems like he's puffing out his chest a bit, but I can't be sure. Is he...showing off for me? Surely not.

Not a single soul in this office has ever flirted with me, let alone come into my office to do it.

There isn't a rule against dating co-workers here.

My grandfather made sure of that, because my grandmother, Maureen, was one of the first female salespeople for the firm and they met here, fell in love, and—the rest is history. I wouldn't be here if he'd implemented a non-fraternization policy.

I swivel in my chair and gaze at Dale.

He fidgets.

I'd peg him at around thirty, definitely on the younger side. Playful and carefree, Dale is ridiculously good at his job. He's also hilarious, and generous, and brings in treats during the holidays and his birthday.

For the longest time, I thought he might bat for the other team, but as his face gets pink, I have to wonder.

Does Dale...

Is he...

...into me?

I study him with renewed interest, nodding as he chatters on about his weekend, casually giving him a once-over. Chest is decent, pecs visible through his cotton dress shirt. Okay arms. His hands are a bit lacking in the masculinity department, but it's not like he lives in the country and can chop wood in his free time. He's not out laying bricks for a living; he's selling ad content and creating copy, for heaven's sake.

I can't fault him for that, but I also don't think I'd bang him.

Yeah, *no*—Dale is too nice.

Is that even a thing?

Too nice—who's ever heard of such a thing?

It's not that I want to date a dickhead, but a little bit of bite never hurt a girl. Unless the guy is biting her bits—huge difference.

The thought makes me tingle downtown, and I mentally locate the vibrator I have stashed in my bedside drawer. Remind myself to stop for batteries on the way home.

Self-care and all that jazz.

Dale is still talking when I dig through my desk and pull out a steno pad—contraband from my grandpa's office. He's old-school and keeps office supplies in his desk, too, and I find myself stealing them from time to time. Rather than the high gloss company stationary in the supply room, I prefer the throwback yellow notepads Gramps keeps in his drawer.

If he notices them missing, he hasn't mentioned it.

Come to think if it, the old coot probably has me stealing them on camera.

He isn't here often—he retired years ago—but he does like to haunt the place now and again by taking his lunch in his office and giving the staff a stroke with his presence. To me, he's just Grandpa. To everyone else, he's one of the most powerful men in the city.

My dad is, too, I suppose, though he's on the finance end of things. I rarely see him.

"Anyway," Dale is saying, wrapping up with, "We usually go out after work on Wednesdays if you want to come."

"For happy hour?"

"Yeah, I guess?"

"Tonight?"

"Yes." Dale laughs nervously, toying with the buttons on his cuffs. The upturned fabric is a different pattern than the pink check; it's a bold, floral print and the perfect contrast.

I like it.

I like him—he's a nice guy. I just wish I felt more downstairs, because it's not easy meeting someone in this town.

"Sure. That sounds good. When I'm done for the day, I'll join y'all at the bar."

Dale rises. "Cool. It's right around the block, so you can walk there then take a cab home."

"Sounds good!"

It takes me hours of going back and forth to complete this project I have Bambi working on. Another several conversations with other team members in the art department working on a few layouts for me. All in all, a very productive day.

I meet Dale and a few people from my team at a bar they've chosen, a dark throwback called The Basement that feels like more of a guys' club than a normal hangout, but beggars can't be choosers and I need the night out.

To network and socialize.

I won't bore you with all the details, but the drinks flow like water. One—okay, *two* vodka sodas in and I'm laughing hysterically at Dale, two guys from accounting, two more from graphics, and one from our entertainment division, sharing pieces of myself and building a few friendships. I can feel them growing as I hug everyone before taking my leave.

Taking my leave? Jeez.

I snort as I nod in greeting at the doorman of my building, giggling to myself because I sound ancient. What self-respecting twenty-four-year-old says 'taking my leave'?

Ugh.

Chuckling again because I'm buzzed and feeling good, I stand rigidly at the bank of elevators; there are twenty-three floors in this building and I live on the twentieth. Not too shabby for my first apartment, and I giddily anticipate the ride.

I doubt there'll be a day where I don't pinch myself for being so lucky.

Fine. Luck has nothing to do with it—I work my ass off and

every living expense comes out of my own pocket.

A hiccup escapes my lips and I press three fingers to my mouth. Crap. I hate the hiccups; they linger for so long.

Another erupts as a guy bursts through the revolving door, balancing a box that, although it doesn't look heavy, appears loaded down with random odds and ends. Gadgets? I can't tell from here, but "Come on, come on" leaves my mouth, willing the elevator to speed things up so I don't have to humiliate myself by being trapped with this gorgeous specimen of a man.

I've seen this guy around, and I don't want the first time I meet him to be in an elevator! When I'm drunk, for heaven's sake, cheeks and nose probably cherry red.

Cue another tipsy hiccup.

And another…

He's heading straight toward me. Okay, maybe not toward *me* specifically, but toward the elevator car, and I hold my breath as the electronics think, silently praying the doors will close before he reaches me.

"Hold the door please!" he calls out, box now somehow balanced on one hand like he's a server at a restaurant, other one outstretched, beseeching me with an open palm. As if he's about to force the door to remain open with the sheer force of thin air and a prayer. "Fuck!"

The box teeters and he careens slightly to the left. Right. A pantomime of a balancing act.

"Sorry?" Drunk me doesn't feel guilty in the slightest about not pressing the button to hold the door for him. Sober me? She'll regret it in the morning.

I shrug as if helpless and hard of hearing, cupping a hand over my right ear. "Say again?"

Hiccup.

He knows damn well I can hear him if his eyebrows shooting into his hairline are any indication. He's genuinely shocked I'm blowing him off. Well surprise, surprise, pal, I'm shocked at myself, too—I'm normally so well mannered!

A flash of irritation mars his brow.

Truthfully, I'm ordinarily a *really* nice person—too nice, my friends have said. My nan calls me a pushover who needs to grow a pair of lady balls, preferably a bigger set than she has.

"Oh no!" I peek through the closing steel doors, the corners of my mouth shifting down into a grimace. "Shoot! I can't... Nooooo!" My voice mimics a sound like I'm fading into obscurity, gets quieter as the guy disappears, an incredulous expression slashing his handsome features.

"I'm melting!" Drunk me adds more drama for good measure, as if I wasn't acting ridiculously immature enough. The doors are two inches from closing. I snap my fingers in front of the diminishing crack between them and add a sassy wink. "So close. Almost made it."

Shoot him some air pistols and blow off the imaginary smoke.

I sigh and sag against the wall when the doors mercifully slide shut.

But dang, he was good-looking.

Tall—really tall, actually—with dark hair and thick eyebrows, eyes so blue I could distinguish their color from across the lobby, almost thirty feet away. His hair was windblown, sculpted cheekbones red from the cold. Dark gray wool jacket with the collar pulled up. Black scarf. Jeans and dress shoes. I didn't need long to get the full rundown on his appearance.

Good-looking men never take long to drool over.

And just as the door shut in his startled face, I saw the traces of a shallow cleft in his chin.

Damn him, I'm a *sucker* for those.

"Huh."

That face.

That handsome, bewildered face.

It's the last thing I see when I close my eyes that night and, let's face it, pass out in the middle of my bed.

4

BROOKS

Weekends are for: alcohol, hook-ups, sitting on my ass. And exercise.

On days I run, when I'm finished, I take the stairs to my apartment, skipping the elevator so by the time I reach my floor, I'm panting like I'm on my last breath, almost collapsing when I shove through the door exiting the stairwell, practically falling into the hallway.

Stumble.

Panting like a goddamn dog, like I've just come from a one-hundred-degree room, wearing thirty layers and running backward on a treadmill.

Feebly grasping toward the direction of my apartment, I sound like I'm breathing through a metal lung and—

"Yikes," a voice says. "Dude, are you okay?"

"Jesus Christ!" I shout, startled that anyone is standing in the hallway. *No one* is ever in the hallway, so this pleasant female voice takes me by complete surprise.

I wipe the sweat dripping down my brow and into my eyes, glancing up into the curious eyes of—

"*You.*"

Just that one word is an accusation, delivered in a special

tone reserved for shock and disgust, for when I'm feeling both at the same time.

Her.

It's the little shit from the lobby—the one who wouldn't hold the friggin elevator for me and let it slam in my face.

Okay fine, elevator doors don't slam. They slide closed slowly. But she punctuated the whole thing with air guns, so that whole "Oh no, I'm meltinggg!" bullshit was just that—bullshit.

She wasn't melting. She's perfectly intact, staring at me as if I were heaving, hunched over, and nearly hyperventilating in the hallway of our apartment complex.

I squint up at her.

This—she is why I'm swearing off women—women like her.

"You? Huh?" Dawning registers on her face. "Oh you mean meee." Her nose turns up. "I'm sorry, do I know you?"

"I think I'm your neighbor."

"Hmm." She taps her chin, thinking. "Which one?"

"The one that lives here?" I point to the door behind me— the gleaming number 2045 that matches her gleaming 2042. The cream doors exactly identical, save for the gold addresses affixed to the centers.

Gold doorknobs.

Gold peepholes.

The place is classy as fuck, and some days, I cannot even believe I live here. Not after the lifetime of shitholes I had to live in growing up, digging myself out of the poverty hole my parents dug us into by never having jobs.

I'm fucking proud of how successful I've become, proud to afford this place.

Except now I have this lippy troll glaring at me from across the carpet of this gilded hall as if I'm the dickhead in this scenario, not her.

"Huh. Didn't realize I had one."

"You didn't realize you had a *neighbor*?"

That's a giant load of crap if I've ever heard one. The hallway is full of doors and she didn't realize she had a *neighbor*? Now she's just being difficult. I know I've played my music a little too loud on occasion, and even though she's across the hallway and we don't share a wall, there's no way she hasn't heard it at least once through the door.

Not unless she's a hermit who never comes out, which I highly doubt.

This girl is polished, poised, and sassy. Definitely comes off as a bit of a snob, and from the way her eyes keep roaming up and down my sweat-soaked body, no doubt she's judging me. Finds me lacking, I'm sure. Not sure how I feel about that—the blue gaze a twinkling gleam I'll catalogue as toying with me.

She's amused, teasing me like a mouse to a cat.

I hate cats.

I'm more of a dog person, and why the hell am I even thinking about that right now when it's not the point?

The girl—this *young woman*—is watching me, and it's obvious she knows my thoughts have strayed. She seizes the opportunity to bail on an introduction.

"Well, nice to meet you. *Bye.*" She tries to slide inside her apartment, but I stop her.

"Whoa, whoa, whoa. Not so fast."

She sighs, sagging against the doorframe. Crosses her arms and rolls her eyes. "Ugh, fine." Instantly, a disgruntled censure commands her voice. "I'm *sorry* I didn't hold the elevator for you the other night. I was *busy* and had stuff in my hands."

Busy?

Stuff in her hands?

Little liar. "You weren't holding jack shit!" Meanwhile, I had a cumbersome box full of crap from the office! "If you're going to lie, at least put some effort into it."

"Fine. I might have been a teensy-weensy bit drunkish." She regards me again, tilting her head. "What was in that box you were carrying anyway?"

"Mail. Packages. Work stuff I had sent to myself."

"What kind of work stuff?"

I narrow my eyes, patting at the perspiration on my forehead. "Are you always this nosey?"

"Actually—no." Her smile is crooked and cute and oddly enough, I believe her. "Normally I don't care a fig about what other people are doing."

A fig?

I shift inside my sneakers, legs cooling off. "I'm working on a project and thought I'd bring some of it home."

"What's the project?"

Nothing you need to worry about. "It's just a project."

"Why won't you tell me what it is? Is it illegal?"

"Why do you care?"

Her shoulders rise and fall in a feminine shrug. "Just curious about what my new neighbor does for a day job. There are a lot of mafia around here, you know."

Jesus Christ. "I'm not in the mafia, and I'm not your *new* neighbor—I've lived here for nine months."

"It's so weird we haven't bumped into each other." She pauses. "So what was in the box?"

"*Oh my God.*" My groan is loud and dramatic as I brace my hands against the wall so I can stretch my calves while we're wasting time blabbering out here.

"Just tell me." Another hesitation. "It was a severed head, wasn't it?"

A severed he—

"If you really must know, I'm one of the principal architects at Witt & Spencer and I'm working on the latest technology for a high-rise development downtown." I'm not proud to say I puff out my chest as I deliver a line I've actually practiced saying in front of the mirror in my bedroom, but what can ya do.

She's suitably impressed, eyebrows rising into her brown hairline. "Well la-di-da, aren't youuu fancy!"

Wait—is she impressed, or is she mocking me?

I can't tell.

"Okay Miss Sassy Pants, where do *you* work?" I want to know the answer, even though I have sweat dripping from my spine to my butt crack. I'm dying to swipe at it, but no way am I digging into the ass of my shorts in front of this chick. I have a feeling she'd never let me live it down.

"I'm over at Margolis & Co."

"Doing what?" She's young—definitely in her twenties—so I immediately peg her as a junior executive assistant, or maybe even a trust fund baby? Seems highly unlikely. This girl isn't nearly snooty enough.

I've been inside that building a time or two, mostly when I was younger, doing architectural tours of the city. That's kind of always been my hobby: scouting modern cities for old buildings and historical sites. I try to see as many Victorian and Art Deco designs as I can before they're inevitably demolished, one by one, to make way for newer, shinier skyscrapers.

The girl hesitates.

"I'm Vice President of Media Development."

Say what now? "What?"

"Vice President of—"

"No, no, I heard you. I'm just surprised. You seem kind of…"

I don't want to say…

"Young?" Now she's leaning against her door, fiddling with the tie on her mauve yoga pants. "That's because I am."

"How old are you?"

Again, her nose turns up. "Didn't your nan ever teach you it isn't polite to ask a lady her age?"

My *what*? "What the fuck is a nan?"

The girl laughs. "Your grandmother?"

"My grandmother is dead." I say it deadpan, to shut her up and to wipe that smirk off her cocky little face.

She blanches. "Oh my G-God," she stutters. "I'm so sorry. I…I…" She's sputtering, turning the delightful shade of red one acquires upon jamming her foot so far in her mouth, she chokes on it. A dainty hand covers pouty lips, her once pale porcelain skin now the color of a ripe beet.

Good.

I wait a few more seconds, letting her squirm.

Then, "I'm just fucking with you. My grandma on the East Coast is probably at some casino gambling away all my grandpa's life insurance money."

Her mouth gapes. "You. Butthole."

Butthole? That's the best she can do as an insult? Shit, if that's the worst thing I'm called today, I'll call it a win.

And it's not even eight o'clock in the morning.

Which reminds me, "What are you doing out in the hallway?"

"My nan had breakfast dropped off for me and I was out here making sure I didn't leave the bag of condiments."

Huh? "Say that again, slower."

"My nan had breakfast delivered for me since I can't be there for brunch today, and I just popped back out to make sure I wasn't forgetting anything."

"Your grandmother brought you breakfast?" I glance at the watch on my wrist. "It's so early."

"She didn't bring it, she had it delivered."

"Why?"

"Um, because I'm missing family brunch today."

"Why?"

She huffs. "I don't want to go?"

I cock my head. "What does Nan-Nan think you're doing instead of going to brunch?"

She checks her nail polish, intently studying her hands. "I told her I already had a brunch date."

"A *date* date?"

"Yes."

"On a Sunday?"

"Yes?"

"And that was enough to get you off the hook and out of a family obligation?" Why am I so impressed?

"I mean, yeah? She's trying to get me married off, so…"

"*Why?*" The shock registers in my own brain, the expression on my face must look pretty ridiculous.

"She's old-school—that's what Nan does."

"Right…" I draw the word out, because this whole conversation is borderline ridiculous. A nan sounds like a character from a damn cartoon movie—and along with cats, I hate cartoons, too. "Are you going to tell me what kind of food she had delivered at seven thirty in the morning on a Sunday?"

"Why?" Her eyes have gone to slits.

"I'm starving." Obviously.

"Should you be eating? You just ran up twenty flights of stairs—won't you want to puke? I mean, you look like you're going to."

Meh. "Maybe, but I'm hungry and I should be eating protein. Got any?"

"I might, but…" She gives me a once-over, eyeing my sweat-soaked outfit, scuffed jogging shoes, and perspiration-drenched headband.

I know I look like I just ran the Boston Marathon, pissed myself running, and barely managed to drag my slack body across the finish line.

"But what?"

"I don't even know you." She's chewing on her lower lip. I can't help but notice that it's pouty and pink, and though there's no makeup on her face, she's really goddamn pretty.

That would matter if I were interested.

Which I'm not.

Besides, no fucking way am I going to lose that bet with the BBS. No. Fucking. Way.

She doesn't want me eating her food because she doesn't know me? Fine. "I'm Brooks Bennett."

A laugh escapes her throat and she sputters, spitting a bit, which is kind of disgusting.

"What's so amusing?"

"Is that seriously your name? *Brooks* Bennett?"

"Yes." I take in her light pinkish yoga pants, soft gray pullover, and bare feet. Toes are painted a soft pink. "What's yours?"

A brief silence. "Abbott."

Abbott. "Abbott what?"

"Just Abbott."

"God, don't tell me you're one of those chicks who's an internet blogger with one name."

She laughs. "I have a last name, I'm just not telling you what it is."

I roll my eyes so hard I feel them in the back of my skull. "I'm not going to stalk you—don't flatter yourself."

Now she's the one rolling her eyes. "I'm not a blogger."

"Well, Abbott *I'm not a blogger*, if you feed me, I'll super appreciate it, and I won't bother trying to search you online later." I have no food in my fridge and make a mental note to have something delivered later so I'll have a meal to eat after work tomorrow. "Give me a few to jump in and out of the shower then I'll be back to bang your door in."

Bang your door in—good one, Brooks.

My pretty little neighbor scrunches up her nose, unsure about whether or not that was a sexual innuendo.

"Fine." She points an accusatory finger at me, and I notice her nails are light pink. "But you're not staying long."

As if. "Fine."

I'm just using her for food, anyway.

It takes me half an hour to wash the sweat from my body and throw on clean clothes before I'm back at Abbott's apartment door. Three loud raps of my knuckles and she's swinging it open with a huff.

"Oh my God—I heard you." She glances up and down the

hall, yanking me by the arm. "Everyone heard you! Chill out and get in here before someone files a complaint."

I hiss at her.

"Don't you dare hiss at me," she gripes, pulling the door farther open so I can follow her inside.

The first thing that registers about her place is how good it smells; a candle glows on a compact table in her entryway, emitting a delicious—

"*Holyshitwhatthefuckisthat?*"

A demon lurks at the far end of the corridor, glassy eyes wide, white fur standing on end, the glow from the living room windows backlighting its stark white fluff, creating an almost supernatural glow. It's eerie, unsettling, and…

…are those *fangs*?

"It's a cat." Abbott takes the keys for my place out of my hand, dropping them onto the round table. Flips on the rest of the lights as she goes deeper into the apartment.

"A cat. Right." I side-eye the beast suspiciously, glued to my spot in the narrow entrance. "But why does it have laser beams coming from its beady eyes?"

It hasn't blinked once, I'm sure of it.

Jesus Christ, this cat looks like Satan's mistress.

"Oh give me a break. Desdemona doesn't have lasers coming from her eyes. She's sweet—look at her." She points to her evil dictator cat, its tiny fur paws rooted to the floor, back arched. "An angel."

"I *am* looking at her. She looks like a holy terror that wants to shred my face off with whatever talons are buried in her hair."

"It's called fur, and would you stop it? She's as sweet as pie."

Doubtful. The cat chooses that exact moment to hiss when I make eye contact.

Little fucker. "What's its name, again?"

"*Her* name is Desdemona. I call her Desi for short."

"Desdemona? That's fucking horrible. Who came up with that?"

"Technically, her registered name is Duchess Desdemona McPurrs-A-Lot, but obviously that's a mouthful."

Obviously.

And who the hell *registers* their cat? Rich people, that's who.

"Right, McPurrs-A-Lot. Purrs. Does that thing purr at *all*?"

"Of course she does, don't you little furball, don't you my precious angel kitty?" Abbott coos to the mangy feline glaring up at me, a satisfied sparkle in its left eye. "She's just wary of strangers."

I'm not convinced, taking another glance at the cat, who now has its white body firmly pressed against the wall at the end of the hall even as Abbott strokes its back.

This cat isn't fucking around. It's out to get me.

"Can I call it Lucifer instead of Desi?"

"No!"

"Captain McPussyPants?"

"Oh my God. *No.*"

"How about Desi McTerrorPuss?"

I like that last one, settling on the nickname even though I know it's going to drive my cute little neighbor nuts—or perhaps because I know it will.

"Don't you dare call her that." She feigns outrage on the cat's behalf. "It's undignified."

Right. Because I'm worried about that.

Not. "Pussy of Terror."

Abbott tilts her head in thought. "Okay, see—now your names are starting to sound like rides at a theme park."

"Pussy of Terror." I laugh. "I dated a woman with one of those once. It was the worst ride I've ever been on," I joke.

Abbott stares blankly, too classy to take the bait of my barb. "If that was a sex reference, I'm choosing to ignore it."

"You do that." It was definitely a sex reference, and I wish Abbott would bite at one of my jokes, because sparring with her is one of the most exciting things I've done all week. And it's Sunday, which is saying a helluva lot.

My week sucked balls but seems to be ending on a high note —free breakfast and company included.

My eyes stray to the white cat now lurking in the corner.

"Do you ever live in fear that he's going to maim you in your sleep?"

"*She*. Desi is a girl. I've referred to her as a *she* at least a dozen times."

Doesn't matter—that pussy is pure evil; I can see it in her tiny, black stare.

Angriest little pussy in the building, I'd wager, not including Abbott's. Ha ha.

"It already hates me."

Abbott laughs, a soft trill as she trails down the hallway and disappears into another room. I follow, cat glare beating on my back.

Fuck. I'm actually scared to look over my shoulder to see if it's creeping along after us. Slinking, sneaking—whatever it is cats fucking do when they're being shady.

I find my neighbor in a kitchen identical to mine, already prying open the refrigerator and leaning inside. She retrieves two bottles of water and hands one over without looking at me, digs through the crisper, and pulls out a brown paper bag with the name SmithStone's on the side.

Speaking of fancy—SmithStone's is one of the bougiest places in town. Expensive and exclusive for a small eatery, I'm pretty fucking sure they don't cater, or deliver, and certainly not so early in the damn morning.

"Desi doesn't hate you." Abbott tears the bag open, breaking the gold sticker sealing it shut and peering inside. "And she won't try to hurt you. She's quite gentle."

Debatable.

"She hasn't attacked you yet."

"Yet?" My heart rate accelerates. "What the fuck does that mean?"

Another laugh, and this one has Abbott bent at the waist in

a giggling fit. "Sheesh, Brooks, you should see the look on your face. I'm kidding! The cat isn't going to attack you. She's way too lazy for that. Take a look at her collar—the little gold plate says Lazy AF."

No way am I touching that thing.

Abbott prods me. "Oh don't be a baby. Take a look."

I shake my head. No. *Nuh-uh.*

"Are you trying to tell me you're a big ol' chickenshit?"

I cross my arms defiantly, like a petulant child. "That's exactly what I'm telling you."

You couldn't pay me to get within five feet of that pussy, and that's a sentence I've never said in my entire life.

Abbott roots around in a cabinet and retrieves two plates; next come napkins and forks. She grabs the paper bag of food off the counter and heads in the direction of the living room at the back of her apartment. I know that's where she's going because it's the same layout as my place.

I find her plopped down on a cream-colored couch, sitting cross-legged and grabbing the remote control for the television. "Wanna watch *House Hunters*?"

No, I'd rather poke my eye out with one of her fancy forks. "Sure." I'm distracted by what's out the window. She has a view of the park, and her windows are fucking ginormous, while mine are…normal.

"Why are your windows better than mine?"

Technically we have the same apartment. Same end of the building. Same floor.

So how the fuck did she get floor-to-ceiling windows?

"Your view is fucking ridiculous." A panoramic overlook of the whole city—the nighttime skyline must be absolutely insane. "What the hell, dude!" I stand and stroll to the window, hands braced on my hips, the green-eyed jealously monster rearing its ugly head. "How much do you pay for this place?"

Translation: *How the fuck can you afford this?*

Abbott's pert little nose tips into the air.

"None of your dang business." She pops open a to-go container and steam rises; four eggs Benedict sit presented on a bed of asparagus and browns, hashed and spiced to perfection.

Well dangggg. Gimme.

I watch hungrily, mouth watering as she scoops out a serving and slides it on a plate. Sets the plate on the table.

Repeats the process, then once again digs into the paper bag. Roots around and retrieves another identical container.

Goodie, there's more!

She eyeballs me like her cat did earlier. "Are you going to sit or not? Because I'm starting the show, and if you're going to just stand there, I'm going to start eating without you."

Grumbling, I kick my shoes off and flop down next to her. Sigh. Give her a sidelong glance. "Do you have any salt or anything? I don't think I can eat veggies without putting something on them."

"Cabinet next to the fridge." She barely acknowledges me, which is more than I can say for Desi McTerrorPuss.

When I stand, the cat does too.

I sit back down on the couch.

Desi slowly lowers her ass to the carpet.

Fuck.

Checkmate.

Abbott notices. "Jesus, are you being serious right now? The cat isn't going to hurt you."

"You're not taking this seriously enough!" I argue, stricken. Man I want that salt. But do I need it? Really?

I make puppy dog eyes at Abbott. She makes puppy dog eyes at the cat.

"Brooks, I'm not going to the kitchen for you."

"Please!" I beg, in a deadlock with Desi. "I'm hungry!"

"If I go to the kitchen, you're still going to be alone with the cat," she warns.

"Right, but at least I can keep an eye on her. She only moves when I move."

Abbott shifts on the sofa, tilting her body toward me, resting one arm on the back of the couch. "I dare you to go to the kitchen yourself and get the salt."

"You *dare* me? What do I get if I actually do it?"

Abbott looks exasperated. "You get the salt, moron."

Fine. Fair enough. "You're sure the cat isn't going to attack me?"

"She hasn't attacked anyone so far today. I think you're safe."

"But it's not even eight o'clock—there's still time." The cat raises its hairy old man brows at me, taunting. "I swear, if that thing does anything…"

Abbott scoops some eggs onto her fork and into her pink, pouty mouth. "You're being so dramatic."

I rise. Point at the cat and tell it to, "Stay."

It stays.

"Huh." I square my shoulders back and puff out my chest, victorious. "Look at that, I'm the pussy whisperer," I murmur, more to myself than to my neighbor, because now she's blatantly ignoring me. Admittedly, she looks quite adorable perched on the couch with a blanket across her lap, nibbling on her breakfast.

She finally spares me a glance.

"Brooks: a regular magician. I'll call you Houdini from now on. How would you like that?"

"Actually…" I rub my chin, make for the kitchen, and quickly grab the salt and pepper from the cabinet. "I'd love it—even though technically Houdini was an escape artist and not an actual magician." I haven't had a nickname since college, and that one wasn't even original—it was just my last name. "What about Copperfield?"

Her eyes narrow. "You're starting to annoy me."

"You're cute when you get worked up. No, seriously, how many people look that adorable with flared nostrils?" I finally relax on the couch, the cat having backed off enough to let me eat. "Like two tiny caves—a tiny little dragon could fly right up in there."

"Stop it right now, *shut* up." Her hand flies to her nose.

"Cool it, I'm fucking with you." The eggs and asparagus go down my esophagus delightfully smoothly, taste expensive, and tantalize my taste buds. "Thanks for the free food."

I'm one cheap son of a bitch who never turns down a handout.

"As if I had a choice? You barged in."

"We always have choices, Abbott with only one name."

"Stop it. I have more than one name."

"Maybe, but you're not telling me what the other one is. What's the big fucking deal?"

Abbott sighs, loud and long. "It's Margolis."

I glance around, somewhat expecting fireworks to explode and sirens to go off with the pronouncement. Or maybe that's what *she's* expecting to happen?

Instead, I dig into my breakfast. "Okay."

There's a long pause, and finally, my neighbor joins me.

5

ABBOTT

Nothing happened when I told him my last name.

I wait for more of a reaction, but it never comes.

Admittedly, I may be hypersensitive to it. *Or maybe you're sheltered, living in a bubble, and only think everyone knows you— or cares—because that's who you surround yourself with.*

I watch as my neighbor readjusts himself on the couch before shoving more food into his face, resting his ass on my soft cushions, and spreading his legs comfortably.

Brooks.

Bennett.

What a doozy of a name—and here I thought mine was hoity-toity.

He's dressed casually in mesh basketball pants and a hoodie, looking cozy and relaxed in my apartment. Looking like he belongs in my living room.

Not long after that firm ass of his hits the couch and he raises his plate, forking the breakfast I've served him, Desdemona pounces like the food enthusiast she is, like I knew the dang cat would. She has no manners and even less patience.

My cat loves food, eggs in particular. And while she might not be keen on strangers or new people, she's a slut for snacks.

I watch, entertained, as my neighbor reacts to the cat, the entire scene playing out in slow motion, more beautifully than I could have scripted it.

Brooks' display is an Oscar-winning performance.

"Holy shit! Holy fuck! I'm under attack, I'm under *attack*!" Brooks screeches from the depths of his soul. "Get it off!"

It literally sounds like he's getting attacked in a pool of sharks and can't climb out of the water.

Wow.

I've *never* heard a man scream like a girl before. Well, once, my twin brother Stuart saw a mouse run through the living room of our lake cottage when we were young. He let out a bloodcurdling scream and had an asthma attack, but we were twelve, hadn't hit puberty yet, and had never seen a live mouse in person before.

The scream emitting from Brooks' throat is one of sheer terror, and I'm shocked a puddle of urine isn't soaking the cushions of my brand-new couch. He needs to take a chill pill.

"Help!"

I yawn. "You're fine."

He squeals, "How can you say that?" and that's when I begin to laugh. "How?!"

He's serious.

Tears stream from the corners of my eyes, streak down my cheeks, and Lord, I know I shouldn't be laughing—because he's freaking out—but there's no stopping it now. "Shhh, calm down. Calm down." I'm sputtering with a snort, tears, and also some spit, doing my best to soothe him. "You're scaring her."

My poor little boo-baby is crouched next to Brooks, torn between her want of a treat and the urge to escape into her kitty house.

"*I'm* scaring *her*? I. Scared her. She scared *me*! What the fuck, Abbott—whose side are you on?"

My eyes fly back to the cat.

Yup, Desi definitely looks terrified—not enough to jump down from his lap, but enough that her ears are pulled back into a defensive position.

I keep laughing at him. He's ludicrous. "Sides? What are you, five? It's a cat, not a person trying to compete with you. Dear Lord, get a grip."

Desdemona's ears slowly slide back into their normal position as I sweet-talk her, waving a little piece of egg in her direction.

Her nose twitches curiously. One tiny paw goes back onto Brooks' forearm and he bristles. Glares.

"This cat isn't normal!"

"Neither is your yelling about it. Let her love you."

Voice having risen four octaves, Brooks has his arms and plate extended over his head like a convict waiting for a pat down from the police, his eyes glued to the animal creeping back onto his lap, her pink nose sniffing toward the plate he's holding hostage.

"No. *Bad* pussy." He holds it higher until Desdemona is forced to retreat from her looting. The savage, greedy little thing. "Bad."

My kitty gives him a pitiful little mew. Pats at his abs with her petite white paw, beseeching.

"*No*," Brooks tells her again.

"You know, cats aren't like dogs. She doesn't know any commands."

Trust me, I tried teaching her how to roll over and play dead the first few months I got her, but she wasn't having it. Occasionally she'll come running when I call out her name, but mostly she gives me the big green weenie.

Desi puts her face on his lap, deciding to wait him out.

She's no fool, probably knows he's afraid and isn't going to budge from that spot.

Animals can smell fear.

"Awww, look at her—she likes you."

Brooks, too petrified to move even an inch, is stiff as stone. Back ramrod straight, arms still above his head. "The feeling is not mutual."

"At least you can stop worrying she's going to claw your face off."

My neighbor studies my face, eventually asking, "You think this is funny?"

"One hundred percent." I cannot lie.

"You're *sick*."

My shoulders move up and down in a casual shrug. "I guess I could have warned you—Desi loves eggs. And popcorn. *Loves* people food." In fact, love is putting it mildly. Any time the gluttonous furball hears the fridge open, she comes stampeding into the kitchen like a tiny herd of cattle.

Brooks stares at me for a good, hard second. "You did that on *purpose!*"

Cannot confirm or deny that one. So, I go with a futile, "You insisted on coming over to be fed. You don't even know me, just invited yourself in to mooch off my nan's giving nature! Do not blame me for any of this."

"You are so full of shit, Abbott—you knew damn well the cat was going to jump on me as soon as I sat down. Don't lie."

"Oh, now I can predict what the cat is going to do? I'm not a psychic."

Desdemona, unsatisfied with the progress she's making by manipulating him with her cute face, rises to stand, climbing farther into his lap. Walks her kitty paws up his chest, furry face reaching for his. Nose practically squished against Brooks' neck, the loud purrs emitting from her belly no doubt vibrating on his chest.

"Jeez, get this thing off me."

Thing? This thing?

I'm insulted for my cat for the second time this morning and come to her defense. "You said you didn't want her attacking you, but you don't want her to love you, either? Make up your mind."

"You should have told me the cat likes eggs."

I check my fingernails for lint. "I forgot."

"Has anyone ever told you you're an awful liar?"

"Yeah, that's what I hear." I pop another forkful of Benedict into my mouth and chew. Swallow. Shrug. "Has anyone ever told you that you scream like a girl?"

He doesn't even have the energy to look affronted. Just tells me, "Shut up, I do not."

I don't chastise him for the bad manners, instead driving my point home to irritate him.

"No, for real. You sound *just* like one." I lean across the couch and reach for the eggs Benny on Brooks' plate. Pluck a bit of egg off for the cat, feeding her from the palm of my hand as Brooks looks on, still breathing heavily. Terrified. "Good kitty. Good kitty witty."

I don't usually talk to Desi like she's a baby; it's mostly for my neighbor's disgusted benefit, because now my cat is purring all up on him and Brooks is hating life right now. Baby-talking the cat likely increases that misery.

I'm not wrong.

"Please take my plate," Brooks begs.

I lean my back against the couch cushions, enjoying his anguish. "Meh. I don't think so."

I fluff the blanket on my lap. It's white and pristine and fluffy, just like the cat curled up on his.

"Please. I think I'm having a heart attack."

Doubtful. "If you were having a heart attack, you wouldn't be complaining right now."

"I'm not hungry anymore."

Yes, he is; he's just being stubborn. "Stop being a pussy."

His blue eyes widen and he mocks a gasp. "How *dare* you throw that word in my face? How *dare* you!"

Speaking of pussies, Desi coils up in his lap and purrs

furiously, snuggled against this newcomer she's decided she loves and adores.

Just like I knew she would.

6

ABBOTT

I'm at work bright and early on Monday, a pep in my step that wasn't there when I left the office on Friday—even after happy hour with my colleagues.

I don't see Dale when I round the corner, coffee in hand, headed for my office, but his secretary is at her desk, fingers tapping away at her desktop. On her monitor is a huge image of an orange tabby cat I can see from here. A framed photo of the ugliest dog I've ever seen sits next to the computer, and my brows go up as I breeze past.

"Morning Ms. Margolis," she greets over the wall of her cubby.

"Morning…" Shit, what's *her* name? Becky? "Beth."

I give her a little wave, pushing my office door open with the toe of my shoe, closing it behind me when I'm all the way inside. Make the extra effort to close the horizontal blinds, which are ordinarily—permanently—kept open.

I pull the thin string until they slide slowly down, creating a blinder for the office staff beyond, who will unquestionably suspect me of looking at porn or having sex on my desk like Sheila in accounting—or Dennis in marketing.

I settle at my desk for an early-morning extracurricular activity.

It takes a little while for my computer to warm up, but when it does, I hunker down in front of it like a spy about to begin her first mission and greedily click open search engines.

B-R-O-O-K-S

B-E-N…one N or two? Shit. Two Ts or one?

I try both.

"Brooks Bennett…Brooks Bennett." I cannot believe I'm creeping online—as if I don't have a million other things to occupy my time. And doing this at work, in my office, feels sketchier still. Like a good old-fashioned stalking session, the kind I used to have in college with my friends when I liked someone.

"You're not getting paid for this and it is a clear violation of company policy," I reprimand myself as some weak tactic to thwart my own efforts. But I persist, already ankle-deep in the fray, already gazing at photos of him—the few that pop up in my search, knowing more will appear when I hit his social media pages. "Dad would kill you if he knew you were wasting company time to stalk your dumb neighbor."

Brooks Bennett is…kind of a tool; logically, I know he is. The cat knows it. That guy probably has more lotion and skincare than I do, and he came over wearing *house* shoes, for Pete's sake. Only my grandfather has ever worn those, and *he's* pushing eighty.

Brooks talked during all the television shows. Occasionally chewed with his mouth open. Talked while he was eating. Scratched his nuts in front of me twice. Brought up all the good times he had in college. His fraternity. And disciplined Desdemona.

But oddly enough, we had a good time together, and Desi both hated and loved him (an excellent sign). We spent the day laughing on my couch, eating breakfast—then ordered lunch, then ordered Thai takeout for dinner. Binged an entire series, watched an entire movie.

It was late when he left my apartment, reluctantly crossing the hall for bed. Though he'd almost passed out on my couch twice, he refused to spend the night.

Whatever—it's not like he had a drive across town; he only had to walk a few feet.

Yet here I am, googling the wiseass during business hours, with my office door closed and curtains drawn like a total psycho.

He's not difficult to find, not with his name combination. The first thing that pops up is a collegiate business organization photograph, taken during his tenure at an illustrious university out east.

Just like me.

Brooks is in a black tux, black bowtie, and he's got a dark mustache.

I lean in closer, pushing on a pair of glasses.

Correction: fake mustache. Felt, from the looks of it, but honestly so hard to tell since the picture is sepia-toned.

What an idiot he must have been, I muse, betting he was probably a giant asshole, undoubtedly hazing all the new pledges as an upperclassman.

Brooks is cute. No—he's painfully handsome.

Crooked, cheeky smile below that dumb mustache. Dark, shaggy hair. Broad shoulders and debonair in a tuxedo, although to be fair, on the bottom he probably wore boxer shorts and not dress slacks.

The rest of the crew look like morons, too—daddy's money doesn't buy anyone class, and these guys look like they just rolled out of bed and stumbled into the photo shoot. Several of them are wearing sunglasses inside. Three of them have cigars dangling from their spoiled mouths.

One kid dons a sombrero.

I move along to the next photo of Brooks, this one from a

hometown newspaper, the article a write-up of the students from his high school who got full-ride scholarships to colleges and universities.

Brooks received four offers, and my heart beats a bit faster.

Good grades, hard worker. Crazy good-looking. Funny.

Maybe not so spoiled after all.

I find his Instagram; he follows a ton of people but doesn't post often. Mostly just food and old buildings? Which surprises me—you'd think an egotistical guy like him would post gym selfies and pictures of himself dressed up, or at fancy bars.

No such posts.

His Facebook is set to private and unsearchable.

I recline back in my chair, steepling my fingers, deep in thought. *Maybe he's not such a tool after all. Maybe there's a bit of substance to him, barring the fake mustache…*

Hmm.

7
BROOKS

I do not have time for this. I do not have time for this.
Get to work, asswipe.
Focus.

"Abbott Margolis—how the fuck is that even spelled?" I'm a smart guy; two college diplomas on my wall prove it. So what the hell am I doing stalking Abbott and why the hell can I not figure out how to spell her goddamn name?

My long fingers hover over the keyboard of my computer, suspended and at a total loss. They can't type without a command, and I have no fucking clue how Abbott spells her name.

It's not like this little Google sesh will amount to anything. It's not like I want anything from her. Besides, my prissy little neighbor seems more like the relationship type, and we all know I'll never be part of a couple.

Not any time soon, anyway.

Sure, I'd like kids someday. But like, when I'm forty.

Not the fucking point, Bennett.
Get back to work.

There is a clock mounted on the wall in my office, and its second hand ticking is the only sound. There's no sound of my fingers typing, nor of my mechanical pencil being dragged along a piece of paper.

Just the ticking of the clock, one second at a time.

Tick.

Tock.

Tick.

My index finger hits the A key. Then the B. O.

T.

Enter.

How the fuck is Margolis spelled?

M-A-R-G-O-A-L-E-S.

Enter.

Nothing pops up. I try again, this time with a new letter combination.

Nothing.

Fuck.

Dammit.

Why am I wasting my time with this? Why can't I spell?

I hit my intercom. "Taylor?"

"Yes, boss?"

Cringing, I lean forward so he can hear me. "I need you to find the spelling of a name for me."

The sound of him shuffling for paper. "Is this the name of a building or the name of a place?"

"Neither."

"Is this the name of an architect?"

"Why does it suddenly sound like we're playing a game of Guess Who or Twenty Questions and you're trying to win something?"

Taylor huffs into the intercom, lowering his voice. "Look, it's barely noon, I can't eat carbs, and I am an intern for an architectural firm. I want to design buildings, but I'm stuck answering the phones up front. I have to amuse myself any way I can." If I didn't know any better, I'd say he was pushing his bangs aside and throwing his head back, à la Cher.

Pure diva.

"So. *Who* am I searching?" He's already clicking away on his computer, no doubt pulling up LinkedIn.

"Calm down." Why is everything an event with this guy? Don't they teach these kids in college how to behave less excitably in a professional work environment? "I don't need you to do the searching for me, I just need to know how to spell a name."

His enthusiasm tapers, the professionalism returning to his voice. "What's the name?"

"First name Abbott, last name Margolis."

If one could hear a set of eyebrows rise into a hairline, I'd be hearing it now. "Alright. Hold on."

"Thanks."

The line goes dead. Minutes pass until I'm impatiently swiveling in my desk chair, abandoning all the precious work that earned me my promotion. For what?

To creep on some chick I'm technically not allowed to chase. Even if I'd met her before I created the Bastard Bachelor Society, I doubt I'd have pursued her.

Yet here I fucking am.

I stare at the intercom system, wondering where the hell Taylor is with the information I need. I can't sit here all damn day staring at the damn clock; I have actual work to do, and if any one of the partners walks in here, I'm in some serious—

"Got it!" Taylor breezes into my office, a yellow sticky note stuck to two fingers. Slaps it in the center of my desk.

"Jesus Christ!" He could have just given me a stroke.

"Your frown lines are going to give you wrinkles." His lips are pursed, eyes boring holes into my forehead.

"I think I can live with that." I pluck up the small square of paper. "Are you sure this is right?"

"Yes. It wasn't hard to find." Taylor leans against the corner of my desk, pencil eraser caught between his front teeth. "Is she a new client?"

I hesitate. "No?"

"Is she a personal project?"

"No!"

"Do you want her to be?"

"Christ. No. She's my neighbor."

"Oh, the plot thickens…" He leans closer, poking my mouse with the tip of his finger, powering up the monitor that had gone black. "Seems super un-neighborly to stalk your neighbor."

"It's not stalking. It's… I want to make sure she's not…" I pause, for lack of adjectives. "That she's not…" When I glance up into his smug face, my head shakes. "Stop making that face."

"What face?" He pulls it again.

"That face—the superior one like you know everything."

"Hey, I know nothing. All I did was get you the information you asked for. Because it's my job."

My eyes narrow suspiciously. "You googled her, didn't you?"

His only reply is a snarky grin.

Fuck.

"Can you get out of here?" I tell him unprofessionally, irritated that he's seen her background first. Because I couldn't figure out how to spell her fucking name and he could. I tack on a "Please" to soften the command.

Except the little bastard doesn't budge from his perch on my desk.

"Nah, I don't think I will. I want to watch your face."

"Why?"

Taylor gives the mouse another—we'll call it a *nudge*—prompting the computer to surge to life. "Go ahead. Abbott Margolis."

He slowly spells out her name, one letter at a time.

"Thanks—I got it. I'm not stupid."

His brows shoot up. *Then why did you need me to find the spelling for you?*

"Shut up, okay?"

Taylor pulls his pinched thumb and index finger across his lips: *My lips are sealed.*

"Was that one B or two?" I ask out loud, though her name is spelled out in front of me, very clearly. Neat and tidy, perfect block-letter penmanship.

The intern rolls his eyes heavenward, and I think it's the first time we've gotten this personal with each other. Which is good —really good. Building relationships at work is paramount and *focus on the task in front of you, asshole.*

"You can relax your face—having your eyebrows permanently stuck into your hairline will cause wrinkles."

Taylor frowns. "Funny. Quit stalling—I have a *billion* things to do."

"By all means, please go do them."

"And miss this chance to snoop?" His tone is indignant. "Pfft, I don't think so."

Abbott Margolis is the granddaughter of media tycoon Ambrose Narcisco Margolis, an immigrant of Greek decent who came to the United States in 1926 and made his fortune through the accumulation of newspaper, television, and magazine networks. Margolis' vast holdings include Margolis & Co., Margolis Worldwide LTD, and TriTelecom Media…

The article continues. Abbott went to the same university I did, weird coincidence. There are photos of her at black-tie events, at grand openings, and on expensive vacations. One or two publicity shots with animals at a shelter, but none of Desdemona.

"Abbott's middle name is Maureen?" I ask out loud, staring at the monitor.

"Uh…" Taylor's voice drags. "That's your takeaway from that article? Not the part about her grandfather being a tycoon or the fact that they practically own this entire city?"

He's being dramatic.

"Shit, look." Taylor's finger pokes at the screen, and I brush his hand away because he's blocking the words he wants me to read.

Abbott is a twin.

One of two fraternal twins, the only grandchildren of A. N. Margolis, they are the only children born to Gustav and Lidka Margolis. Abbott and her brother, Stuart, are both employed by Margolis & Co., located at 1611 West Broadway, Chicago, Illinois.

The article goes on to talk about her father, mother, and brother. Their birthdates. Other living relatives associated with the corporation. Where they attended college, where they're employed now.

"Gross. Talk about living in a fishbowl," Taylor finally says. "She's way out of your league."

He hasn't seen her in pajamas, sitting cross-legged on her couch, eating Thai food with her fingers, but—whatever. "We're not dating."

"Then why are you creeping on her?"

"I'm not."

His perfectly manicured brows shoot back up. "Then what's all this?"

My sigh is loud enough to wake the dead.

Taylor leans over, elbows resting on the desk in front of the computer monitor.

I click the browser window closed and shove back in my desk chair. "Don't you have shit to go do?"

"Yes, tons. Oodles of it. But this is way better."

"I don't need you hovering."

"Does that mean you plan to keep digging once I leave?"

No. *Yes.*

Maybe, but I wouldn't admit it out loud.

"No. I have shit to do, too." Shit involving this new development, because I have a meeting next week to present my ideas to the investors.

One day, I'm going to be the one building and investing in my own projects...

"Whoa, someone suddenly looks serious…"

I give him a look. "Are you still here?"

"You're the one who called me in to begin with."

"Right, but I've told you to leave twice."

"Not technically."

Jesus, this kid is worse than I was at his age, and I remember being a huge pain in the ass when I was an intern—but I don't think I would have sat and hassled a senior designer.

"You need to know when you're wearing out your welcome."

"I do, but you're being passive-aggressive and I'm taking advantage of your weakness."

"I'm being passive-aggressive?"

"Yes. Davis would have told me point-blank to get the fuck out."

Alex Davis is my peer, a talented architect, and quiet as a church mouse. No way in hell does he say things like 'Get the fuck out.'

"He talks like that?"

"Sometimes, yeah—when he's trying to get stuff done."

"Okay, well in that case, get the fuck out."

Taylor tilts his head. "It doesn't have the same impact when you say it."

"Get out!"

I need to be alone with this new information about Abbott. Answer a few emails, text a few people back.

I have my eye on a few acres in the country, just outside of town, for the four-wheeler I'm going to win once I'm the last man standing in this bet.

Which reminds me—I should see if the guys are free to get together for a drink at some point soon. Real soon.

I make a note on a sticky and slap it on the wall above my desk.

Taylor is hovering.

"Why are you still here?"

He chews on a fingernail. "Just checking to see if there was anything else you needed? Help doing some basic math, perhaps an estimate? A calculation or two…study for the spelling test?"

I present him with my back.

"How about a coffee run, then?"

This perks me up and, resigned, my shoulders sag. "Medium iced coffee?"

"On it." I hear him retreating.

"Hey Taylor?"

He pauses, footpads halting on the carpet.

"Thanks."

He smiles. I can't see it, but I can hear it in his steps as he bounds away.

Ugh. I hate when I'm nice…

* * *

"How's it been going?"

Phillip is the first person to speak when our asses are seated around our favorite table in The Basement, three cigars tucked inside the breast pocket of his sport coat, drinks already ordered.

We're all still dressed for work, having come straight from our offices, one week after the conception of the BBS.

"Shitty. My boss is being a fucker," Blaine bitches, studying a menu, eyes skimming the appetizers.

"Maybe he just needs to get laid," Phillip suggests, pulling the cigars out and setting them in the center of the table.

Blaine laughs. "He's got to be in his sixties—no *way* is he getting laid."

"Trust me," I argue, siding with Phillip on this issue, "that dude is getting laid. He's rich, drives a Bentley, and has a penthouse on the water."

"What do women call those?" Phillip stares up toward the ceiling, searching for the proper term. "Silver foxes?"

Blaine's face contorts. "Dudes, shut the fuck up."

I throw my hands up in surrender. *Don't shoot the messenger.*

"I'm being serious. You're probably getting less action than he is."

"That makes me want to throw up in my mouth. Think about how shriveled up his dick is."

"No, no—think about how shriveled *your* dick is going to look when you're his age," I suggest.

"My dick is never going to be shriveled!" Blaine pronounces, a bit too loudly for a guy who's still completely sober.

"Yeah, you're probably right—your dick is way too small to shrink. Did it actually fit inside Bambi?" I rub my chin, pondering.

"Fuck. You."

Not gonna lie, I've seen Blaine's dick, and it's embarrassingly small for a guy who claims to have fucked his way through the city.

"You should call your finance guy and invest in penis pumps —they always say you should invest in things you believe in and would use."

He scowls, slouching lower into his red, velvet-covered chair. "I hate you both."

"No you don't," I tell him matter-of-factly. "You hate your pee-pee."

"Can you please stop talking to me about my dick like I'm a child?"

Phillip sighs. "Fine. Let's talk club business."

"It's a *society*," I remind him, fully aware that my reminder is annoying and unnecessary. I'm right; they both glare.

"What I was saying was—I have something for you guys."

Blaine and I both lean forward because Blaine and I both like presents, watching, spellbound when Phillip reaches behind his chair and produces a brown paper bag.

"What's with the shopping bag?" Blaine immediately asks, impatient. As if we're going to be kept in suspense all night.

I shush him, excited.

"Who's ready to see the smoking jackets?" Phillip asks,

giving the paper bag a few squeezes. It makes a crinkling sound, squishing everything inside.

I scowl, not wanting my shit wrinkled, while Blaine enthuses, "Jackets already? Dang, I thought it would take a few weeks!" He reaches over and punches me in the forearm. "Maybe Lisbeth has a secret thing for you after all."

Phillip glares. "Shut the fuck up about that. He's not sleeping with my sister."

"Un*less* she wanted to sleep with me. Then I'd definitely bang her."

"No one is banging anyone in my family, you got it?"

"No."

"Do you want your fucking jacket?"

"Yes."

"Then shut the fuck up about it."

I cross my arms, pouting. "Fine."

"Now, as I was saying—"

"Drumroll please!" Blaine cannot contain himself, rolling his tongue and banging on the table with his index fingers like he's playing a set of drums.

The suspense is killing him.

"I want to punch you in the vagina so hard right now," Phillip threatens, all the wind sucked out of his sails.

I pop a walnut in my mouth and chew. "Now now, girls, violence is never the answer."

"Do you assholes want to see the jackets or not? Because I'm not going to sit here and—"

"Oh calm down," Blaine interjects. "You're so damn sensitive. Hurry up and show us. I'm tired of waiting."

If Phillip could shank someone with his eyes, Blaine would be dead on the ground, bleeding from a stab wound to the rib cage with no one to resuscitate him.

The brown paper bag sits on our friend's lap, stapled shut at the top and mocking us. This is the reason we're here—these jackets. This comradery. This group.

"I feel so much freer now that I don't have to worry about dating," my friend says, breaking the seal on the bag and peering inside. "These are so fucking cool."

"Didn't you check them out already?"

"Yeah, I was wearing mine last night," he admits.

"What the fuck!"

"What? I couldn't help it. Lisbeth had them shipped two-day air, and I couldn't resist." He lifts the first one out and strokes the velvet fabric. "They're so pretty."

They really are.

He holds it high, turning it to face us.

"She didn't have time to get the pocket embroidered—we can decide to do that once we have a logo or whatever."

Shit, we should probably have a list of things we need to do to run smoothly, but for now, having the jackets and a meeting location is enough. The rest can come later.

The jacket is blue, a deep navy velvet. Better than Hef's famous red one, with gold stitching lining the hem and the pocket on the right breast. Perfect for a cigar, a handkerchief, or condoms—for those of us who are actually having sexual relations.

I stand. Reach for the jacket and ask, "May I?"

It gets handed to me and I open it, sliding one arm in then the other, fabric gliding smoothly over my arm. The inside is satin—the same blue as the velvet—and cool to the touch.

"How did she get these so fast?"

"Don't know, don't care."

"How much?"

"Uh, I didn't ask. She said she'd invoice you."

My brows shoot up. "Me?"

"I mean, we'll split it, but yeah—she said she'd email you an invoice, including the cost to expedite procurement."

That bitch.

"So Lisbeth is bending us over." It's a statement, not a question, because his sister is bending us over and fucking us up the ass on the cost of these jackets. I would bet money on it.

I already have, in the form of my grandpa's season tickets.

"Basically fucking us up the butts."

"Lovely."

I slide my other arm in and adjust the garment over my dress shirt.

"Wow dude, that is so fucking neat. I wanna try mine on!" Blaine hops up out of his seat. "This is almost worth dumping my girlfriend over."

I glance at him over the sleeve of my sweet new smoking jacket. "How did that go over, by the way?"

"Not good—she was super pissed. Like, I thought I was going to have to file a restraining order." He's happily sliding into his coat. "She'll get over it."

Phillip is putting his on now, too. "I feel like all my problems disappear when I'm wearing this."

"Same," Blaine agrees. "We look so handsome."

"Where's a mirror? I wanna see what it looks like."

We abandon our seats in search of a mirror, locating one on the far end of the bar, affixed to the wall. The bartender eyes us with amusement as we shuffle to stand in front of it, squeezing in and fighting for room.

"Look at us. Just look." I gesture to our reflection, at how majestic we look, the three of us peacocking in our finery.

Murmurs abound.

"Damn we look amazing."

"You're one handsome devil, Brooks Bennett," Phillip tells me over my shoulder, standing behind me. Runs his hands along my shoulders, smoothing out the wrinkled fabric. "One sexy son of a bitch."

"I'd fuck you," Blaine decides out loud.

"I'd fuck you, too," I tell him.

"I'd fuck *both* of you," Phillip chimes in loudly. "And I'd fuck myself." He runs a palm slowly down his bicep, admiring his arms in the mirror, turning this way and that. "Look at this velvet. It's so silky smooth."

"Like a freshly waxed pussy," I agree, stroking my own chest.

"Nay," Blaine argues. "*Better* than a freshly waxed pussy."

The bartender clears his throat.

We stand idle, murmuring our approval at the fine fabric, the gorgeous cut and fit of our new smoking jackets.

"Philly, you still got those cigars?" I ask, never taking my eyes off my own reflection, hand tucked neatly in the breast fold, thumb exposed like I've seen a few royals do in the tabloids.

"I do."

I extend a palm. "Hand me one, would ya?"

Nearby, the bartender—who's obviously been eavesdropping on us this entire time—stifles our fun. "Gentlemen, there's no smoking in the club."

"It's fine. The only smoking he does is from out of his ass after sex," Blaine jokes, jostling me with a jab of his elbow. "Which is almost never."

"He's not a fan of the ladies." Phillip joins him in roasting me. "We're going to check his man credentials after this, as we're not sure there's anything between his legs anymore."

"What the fuck, you guys?"

"Men-only club—sorry, *society*. No dating. No women. No commitments." Phillip pops an unlit, uncut cigar between his lips and fingers the lapel of the jacket. Debonair and cool. Ticking off reasons he considers me a douche.

"Hey, we all decided to do this together—you wanted a jacket."

He touches his, lovingly caressing the precious material. "I do like it," he concedes with a smile. "I'm also gonna win me season tickets and a timeshare, *and* keep my four-wheeler."

"No you're not," Blaine counters. "I am. No one is getting my prizes."

"They're not prizes—they're incentives for following the guidelines set forth by the BBS." If I have to keep correcting them, reminding them what the club is for, I'm going to lose my mind. "Besides, I'm gonna buy me some land so I can drive my newly acquired four-wheeler on it."

That's how determined I am not to fail, and to remain solvent. My focus is on my job—and nothing else.

"Land? You're not serious."

"As a heart attack. Where else am I riding the damn thing? I can't drive it around the city—I'll get arrested." I turn my chin to the left. "Damn this color looks good on me."

"Don't do anything hasty. I broke up with Bambi, and Phillip here hasn't had sex in a *week*."

I roll my eyes. "You can have sex, dude. You just can't date the same person."

Phillip shrugs his shoulders. "For me it will be good not to mix those things up. Sometimes I confuse sex for affection, and if I get emotionally involved, then I lose."

That's true—he does confuse sex for affection more often than not. Once, he went on three dates with this girl Abby and when she passive-aggressively gave him the red light on any future, he thought there was still hope to win her back. All because she let it slip that she loved him while they were fucking —but then dumped him. Anyway, he chased her like she was his soul mate, making an ass of himself, concocting all these scenes to get her attention.

And they'd only gone out three times.

He puts his arm in the air, fist raised high. "Balls to the wall."

I put an arm around his shoulder and pull him in. "Balls to the wall, buddy."

8

ABBOTT

I love my grandmother.

I love my best friend.

What I don't love is having coffee with them at the same time.

I sigh, stirring a packet of artificial sweetener into my cappuccino, bored and deserted—at the moment, they're more interested in talking to each other than they are in talking to me.

I sigh again, louder this time, infusing the sound with a higher pitch so it travels.

"Alright." Nan sets her tea cup on its saucer, lips curved in a half-smile. "Is someone feeling neglected?"

She knows me too well.

Sophia reaches over and tweaks my cheek between two fingers, pinching it as if I'm a child and laughing at me. "Aww, you hate being ignored, don't you?"

Yes, and they both know it. "Y'all always do this when we go out."

"Well, Nan and I haven't seen each other since summer and we have tons of catching up to do, so stop pouting!" Sophia argues, snatching a macaron from the three-tiered tray in the center of the table.

We've gathered for tea—one of my favorite afternoon delights, Nan holding center stage—and I choose a few delicately decorated cakes and sandwiches to set on my plate.

Bite into the corner of a cucumber sandwich and die a little inside from how delicious it is.

Yum.

"Okay dear, tell me your news." Nan lifts her tea cup again and takes a dainty swallow.

"I don't actually have any news." I just wanted attention—is that so wrong?

"That's not true." Sophia gives me a meaningful look. Raises her brows and mouths, *Brooks.*

My head shakes. *No,* I mouth back.

Tell her, Sophia insists. *She's going to find out eventually.*

There is nothing to tell! I want to shout, because it's the truth. *WE ARE JUST FRIENDS.*

Sophia's palm hits the table. *Stop it.*

I scrunch up my face. *No, you stop it!*

"So, Abbott met a nice young man in her apartment building and they've been spending some time together, Nan."

Nan perks up, a pâté sandwich paused halfway to her lips. She returns it to her plate, removes the white linen napkin from her lap, and dabs at the corner of her mouth.

"A young man?"

I groan. "Thanks a lot, Sophia."

My best friend smiles happily and sets to stuffing tiny finger foods into her traitorous mouth.

Rude.

"There is no young man, Nan. Don't get your hopes up."

"But you *have* met someone?"

"*No.* It's just some guy who lives in my building—nothing more, nothing less."

"But he does live in your building." Semantics are not lost on Nan—she has a penchant for details and parsing out specifics.

"Lots of people live in my building, and some of them are male."

"Abbott Margolis, don't get cheeky."

"I'm not!" I say to her. Then to Sophia, I hiss, "This is all your fault."

Sophia shrugs, chomping on a miniscule slice of cheesecake. If anyone loves these little high teas more than me, it's my friend. She will drop everything to sip champagne and eat dessert, no matter the day of the week or the time of day.

"Does this neighbor have a name?"

"No." The last thing I need is my grandmother catching wind of any form of a relationship between Brooks and me. She'd latch on and start digging, drawing conclusions she has no business drawing since he and I only just met.

"His name is Brooks," Sophia says at the same exact time I deny Nan the information, and I groan. Damn her, she always does this!

"Brooks, hmm?" Nan sips her tea, the innocent expression on her face anything but innocuous, the wheels in her crafty brain no doubt spinning.

Nan cannot stay out of anyone's business; her business is meddling.

"Is he on your floor, or just in the same building?"

"I'm not sure."

Nan studies me above the rim of a champagne flute she's just lifted from the table, grasping the stem with two manicured fingers.

Narrows her steel gray eyes. "I don't know why you're being so tightlipped—it's not like I have any vested interest in the matter." She purses her lips and takes a sip of bubbly.

"If there was something to tell, I would tell you. Brooks and I are just friends—that's it."

My best friend gives my shin a swift kick and I flinch, my grandmother pretending not to notice any of our halted actions

—but the truth is, she has noticed everything, and she isn't going to let this go.

9

BROOKS

Abbott: *Hey buddy. Quick question.*

The text from my perky little neighbor comes first thing in the morning, on a Monday, my phone pinging on my desk as I drag a technical pencil along a giant sheet of drafting paper. Long, straight lines that will someday be an exterior wall are truly a thing of beauty.

I stare at the text, reading it again, the reason she nagged for my phone number last night now about to become clear.

Buddy? What the hell?

Granted, she's my neighbor—not really a friend, though if I had to guess, I'd say we're headed in that direction. Still. Being called buddy stings just a little, as if she doesn't think I'm sexy and doesn't want to bang me. No girl calls a guy bud or dude unless they are friend-zoning him.

Me: *What's up, bro?*

I chuckle at that and wish I could see her face to gauge her reaction.

Abbott: *I'll be gone the entire day today and have late dinner plans, so I have no idea when I'll be home. I put out enough food for Desi to graze, but if you could check on her to see if her water is clean, I'd be forever grateful.*

Abbott: *She's been an asshole the last few days, tipping the bowl over.*

Me: *The cat is an asshole? Shocker.*

Me: *I'd love to help you out, but how do you expect me to get into your apartment? I might be a magician, but I have no experience with breaking and entering. This isn't Harry Potter—I can't just walk through walls.*

Abbott: *INCIDENTALLY, I left you a key at the front desk...on the off chance you were available to pop in. If you're busy or won't be home, I totally understand. But if you could spare one hot second to check on the cat...*

Me: *That cat gets more attention than I do.*

Abbott: *Whose fault is that? Are you one of those guys who doesn't want a commitment but who also wants girls falling all over him?*

Yes. One hundred percent.

Me: *No.*

But yeah. Totally.

I've always been that way, since the day I discovered girls have tits, plus vaginas—and when I slid my dick into a vagina, it felt like nothing I'd ever experienced before. Heaven.

Orgasmic.

The problem was: no woman has ever made my heart feel the way her vagina did—all warm and tingly and euphoric and hard. Therefore, I've never wanted to commit myself to one woman.

I came close with Kayla.

Abbott: *So can you?*

Me: *Sure, why not? Just check the water, right?*

Abbott: *Yup, that should do it. Make sure Desi hasn't gone crazy, ha ha. KIDDING. She'll probably be sleeping in the window. If she doesn't run and hide when you walk in...*

Me: *Great. The cat's going to play hide-and-seek. As long as it isn't planning a sneak attack, I think I can suffer through three seconds of checking on her bowl.*

Abbott: *If you're tempted to play with her, I won't be mad.*

Me: *THAT'S not happening. Dream on.*

Abbott: *I figured, but just had to say it. I keep forgetting you're scared of a ten-pound cat.*

Me: *I'M NOT SCARED OF THE CAT!*

Even though I am scared of the cat, just a little. I don't trust the fucking thing. It looks like that damn cat from the movie where all the cats are evil and try to take over the world, whatever that stupid movie is called.

Abbott: *Thanks, Brooks. I owe you one. Next time you need someone to grab your mail or whatever, I'm your girl.*

If I ever went anywhere, yeah, that would be swell.

Me: *Don't worry about it. I'll grab the key and let myself in this afternoon.*

Abbott: *That's perfect!!! Thanks!*

I plunk the phone on my desk, upside down so there are no further distractions, and add *Check on Desi the Terror Pussy* to my ongoing list of shit to get done tonight.

Cat. Dinner. Laundry. Basketball game on TV.

Big night in, most likely with a set of blueprints and a bowl of popcorn.

No women.

No sex.

No distractions.

I stay productive most of the day and, at roughly three twenty-five, look at the clock then the side of my hand, which is covered in lead from sliding my fist over pencil markings. I push back my stool.

Stomach grumbling, I quietly put my things away, storing my expensive measuring devices and writing tools, and click off the light on my drafting table.

Grab my coat and give the room a once-over. Nothing amiss or out of place, I flip the overhead light off and call it an early day; I have a cat to check on.

Cutting out early isn't the norm for me, and a bit of guilt churns in my gut as I pass Taylor's desk.

"Oooh, going somewhere? A hot date you have to shave for?"

God this dude is so random.

"It's just been one of those days, so I'm checking out. I'll finish this up at home." I give the rolled paper, stored inside a hard tube and tucked under my arm, a solid pat. "Game is on tonight and I have some errands to run first."

"What kind of errands?"

My brows go up. What kind of errands does he think I'm doing? "The normal kind?"

"Like grocery shopping?"

"No."

Taylor narrows his eyes. "So like, the post office?"

Huh? "No."

"Grabbing your dry cleaning?"

"No." I sigh, setting down the plastic storage tube. "Why do you care?"

"I don't. I'm just curious."

That's caring. "If you really must know, I have to check in on my neighbor's cat."

He sits back in his rolling desk chair and crosses his arms. "You're running home two hours earlier than usual to check on a cat?" Now he's looking at his fingernails. "Don't cats usually fend for themselves or whatever?"

I thought so, too, but if Abbott wants me to check on McTerrorPussy and it only takes a few seconds, what's the harm in helping her out?

"It's not your average cat."

Taylor considers this information. Then, "Wait—is this your *neighbor* neighbor, or just a neighbor?"

What the hell is that supposed to mean? "It's a neighbor."

"Is this neighbor a man?"

Jesus, the way he says man makes me shake my head. "No."

"Is this neighbor a hot little brunette?"

Sigh. "Yeah, I guess."

"Doesn't she have, like, thirty servants to babysit the cat?"

"Because she's from a wealthy family? Her apartment is the same floor plan as mine."

With a better view, nicer appliances, more expensive furniture, and artwork on the walls that's probably authentic and not a bunch of knockoffs from a discount store.

Other than that…

Our shit is mostly the same.

Mostly.

"So you're racing home to watch her cat?"

"No, I'm going home because I'm tired and can work from my living room, and the basketball game is on tonight."

A pen materializes from nowhere and gets tapped against Taylor's pointy, intrusive chin. "You better be careful or you're going to end up falling in love with this girl."

That—that makes me laugh out loud, and the sound reverberates through the reception area with its polished marble flooring and tile walls.

"Take a picture of her apartment for me, would you?" Taylor's request has me scowling.

"What the fuck, dude—no."

"Bring me a lock of hair! Maybe I can become the next Margolis heir if I clone her."

That makes absolutely no fucking sense, but oddly enough, I kind of get where he's trying to go with that whole idea.

"Bye Taylor." I walk to the elevator bank and punch the down button with my knuckle.

"Take a mental picture at least. I'm going to have a million questions tomorrow—don't disappoint me."

"I'm sure I will." I'm sure Abbott Margolis has had people betraying her confidence her entire life; I don't need to be tacked on to the end of that list. Wouldn't want to be.

It's not that I'm feeling protective of her, but she's a nice girl. Clearly wants to fly under the radar, and I don't actually give a crap how or where she was raised as long as she acts like a decent human being.

Which she does.

So, I'm checking on her cat, following a twenty-five minute commute from the office.

After presenting my driver's license to the newbie manning the front desk in the lobby, I grab the key to her place and dump my work in my own place.

Change out of my work clothes, too, throwing on sweats, an NBA T-shirt, and flops. Pad across the carpeted hallway and let myself into Abbott's apartment.

The lock unlatches easily, and I turn the gold knob. Push the door slowly—not sure why. I know she's not home, but for some reason it feels like I'm about to invade her privacy. Her inner sanctum? It's weird, so I move slowly, not rushing.

I also kick my flops off because entering her place with shoes on also feels wrong?

Whatever.

"Here kitty, kitty."

Why the hell am I calling the cat? All I need to do is check its water bowl.

Wait—where is the water bowl?

I make my way toward the kitchen, head peering around the wall to the cozy galley, metal feeding bowls tucked neatly beneath the lower cabinets. One is full of food, the other…

Is empty.

A wet mess beside it.

Well shit, the little bastard did empty its water bowl—which has an engraved plate on it that reads *Duchess Desi.*

Groaning, I grab the hand towel that's hanging from the stove and lower myself to the ground so I can soak up the water. Just as I start swishing the terrycloth around on the sleek tile floor…

"Don't move, scumbag."

An older woman's voice from somewhere above me tries to sound menacing.

What the…

I turn my head to look over my shoulder.

"I said don't move! Are you hard of hearing?"

Seriously. What the actual fuck?

"Abbott sent me. Who the hell are you?"

This time I do turn around, standing in one motion, facing the intruder. A woman is standing in the doorway of the kitchen, holding a large glass vase in one hand, Desdemona tucked protectively under the other.

"Wait a second, are you *stealing* the damn cat?" I accuse, stepping toward the pair of them to snatch the purring feline.

Little traitor. Of course it's friendly with a thief.

Is this woman nuts?

She doesn't look like a nutjob, or a schizo. I've certainly never seen her in the building before—though that isn't saying much because I'd never laid eyes on Abbott until very recently, either.

"Am I stealing the—are you out of your mind?"

"Just give me back the cat and get the hell out of here before I call the police."

"I beg your pardon?" She is affronted, still holding the vase, still holding Desi.

"I *said*, give me the cat and I won't call the—"

"Young man, I'm not hard of hearing. Who the hell are you and what are you doing in my granddaughter's apartment?"

Granddaughter's apartment.

It's then that I really take a good look at the older woman. She's in her sixties or seventies, wearing an expensive baby blue suit. Striking silver hair that's been professionally styled. Large diamond rocks in her ears and…

My gaze travels south, to the hand cradling Desdemona.

Larger rock on her ring finger.

Shit. This must be a Margolis.

Maybe even *the* Margolis.

Fuck.

Shit.

"I'm here to check on the cat. Abbott won't be home until late." I root about in my track pants and produce the key. "See? I have a key."

Her perfectly manicured brows rise to her hairline. "You have a *key*?"

This information interests her, and she stoops, bending her

knees to a near curtsy to release Desi to the floor. The cat, being a snoop and in no rush to hurry off, sets its ass on the tile in front of Abbott's grandmother and stares at me along with her.

"She needed a favor."

"A favor?"

Why is she repeating everything in that weird tone—like everything I've just said is groundbreaking and intriguing?

You have a keeey?

A favorrrrr?

"Yes, ma'am."

The vase gets set down on the counter, and the woman leans a bouclé-covered elbow on the cold granite. "What's your name?"

"Brooks Bennett, ma'am."

Her regal head gives a nod. "I'm Nan."

"Nan—the giver of Sunday brunch and eggs Benedict." The words fly out of my mouth before I can stop them. Should I have said all that? Shit, what if she gets the wrong idea about what I was doing here Sunday morning? "I met Abbott in the hall the other day—I didn't spend the night." That sounds just as bad. "I mean…we just met Sunday. I didn't know her before that. We ran into each other in the hall and I invited myself in."

Creepy as fuck—that's how you sound, Brooks. What the hell? Get a damn grip.

A true interrogator, Nan looks on silently, letting me hang myself with the word vomit spewing from my mouth.

"We talked because I had breakfast here. I ate your food. I didn't just force myself in—she was going to invite me."

I think.

"I see." That's all Nan says, picking up the vase and disappearing back around the corner from where she came.

I follow and find her in the living room, setting the vase on a hutch, a small bouquet of freshly cut flowers resting on its surface.

Nan goes about arranging them like I'm not in the room, freaking the fuck out.

What's the big damn deal? Abbott has a grandma and she took you by surprise—so what? Get over it and get the hell out. Text Abbott that Nan took care of the cat and move on with your life.

Over and done.

"Are you going to stand there rudely with your hand down your pants or are you going to grab some of these and help me?"

Hand down my pants?

What the fuck.

Nan is no shrinking violet, nor is she a washed-up socialite.

"Sorry."

Nan hands me the stem of a daisy and says, "These are Abbott's favorite. They're small and white—dainty and petite, like she is. Not like the large Gerbera daisies that are more popular."

I'm not sure why she's telling me this, but I jam it inside the vase next to a pale, white rose.

Nan tsks, slapping my hand away. "Put some thought into it. Placed in the right spot, this little flower will shine."

Wait…is she actually talking about flowers? Because if not, that was one hell of a metaphor. For a split second, it occurs to me that she might be talking about her granddaughter. But what the hell do I know about anything?

"Now, tell me again what you're doing in the apartment, and how long you've had a key."

I'm scared to put the flower into the vase for fear I'm going to get rapped on the knuckles again. "Um." Tentatively, I fit it snuggly, sliding it in next to the roses. "Like I said, I'm here to check on the cat. Abbott has some dinner thing tonight and…"

"That cat is Satan," Nan murmurs, interrupting me, and I'm not sure if I'm hearing her quite right.

"Sorry?"

"I said—that cat is a menace. I can't believe the little terror let me pick it up." Nana searches the room, locates the cat on the dais, and glares. "I bought her that creature, and look how the little son of a bitch repays me."

Holy shit.

Whoa—I've never heard a grandma cursing this way, let alone one who looks like Grandma Margolis. Nana? Nan? Whatever her name is, she's one classy broad, and I can't believe she just called the damn cat a son of a bitch.

I laugh. "That's putting it mildly. I thought it was going to scratch my balls off the first time I was here."

"Oh? And when was this?" She's casual, nonchalant in a way that screams, *Give me all the details and don't leave anything out.*

"Last weekend, we bumped into each other for the first time in the hallway, and she had all this food so I weaseled my way into an invitation to eat most of it." I give Nan the side-eye.

Abbott's grandma nods and hums, not taking her eyes off the floral arrangement. "Then what?"

"Then…um…" I rack my brain for some details. "Then this morning she texted me to ask if I could come check on the, uh —Pussy of Terror, and I wasn't busy so here I am."

There. I said it. I threw down the P word to get a reaction from Nan, and now I wait to see how she responds.

A smile tips the corners of her maroon-lined mouth, and another chuckle escapes her lips. "I like that. Very clever."

Clever? More like vulgar, but whatever—I'm not going to argue with the matriarch of a powerful American family. I'm a moron sometimes, but I'm not a complete idiot.

"So, you're here delivering flowers…?"

Nan places the last one, stepping back to survey her work. "I was in the neighborhood, so I thought I'd stop by."

"And you have a key."

"That little detail can stay between you and me, can't it?"

"Nan! You sneak! Are you telling me Abbott doesn't know you sneak in here?"

Nan shrugs. "She must know—how do you think she

supposes flowers just appear?" She fluffs the arrangement. "Elves? Please, don't be foolish."

"How often do you pop in like this?"

Now she turns to face me. Narrows a set of brilliantly blue eyes. "Are you suggesting I pop in unannounced when I'm not welcome?"

"What? No!" I mean, kind of, yeah. "What if she's—you know…getting busy and you walk in?"

Nan scoffs, hefting the full vase off the hutch. "My granddaughter does not get busy."

"How do you know?"

"*Please*—I would know." Her tone is offended as she pads across the room in heels, setting the flowers in the center of the small dining room table. "Besides, if she were getting busy, she wouldn't need all those toys in her bedside table, would she?"

Did she just say Abbott has toys in her bedside table?

Like—as in, sex toys? Vibrators and dildos and shit? There is no way her grandmother would just let that fun fact slip, and she should definitely stop using terminology like 'getting busy' before my brain explodes from this entire conversation. It's too much to hear the words coming from this woman's mouth. But then…the rest of what she just divulged clicks in my brain. I stare, mouth gaping.

"Who do you think bought them?" She fluffs her coiffure, plopping down on one end of the sofa and crossing her legs. "I'm not just a regular nan. I'm a cool nan."

Okay, *now* my jaw is dropping. She *bought* her granddaughter sex toys? What the hell kind of grandma is this?

Eyes stray down the hall, toward the bedroom… I want to know what's in that bedside table.

"Sit," she demands, pointing to the opposite end of the couch. "Let's talk."

Let's not. Nan isn't the boss of me. I do what I want.

"Sit," she repeats.

I sit.

"So. Brooks." Her fingers entwine, resting on her knees. "You live across the hall?"

"Yup, directly across—Abbott has the better view." Ha ha.

Nan's smile is slow. "Indeed."

Um…

"What is it you do?" Her features are sharp and directed straight at me. "Please don't tell me you're a travel blogger, or in finance."

My posture straightens. "I'm an architect."

"Ah!" She's delighted. "Residential or industrial or…"

"Mostly hotels, resorts. High-rise apartments. Some neighborhoods." Why do I feel like I'm being interviewed?

"Any pets?"

"No."

"How do you feel about cats?"

We both look at Desi. "They're tolerable." At best.

"Are you seeing anyone?"

This makes me laugh, and before I can stop it, a loud one bursts out of me. "Uh—no."

"What's so funny about that?"

"Um…nothing?"

Nan sinks lower into the cushions of Abbott's couch, taking me in. "Ah, I see. You're one of those confirmed bachelors who has no intention of settling down." She plucks an imaginary piece of lint from her expensive suit jacket. "Well." She waves her manicured hand around dismissively, diamond ring sparkling, bracelets jingling. "No matter."

No matter? *What does that even mean?*

Nan is a piece of work.

"I don't want a girlfriend." Been there, done that.

"No one really does, darling." Nan smiles, but she's patronizing me. "You young people and your ambitions. So admirable."

Don't get your hopes up, lady. I'm not a piece of meat dropped onto a plate for your precious granddaughter.

"I *don't* want a girlfriend." I cannot stress it enough. And, technically, I can't have one. So even if I met someone right now, I couldn't do it—I'd lose my inheritance. Er, Jags seats.

I change the subject. "What does Nan stand for?"

She stares at me like I have half a brain. "Nana. Grandma. Granny." She's listing off all the synonyms for grandmother, and a slow heat creeps up my neck, to my cheeks, because I should have known better than to ask. Now she must think I'm a fucking idiot. "Gram-Gram. Nanna Banana."

Alright, alright. I get the point.

"When Abbott and her twin brother—did you know she's a twin? Anyway, when they were toddlers, Abbott refused to call me Grandma. For whatever reason, she couldn't say it. Glamma was also a big no, no matter how hard I tried to make that happen. So we came up with Nan."

Nan is definitely a badass Glamma, that's for damn sure.

* * *

THE LOUD KNOCK ON MY APARTMENT DOOR HAS ME listening for another, the water from the sink in my bathroom almost drowning the sound out.

I cut the water and strain.

Another knock.

Wiping the toothpaste off my face with the back of my sleeve, I weave through the apartment and yank the door open without looking through the peephole to see who's on the other side.

Abbott stands there, wearing the same pink yoga pants she had on this weekend, bottle of wine in one hand, glass in the other.

Whoa. I didn't realize she was a lush.

I move so she can scoot through.

"So, this is where you live?" She strolls inside like the Queen of Sheba, head craning this way and that, giving all my dumb shit a once-over.

I bow with a dramatic flair. "Do come in."

She ignores my over-the-top gesture, still glancing around. "What are you up to?"

"Watching the game." Brushing my teeth, getting ready for bed, snacking, scratching my balls—the usual.

"We should go to one." Her comment is offhanded as she fingers a vintage baseball, signed by the championship-winning '82 Jags.

"We should?"

"Yeah. I love watching baseball, especially at the ballpark. Don't you?"

"Sign me up. I love the Jags stadium."

I fail to reveal I have season tickets. I fail to mention the Bastard Bachelor Society bet, in which my season tickets are bounty, up for grabs. I fail to mention that my tickets are pretty decent seats, considering my humble roots.

"My company has a box suite I can probably get permission to use."

Never in my life have I been invited to watch a baseball game from one of those fancy, company-owned suites you always see on TV when the games are being televised, and I'm not stupid enough to pooh-pooh Abbott's offer to sit in one despite owning my own seats. Just once in my life, I want to know what it's like to be in one of those sky boxes, from the vantage point where I can see everything inside the stadium. All the action. Each and every play.

"The kind of suite with food?"

"Yes, there's always food."

"Is it free?" What can I say? I'm cheap and love a handout.

"Yes." She laughs. "I mean, the company has to pay for it, but yes, it's free." She makes air quotes around the word free and pads to my kitchen with bare feet. Sets her bottle of wine on the counter and pops open the fridge, digging around, finally settling on a container of cottage cheese (so random) that's probably expired and a half-eaten jar of peaches—also probably expired. "You don't have shit for food in here."

"I know. That's why I need *your* free food. Also, be careful—you'll most likely get salmonella from what you're about to eat. This is your fair warning in case you get it in your head to sue me for food poisoning."

"Har har." Abbott moves to the living room, makes herself at home on the couch, even going as far as covering herself with one of the few throw blankets I have lying around.

"Make yourself at home."

"Aw, thanks." My remote control is in her hand and she's pointing it at the television, about to change the station. *What the hell!*

"When I said *make yourself at home*, I didn't say change the damn station." In three strides, I'm taking the remote back, burying it beneath a couch cushion like a squirrel stashing a nut; I'll probably regret the move later when I have no fucking idea where it disappeared to, but for now, it works. "How was dinner?"

"Long and boring." She yawns and stretches, the motion pulling the fabric of her top taut across her breasts. "You know how those things go—everyone older talks over you, and everyone else just pretends to know what the hell they're talking about. That whole *fake it till you make it* bullshit the company is filled with." She stretches again, arms lifted above her head.

Avert your eyes, asshole.

"So I'm stuck in between these blowhards—one called me *Kid* four times—and the other…" She shrugs, peeling back the foil top of the cottage cheese, then licks her fingers. "The other one kept elbowing me in the boob."

I eye up her boobs.

"Stop looking!" The blanket gets pulled up further, a shield against my suddenly perverted eyes. Guess nothing is safe when you haven't had sex in ages. "Jesus, this is my safe place."

Her safe place? I don't even know what that means. "What the heck does that mean?"

"It means I came over here because I wanted company and I know I don't have to worry about you hitting on me because we're just friends."

Well fuck.

Friend-zoned?

I already decided to friend-zone her—where does she get the audacity to friend-zone *me*? Doesn't she realize the pecking order here? It starts with me. Me, at the top, hen-pecking away and deciding who gets what.

I do the zoning in my relationships. Me.

Not her.

I open my mouth to argue but am immediately silenced because a spoon is jammed into my mouth, laden with cottage cheese and peaches, and I sputter, caught off guard.

"Taste this—isn't it good?" I have no choice but to chew and swallow, choking down the combination of mealy and fruity with a grimace on my face.

"What the fuck, Abbott? Warn a guy before you jam something down his throat."

"Why? Guys never warn you before they try jamming their business all the way down your throat during a blow job."

Whoa, whoa, whoa—holy fuck now. What?

Abbott doesn't see my shocked expression because her gaze is fixated on the game that's playing on television. First she friend-zones me, and now she's casually bringing up blowies after ramming food into my gullet?

Who is this chick?

Her cute little feet go up on my coffee table, the fuzzy slippers she just slid on winking at me.

She wiggles her toes.

"So what about you—why are you still home?" Her question is half-assed, arbitrary, just making conversation. "Don't you ever go out?"

When I don't respond, she glances at me across the silence.

"Of course I do. Don't you?"

"I went out tonight."

"Yeah, with work people. I bet the average age was 35 to 40, and don't lie and say it wasn't."

"Fine. I won't lie and say it wasn't. Besides, I already told you everyone there was way older. But it still counts because I went out and I didn't *want* to."

"So that doesn't count."

"How does that not count as going out? It was a bar! We had drinks! I am half-baked!" She holds up the cottage cheese, giving the container a little shake, as if her bad choice in snacks has anything to do with her sobriety. She lowers it. "Why is it such a big deal that I like staying home? I have all my crap here." She spreads her arms wide to emphasize her point.

"This is my apartment," I remind her.

"Mi casa es su casa."

"My house is not your house."

"Mi stuff es su stuff."

"Knock it off—my stuff isn't your stuff, either."

"Eh." She readjusts her feet. "We're franz now. This is how we roll."

"This is *not* how we roll. Leave my shit alone." Now I'm irritated. "Take your feet off the coffee table, and stop saying we're friends."

"I'm wearing slippers. Stop being weird."

"You can't take my shit, and you can get your feet off my table. Have some manners."

She pulls her feet off the furniture. "Why are you being such a baby all of a sudden?" Her food gets set on the table and she turns to face me on the couch with a pouty huff. "You don't have any shit I want anyway. It's all boring guy junk."

"Good." Jeez, if this chick makes me roll my eyes any more than I already have, my eyes are going to get stuck upside down in their sockets.

Abbott folds herself up on the couch like a pretzel, holding her knees, snuggling under the blanket. "So, what about you?"

"What about me, *what*?"

"Don't you, I don't know, date and stuff?"

The way she says *and stuff*… "Yes, I date and stuff."

"Oh." She fidgets with the ends of the blanket, pulling at the strings one by one, rubbing the soft fleece between her forefinger and thumb. "When's the last date you were on?"

"I don't remember."

"If Brooks Benny was going on a date, where would he take her?" She shortens my last name from Bennett to Benny and it's kind of cute. Kind of.

"Just for drinks. Nothing fancy."

"Why?"

"Because if it doesn't work out, I haven't blown a wad of cash on dinner. That's guy code."

"That's…terrible. If I'm going out with someone, I want them to make an effort."

"Yeah, well—we're probably not running with the same caliber of people."

She pulls back, confused. "What does that mean?"

"We pull from a different pool of people." I reword the sentence, as if the point I was trying to make was obvious.

"I still don't get it."

I sigh, hating that I have to be blunt. "Abbott, I googled you —I know who you are and where you come from, and I know you don't just hop on a dating app to find a date. You probably date trust fund babies and hedge fund managers, not someone you've swiped right on."

Her pretty face contorts. "First of all, stop judging me. I hate when people do that—you know nothing about me. Second of all, those are the furthest thing from my type. Gross."

"So what is your type?"

"I don't really have one. All I can say is I usually meet people the old-fashioned way, at a coffee shop or whatever."

"When's the last time someone took you out for dinner and not just for drinks?"

She studies her fingernails. Tonight, they're a metallic gold. Flashy and so unlike her. One delicate shoulder lifts and falls. "Three months ago?"

"Say that louder. I thought you just said three months ago."

"I did." Her eyes are glittery daggers. "So what if it's been a while? I've been busy." She graces me with a quick once-over. "What makes you the damn expert on dating? You're not even seeing anyone."

"Let's just say I haven't had any complaints, even if I've only had one- or two-night stands in the past few months." To take the edge off. Meaningless sex with women who meant nothing to me. Women I slept with hoping I'd feel something.

"Um…"

"I know what women want," I pronounce arrogantly, because let's face it—I know what women want.

Abbott laughs, falling back against my couch, the loud cackling sound coming from her throat an insult to my ego. God she's being such an asshole.

"What's so damn funny?"

"You. Did you just say *I know what women want?*" Her voice lowers as she mimics my masculine voice. "Like, did those words actually come out of your mouth?"

"Stop making fun of me. I have a proven track record."

"Oh, you have a proven *track* record!" She finds this so amusing she has not stopped laughing at my expense. "Is that a fact? How so?"

"The last two women I had drinks with wanted to marry me, so…*yeahhh.*"

Abbott reaches behind her and lobs a pillow in my direction. It misses my head, but only by a fraction of an inch.

"They did *not* want to marry you." Her disbelief wounds me.

I pretend I didn't hear her, hand shooting up as if I'm swearing an oath in front of Congress. "Scout's honor."

"You can't say Scout's honor unless you were an actual Scout." She studies me, head tilted. "Were you?"

"No." My parents couldn't afford the small fee it cost to join.

"Well then, it can't be true. You were never a Scout, so…"

God, I just want to wipe that smug look off her damn face.

"For your information, smartass, I have the Nan stamp of approval." I throw down, no longer fucking around. For whatever reason, talking about relationships with Abbott and the kinds of dudes she does and doesn't date has me feeling some kind of way—and I'm not loving how my stomach is churning at the moment.

That has her attention. "Say again?"

"I have the Nan stamp of approval."

"What the heck does that mean?"

"It means, I met your nan, and your nan loves me." I deliver this news as casually as possible, but deep down inside, I'm doing a celebratory dance, jumping and leaping on the couch and bouncing on the cushions, because the *look* on her face is priceless.

Disbelief and annoyance and bewilderment.

Translation: Abbott is not a happy camper.

"When? *How*?" I can see clear up her pert little nose, her nostrils are that wide from flaring. "Is that where the flowers in my apartment came from? Was Nan there today?"

"A magical elf sure as shit didn't bring them." And it sure as hell wasn't me.

Oh shit. She didn't actually think I brought flowers when I went to check on the cat, did she? She had to know that ridiculous arrangement, which must have cost a bundle, did not come from me. Right?

Oh shit. Maybe she did think they were from me.

Abbott's beautiful face blanches. "Oh."

Yeah, *oh*.

Fuck. Now I feel doubly terrible, though I did nothing

wrong—except break Nan's confidence by telling Abbott her grandmother let herself into the apartment.

"Did you know your nan has a key?"

"Yes, of course. Everyone has a key." She rolls those blue eyes. "Though Nan is the only one who lets herself in unannounced. She thinks I don't know—as if I wouldn't notice a stocked refrigerator, or new decorative pillows on my bed." A delicate snort escapes her nose. "She tries so hard to be sneaky, and I pretend not to notice."

"Why is she always stopping by? You're a grown-ass woman."

"True. I think she just wants to feel relevant. Needed? Her children are all grown and she has all these big, empty houses. I don't think her friendships are… They're the society type. Fake. Botoxed." My neighbor leans forward to retrieve her cottage cheese and spoons a mouthful. Chews.

Swallows.

"It's not just me. Nan's best friend has a granddaughter, who's also in the city, and Nan breaks into her pad, too." Her back presses against the couch cushions and she props her feet up, barely sparing me a glance. "Basically she steals keys, gets copies made, and breaks into our places. My brother has a house in the burbs and she does the same shit to him, too. We all just look the other way. It's cute. I've never had her bust in on anyone, though. What did she do?"

"She was going to crack my skull open with your vase."

"Tiny Nan?"

"Tiny Nan would have clocked me good—I could see it in her beady eyes." I put my feet up too, the charade of being clean and tidy and proper long gone out the window. "But she was holding the cat under her arm, so if I had seriously been robbing your place, she wouldn't have stood a chance with the one-armed vase toss."

"She was holding the cat?"

"Yeah—protecting it or whatever."

Abbott covers her mouth with a hand. "Holy Hannah, that is so cute."

"That cat is not cute."

"I'm not talking about the cat—I'm talking about the fact that my grandma was protecting the cat from a robber. If that were me, I would be all, 'Every man for himself! Deuces, Fluffy.'" Her hand rises and makes a peace sign.

"Seriously? You'd abandon your beloved cat?"

I can't believe what I'm hearing.

Pampered Desi McTerrorPuss, left to fend for herself?

"My cat would have been fine. I've seen her fly into defense mode. Actually, the more I think about it, the more I'm convinced Desi would hide in a closet. Either way, she would have been safe."

She talks about that cat like it's a human being, but what I really want to nag her about is her grandmother. "Enough about the cat. Don't you think someone in your family oughta have a talk with her about safety?"

Abbott chuckles. "Don't be so naïve. My grandmother knew exactly who she was going to find when she snuck into my apartment."

"Who did she think she was going to find?"

Abbott levels me with a stare. "You."

10

BROOKS

"Mr. Bennett! Mr. Bennett!" My name is being called as I march through the lobby of my building and pass by the security guard at the front desk.

I hesitate, unsure. Mr. Bennett? Surely he isn't speaking to me. My office is in a high-rise, located in the heart of the city, eighteen stories up—I've never met the doorman, the security officer, or anyone who works on the ground floor. The fact that one of them is calling my name gives me pause, and I spin on my heel, questioning.

"Me?" I point to my chest like a goddamn imbecile.

The man is dressed in a navy officer uniform, security patches emblazoned on his chest and biceps, his hat dipping low over his heavy brow.

Portly, sweating, and gesturing me over with a few meaty fingers.

"Good morning, sir."

"Good morning?" I wish he'd get to the point before my heart rate accelerates to an even more rapid pace.

"Are you Brooks Bennett, sir?"

Every time he calls me sir, my posture straightens and my chest puffs up with a bit more importance. I shift the weight of the blueprint I'm squishing under my armpit and stick it under the opposite arm.

"I am."

"Would you mind showing me some form of ID? We have a package here for you."

That's weird—I don't remember ordering anything…

My arm goes to the back pocket of my pressed gray slacks, and I pull out the black leather billfold holding my driver's license, slide it out. Flash it at the security guard and wait a millisecond while his eyes flit back and forth between my photo and my face.

"Thanks. Give me one second."

He disappears for a brief moment, reappearing from the storage room behind the front desk with a package, setting it on the counter.

Package indeed.

Not in a postal envelope or standard-issue box, this delivery isn't something that was mailed to me. Guarantee it was hand-delivered. It's not wrapped in discreet brown paper and taped up, nor is it slapped together haphazardly. Nope. This box is black *lacquer*, a high gloss, with nothing but my name and place of employment handwritten in gold, metallic ink.

What the…

"Hell is this?"

The man shifts on his feet, and now he's staring at it too. "I wouldn't know that, sir."

Yeah, no shit. I'm aware that you don't know what it is—the question was rhetorical.

He watches, anticipation evident on his face, but I'm about to disappoint him.

"Thanks. I'll take this to my office."

"Very good, sir." Okay, now he sounds like a butler from the Plaza, or like he's on one of those shows about a British household with all the servants…what's it called? Bromton Dabbey?

Whatever. It's boring.

I pluck up my box, surprised to discover how light it is. Give it a shake.

Not much jiggles around on the inside, so lacking in weight or sound there's a possibility it's completely empty. I won't know until I make it to my desk, so I hustle, making haste to the elevator banks, down the hall past Taylor's prying eyes, and shut my door like a rat about to devour a stolen sewer cake.

I pry the top off slowly, prolonging the inevitable, relishing the fact that I have an unexpected present, something I almost never receive, not even during the holidays.

We never had the money.

We were that family who needed assistance from their electric company so the power wasn't shut off for an unpaid bill. We were that family who was adopted by other families during the holidays, except I never received toys. It was always socks and shirts and pajamas. Shit we needed, never anything we wanted—which I understand now that I'm an adult, but I resented it as a child.

So I take my time, loving every second of this moment, a grown man with a valuable prize, a beggar on the street hoarding his possessions.

My hand riffles through gilded tissue paper, feeling around for the treasure buried at the bottom of the sea. With every unfruitful swipe, my hopeful little heart loses some steam.

Until.

The tips of my fingers hit a hard square—an envelope? I grasp at it, pulling it through the paper, shaking it loose as tissue falls.

It's a gift card for one of the most expensive restaurants in town, a place impossible to procure a reservation at. Along with that, there's a gift card for SmithStone's.

The sums are embarrassingly high, and I shift uncomfortably in my chair, unsure about how I should react. I can't call anyone to thank them. I can't call anyone and tell them the gift is too much—not just the amounts but the whole gesture.

There is no enclosure card. No note. No sender.

Nan.

Has to be. No one else would send a gift card in this amount; it's beyond ridiculous, and I only know one person this extra. Well, besides Lisbeth, Blaine's sister who hates me and was able to get us the smoking jackets.

Why?

Why would Nan do this?

I barely know the woman—I barely know *Abbott.*

It takes me no time at all to google her now that I have the proper spelling of her name, the yellow sticky note Taylor scribbled it down on still stuck to my computer monitor.

No time at all and I'm looking her up in the company directory at Margolis & Co. No time at all and her secretary—yeah, she has her own fucking secretary—is putting me through.

"Abbott Margolis speaking." Her voice is crisp and professional, though there is no doubt she knows it's me. I wouldn't have gotten through to her otherwise. All her calls are screened.

I don't waste time with idle pleasantries.

"I think your nan sent me something."

"How did you get this number?" I can hear her eyes narrowing at me, imagining she's toying with the phone cord, seated behind her desk. Maybe chomping on a bagel since it's early and she seems like the type to grab and go.

"You're so hard to find? *Please.*" I scoff at the notion.

She hmphs, ignoring me, then I hear her swallow. "I'm sorry, you were saying something about Nan sending you something?"

"Yeah—I got a package at my office, and I'm pretty sure it's not from you."

"Don't insult me." Abbott snorts. "I'm not above sending people random gifts—but you're right, this one definitely is not from me."

This piques my interest, and I latch on to the idea of her sending me something. "So what you're saying is you'd send me a present."

"That's not at all what I said. Would you please focus and tell me what was in the box?"

"Can't." I throw a paper airplane into my wastebasket. "You already said you're not above sending me nice gifts." I pause as it hits the wall and lands on the floor. "What kind of nice gifts?"

"Your ego couldn't handle me sending you something thoughtful. I'd never hear the end of it."

"That's not true—no one ever gives me anything, so I doubt I'd be a dick about it."

"Well, *some*one did—probably my nan. So…what is it?"

"I think she's my nan, too." I crack the lid on the box and peer inside.

"Did you just call her *your* nan?"

"Yup." I pop the *P* for effect, knowing it's going to irritate the piss out of her.

I hear her lips purse. "You're ridiculous."

"I've been called way worse."

"Oh my God, Brooks, would you tell me what she sent you? I have actual work to do!"

Jesus, why's she getting all pissy? "Patience! Patience…"

"I'm *literally* going to choke you."

"I'll choke you if you want me to. All you have to do is ask." I smirk and palm the gift card in my right hand, thumb pressing into the outer corner.

"Shut up."

"Did you just roll your eyes at me?"

A soft chuckle reverberates on the other end of the line. "I might have."

She totally did.

Adorable.

I haven't known Abbott long, but I'm already well aware of her many tells:

1. When she's frustrated, she tells me to shut up.
2. When she thinks I'm amusing but doesn't want to admit it, she rolls her eyes.
3. When she's trying not to laugh at me, she snorts.
4. When she's trying not to touch me, she puts something in her mouth…

Speaking of putting something in her mouth…

I squirm at my desk, lifting my ass so I can readjust the crotch of my slacks, then settle back into the conversation. I already know Nan likes me—as evidenced by the polished black box sitting in the center of my desk.

It's her granddaughter I'm not sure about.

Women don't usually treat me like this, even women I have no interest in. Typically they're more…shit, what's the word I'm looking for? Needy? Clingy. Fake. Coy. They play hard to get, but I'd bet money that's not what Abbott Margolis is doing. No—this girl is all class, and for whatever reason, she's not romantically into me.

I can't recall a time I haven't been able to make a girl wet for me, and I wonder how long it would take with my neighbor.

Stop, Brooks—fucking around with the girl who lives directly across the hall is the dumbest thing to enter your mind.

Fine, so maybe it's not the dumbest idea I've ever had—there have been plenty of others. Like the time when I was sixteen and found a wad of cash in my mother's rusted coffee can. A few boys and I took ourselves down to the seedy strip club in town, an old, converted warehouse where they'd let anyone through as long as they had money in their pockets. It smelled like stale beer, cigarettes, and disappointment.

I took that wad of cash and got a flash of my first pair of tits that day—then got grounded and received a beating for my efforts, too.

My parents had needed that money, and I'd spent it on strippers.

But come on, I was sixteen—where else was I going to get the opportunity to see boobs? I was a late bloomer, not coming into my own until college. Skinny, lanky, and awkward with plenty of acne, the unhealthy cafeteria food at university bulked me up in no time. The freshman fifteen done my body good.

"Brooks? Are you there?" There's a pause. "Hello?"

"Huh?"

"Honestly, Brooks, you called me—not the other way around."

"Shit. Sorry, I just remembered something."

"Mm-hmm." She hums into the receiver, the sound amplified by the old-school telephone system.

"Right. The package—sorry." I spin in my swivel chair, replacing the gold tissue paper and putting it back inside with an "*Ooh*" and an "*Aah*." There. All pretty again.

Abbott sighs. "Don't just moan into the phone like a creep, dammit—tell me what it is!"

I'm taken aback. "I sounded like a creep? Dang, I thought I was being sexy." For real though.

"Not even a little." There's a tapping noise, as if Abbott is smacking a pencil against the surface of her desk. "If that's your idea of sexy, it's no wonder you're single."

Now is not a good time to mention the Bastard Bachelor Society, and if she's hoping to sink her female talons into a guy, she has a better chance with someone else. This gentleman is unavailable for courtship.

"I must be losing my touch."

"You had a touch? Huh. *Weird.*"

"Is it necessary to be such a smartass?"

"I don't know, is it?"

"Stop doing that."

"Doing what?"

"Answering a question with a question."

"I only did that once."

Once was enough. "What are you doing for dinner tonight?"

There, I changed the subject, knowing she loves to eat and loves to talk about food.

"Leftovers, probably."

"What kind of leftovers?"

"I don't know, maybe the chicken I had at dinner the other night. I might fry that up with some eggs and whatever vegetables I can find."

"That sounds disgusting."

"No it doesn't! It's literally all chicken by-product and vegetables, you moron."

"It's not fresh. Nan got me gift cards for SmithStone's and another one for Flocke and Brow, so I'd rather eat that."

Abbott emits a low, impressed whistle. "Oh, so you're a snob now?"

Do I sound like a snob because I don't want her leftovers? Probably, but blame it on a lifetime of being hungry and not having enough to eat. In a way, I feel entitled to be a picky eater now that I can afford groceries.

"No, I'm not a snob—just not in the mood for leftovers, that's all."

"Oh, now that you have those gift cards burning a hole in your polyester pockets, you're hot shit, eh?"

I glance down at my lap, at the gray slacks I had professionally altered and that cost more than I used to make in a week working at the coffee shop near campus when I was still a student. "These are a wool blend."

"Brooks, I'm only teasing. If you want to have dinner with me, just say so." I can practically hear her twirling her hair.

"I don't want to have dinner *with* you." Can't. "But since we both have to eat, we could do it in the same room."

"Wow. How romantic."

"I'm not asking you on a date." How can I make this any clearer? "I just don't want your slim offerings."

"I wasn't offering to feed you! Not once! You asked what I had planned for dinner and I told you I was having leftovers.

Stop twisting everything I say to suit your goals. And if you want me to come over for dinner, just say so."

"I don't want you to come over for dinner."

"Okay then. I won't."

I hesitate, feeling like a world-class dipshit. I mean, she's amazing and I love spending time with her—is it necessary for me to completely shut her out? After all, can't we all use a few good friends?

Plus, her apartment is better than mine; her fridge is completely stocked, thanks to our nan; she has fresh flowers so it smells really good; and her view is insane.

Barring that horrible fucking cat, her place wins top prize in every category.

"Should we order food and eat it at your place? I have these gift cards—go online and pick something out."

"Are you telling me what to do? You're so bossy."

"Do you want mystery chicken combo, or do you want Flocke and Brow?"

"Do you honestly think *that* place is going to deliver?" Abbott snorts again—so unladylike. "You're out of your mind."

"Please. I intend to drop Nan's name all over town like a bad habit—dinner will be on your doorstep at six."

"Are you sure you wouldn't rather use the gift card to go to the actual restaurant instead of eating at home? Where's the fun in that?"

She has a good point, but I'm about to make a better one. "Because I'm all peopled out and you make me laugh."

I can see her defenses melting like warm butter on a hot summer day. I hear her smile. "Make it seven and you have yourself a date."

"You have yourself a *deal*, not a date."

"Sure, surrre, whatever you say, lover boy."

Fuck. "No flirting tonight. We're just friends, remember?" She's the one who said it, not me, and it's best that I remind her of that. Shit—it keeps me in check, too.

Abbott is funny, cute, successful—it would be too fucking easy to fall in love with her...

"If you keep bossing me around, I'm going to put the cat on your lap when you sit down."

I hiss. "You wouldn't dare."

"*Try me.*"

11

ABBOTT

Brooks arrives before the food does, and Desdemona and I are on the couch when the first knock of the evening sounds through my compact but stylish apartment.

I breeze down the little hallway, checking my reflection in the mirror hanging above the small table I normally use for my keys, mail, and purse. My dark hair is down, wavy, and looks amazing against my baby blue sweatshirt. It's velvet and ridiculously soft, so—not your average sweatshirt, but casual enough that it doesn't look like I'm trying.

I've thrown on a pair of dark, charcoal gray leggings. They have a hint of sheen and are skintight. Bare feet.

He's not going to notice what you're wearing, Abbott. Why did you even bother? Nervously, I push my hair behind my ears. It's *meh*. Pull it back down, giving it a fluff. A few strands fly up from static, and I curse. "Stop. He's going to know you were fussing."

Why am I fidgeting? It's just Brooks.

Just Brooks? Is there such a thing?

Brooks is clever and…

…and has my stomach twisting into a knot. I take a few breaths as I continue fretting in the mirror, running a hand down my silky hair, finger combing it for the umpteenth time. Ruffle it to give it volume. Smooth it back down.

"*Ugh!*"

Okay, so he's not *ha ha* funny, and let's get real here—he's definitely not funnier than I am.

What he is, though, is heart-stoppingly handsome. Maybe not in the classical way; certainly there are guys who are far better looking. Still, something in the way he carries himself has had me lying in bed the past few nights, staring up at the ceiling in my bedroom, daydreaming.

Remembering his face as the elevator doors closed on him. His expression when he blew through the stairwell door, flushed and breathing heavy. The way he looked when Desi hissed at him the first time they met.

I glance behind me to check for the cat as Brooks knocks for the second time; this time, I'm ready, yanking open the door too hard. Too eager. Too flushed. Too done up.

Ugh, I hate myself right now.

"Sup, buddy?" He gives me a nudge when he bounds into my tiny foyer, kicking off his sport sandals next to the door, giving them a tap so they're off to the side.

His nose goes in the air, sniffing. "I don't smell anything," he muses. "Why don't I smell anything?"

"It only took you fifteen minutes to change—what, are you expecting Superman to deliver the food?"

"Kind of. I mean, I said Nan Margolis no less than four times in a five-minute conversation with the manager of Flocke and Brow."

"The manager?"

"Manager approval is the only way to get anything delivered from that place."

I shake my head with a smile on my face, closing the door behind him. Trail along after when he goes to the kitchen, puts some ice in a glass, pours himself a water. Takes a second one out and repeats the process for me.

"Water okay?" He finally glances at me over his broad shoulder. He's wearing a navy Henley and gray lazy pants, the kind that make his ass look round and thighs muscular and—

"Earth to Abbott?" He's holding the glass out in front of my face; I hadn't noticed because I was objectifying him sexually. "Hello?"

Oops. "Thanks."

When I reach for the cup, my fingers cover his and I shiver. Shake it off because he isn't into me that way, sees me as a friend, and I'd do best to remember that.

Thankfully, the awkward moment is interrupted by another knock. Brooks flees to the door. "Thank God you're here—I could eat the ass out of a dead skunk," is his greeting.

I poke my head around the corner in time to see Brooks slide a twenty-dollar bill into a young man's hand then send him off with a pat to the bicep. "Thanks, man. We appreciate it."

We.

My ovaries clench.

He didn't mean we as in we, *Abbott. Calm down. Get a grip.*

Still, seeing him slide that kid a fat tip has my girl parts hot and bothered. I love a guy who is generous, and Brooks just showed me a layer of himself I've never seen.

Realistically, it's because other than hanging out in this apartment, we've only been in his. We've never been in public together. Never been outside, never gone to a coffee shop or a restaurant.

I sigh.

Oh well.

Resigned to the fact that I'm probably not his type, I shuffle into the kitchen and start pulling out plates. Forks. Knives. Napkins.

Brooks is buzzing from excitement (and hunger) when the bags get set on the counter—two loaded, top handle bags with ribbons securing them closed and the food safely inside, piping hot and fresh.

Soon, we're prepping our plates, loading them up with pasta and ribeye steak and vegetables, desserts of key lime pie and crème brûlée left inside the bag and placed in the fridge. Shortly after that, we're settling into our spots in the living room—me on one end of the couch, him on the other. The same spots we occupied the other time he came and crashed at my place.

Almost like we've settled into a routine, natural and…casual. It's nice.

"What are you into?" He's looking at the television, so I'm not sure if he wants to have a conversation, or if he's just being polite.

I wait until he makes eye contact to ask, "What do you mean—like, what are my hobbies?"

"Sure." He shrugs. "What are your hobbies?"

He's twisted his body to face me, legs up on the sofa, plate balanced in his lap.

Sure? Was that not what he meant? Why would he say it like *that*? "My hobbies. Uh, let's see. I collect…" I stop myself, because he's not asking what I collect. He wants to know what I do for fun, outside these walls.

I think. Gather my thoughts and a forkful of dinner, then continue. "For fun I love walking through the city in the evening, just as it gets dark, with a hot cup of tea. Especially when it's cold out." Is that lame? "Oh—I also love antique shops." Shit, I sound like Nan. Those are her hobbies, which, I suppose, would make sense since she helped raise me. "I love shopping, but not for myself. I love giving presents. And, um… hmm. I don't know, baseball."

Brooks' brows shoot up. "You? Baseball?"

"Sure, I mentioned it before. Plus who doesn't love baseball?"

"I can list a thousand people who don't," he quips arrogantly.

"Please, you don't know a thousand people," I shoot back, stabbing a carrot with the tines of my fork. "But you're right, I bet not a lot of women you meet are the type who like baseball."

He already knows my family has a suite at the stadium, and if he wanted, we could use it for any game he wanted to watch in person. He would be fed and could see all the plays from the best seats in the place.

I feel myself blushing. "I do really love baseball. My grandparents—mostly Grandpa—took me when I was a kid. My brother hated it, but I always loved it." It's been years since I've been to a game, but I doubt I've lost my zest for it—the loud thunder of the stadium during a scoring play, the cheers during a stolen base, the boos.

The hot dogs.

My stomach growls and I take another bite. "What are your hobbies?"

"Baseball. I like sports."

"Do you like watching them in bars?"

He nods. "Fuck yeah. Who doesn't?"

"In this city? Plenty of people." You'd be hard-pressed to find a dingy sports bar in this city of snooty people, but I have a hidden gem I've been known to kick back in on game day. "I know a great place to watch in if you don't want to hit the stadium. We should go sometime."

"What's it called?"

"I can't tell you." I nibble the end of a piece of asparagus.

"Can't, or won't?"

"Yes."

"I *hate* when you do that." He's frowning, cramming a hunk of meat into his mouth.

"I've literally never done that before."

"But you will, and when you do, it's going to annoy me."

"Noted."

Note to self: repeat that specifically to annoy him.

"Can I ask you something?"

I hate when people start sentences that way. I also hate

Now, don't take this the wrong way and *No offense, but…* So when Brooks faces me, plate on his lap, expression earnest, I cringe a little inside as I crunch down on my food and chew, no idea what he possibly wants to ask me.

"I guess so?"

"Why did you friend-zone me?"

Not what I was expecting. "Did I?"

"Yes. You've called me dude, buddy, and friend at least a dozen times."

"So?"

"So—girls don't friend-zone me. I friend-zone them."

I set my plate down, resting the fork along the edge, placing the utensils in the perfect ten and two position. "How long has this been driving you crazy?"

"Since you called me buddy when you asked me to check on the cat."

"Did I though?"

"You did and you damn well know it."

Jeez, why is he so bent out of shape about it? He hasn't made a single move on me, nor has he flirted or done anything else that's led me to believe he was interested. "Do you want to date me?"

"God no."

"Then why are we having this conversation?" Is his ego so fragile that he can't handle me not falling at his feet? He's handsome and smart and successful with no shortage of women throwing themselves at him—what does he need me for?

"I was wondering."

"You and I both know I'm giving you exactly what you want, so stop bitching about it." I will never be the kind of girl who allows herself to be a notch on someone's bedpost.

No matter how my feelings for him are changing.

* * *

"You're awful quiet—what are you looking at over there?" Brooks has been quietly chuckling at his phone for the past few minutes. First he went on it to check a work email he'd been expecting, and ever since, something else has piqued his interest.

He almost never sits and plays on his phone.

The past four nights we've spent together, either on his couch or mine, bingeing our favorite shows and sharing dinner. It's strange and oddly satisfying. Last night he was two hours late; showed up a bit drunk, reeking like cigar smoke and chattering about his buddies and bad decisions. I cannot for the life of me imagine what his friends are like, but if they're anything like him…they do some stupid shit.

He's smirking to himself, as if he has a secret. Something he can't—or won't—say out loud.

Is it a girl? Is he seeing someone?

His lips part. "I get these daily emails from Millennial Dictionary, and this word of the day is fucking hilarious."

Millennial Dictionary is basically a modern take on the dictionary where readers and visitors are able to add definitions. A huge majority of the words are slang, gutter talk, or dirty.

"What's the word of the day? Care to share with the rest of the class?"

Brooks grins. "I don't think I can say it out loud."

I feign irritation. "How old are you? Grow up and read the dumb thing out loud."

"Okay, but if you're insulted, remember you're the one who wanted me to read it to you."

Is he serious? "You're over there giggling like an idiot, and you think I won't want to know why? Hurry it up before I lose interest."

"Fine." He raises his phone and adjusts an imaginary pair of reading glasses set on the bridge of his beautiful nose. "Word of the day: sloppy toppy."

I feel my nose wrinkling. "What the hell is a sloppy toppy?"

"A wet blow job. With, uh—lots of drool."

"That's…*porny*."

"Tell me about it. Disgusting, right?" He wrinkles his nose, as if the notion of a wet BJ is unbearable.

I don't believe for one second Brooks Bennett thinks a wet blow job is disgusting. Still, he says it with a straight face, lowering his phone and shrugging as he sets it on my glass coffee table.

I'm still holding the carton of shrimp with bora in my hands, and I spear one with the tip of my fork. It's poised in the air, in front of my face when I say, "Know what a nice gift would be for your one-night stands? A box of tissues to wipe the spit."

"One of my one-night stands? Uh, you have way too much faith in my ability to get laid these days. But that actually would be nice! And *so* thoughtful—according to Millennial Dictionary, they're super fucking sloppy. Tissues would be a nice touch." He leans over, peers down into my carton, and steals a shrimp. "Generous, even."

"I wonder if there are recommendations anywhere for bibs with the highest rate of absorption—in the long run, that might be cheaper than constantly buying boxes of tissues."

"So, a blow job bib? Now there's an idea."

A blush colors my cheeks at the compliment. "I'm nothing if not practical."

"Maybe you're onto something here—something to keep her clothes from getting cum on them that allows for easy cleanup? Not everyone swallows."

"So true," I agree with a nod, the visual of giving Brooks a blow job suddenly entering my mind and making me blush harder. Jeez, I have seriously got to give dating another shot— if I'm lusting after Brooks, I'm in a drier drought than I thought.

Brooks tilts his head. "Possibly sold at a novelty store?"

"A blow job bib really is genius. We can sell those to all the sex shops and make a bloody fortune. We can plan the whole thing out on a cocktail napkin." I look around my living room. Not a cocktail napkin in sight.

"You said cock." My neighbor laughs like a ten-year-old boy who's into potty humor.

"No more socks or paper towels necessary for a sloppy toppy —that could be our slogan." We just keep going and going, the endeavor taking root and making us both laugh as we shout out slogans and products and marketing ideas.

"Fuck, maybe I should quit my job and start a business with you. Who needs to design buildings and create entire communities when we can change the landscape of the sex industry?"

Duh. "Honestly, Brooks—I doubt we'll even need investors. Just a little seed money—get it? Seed? Semen."

We both laugh drunkenly, though we're both completely sober.

Brooks hoots. "A bit of scrap fabric and a dream. Ah, I can see it now."

That gives me another brilliant idea. "What if we threw in a free hair clip with purchase? Or like, a hair tie."

"Jesus Christ, yes. Fuck yeah to the hair clip. God, it's not even nine o'clock and we've already built an entire business off of blowies before putting on our pajamas. We're brilliant. We could build an EMPIRE!"

I throw myself back into the couch cushions, emitting an evil laugh, not unlike an evil queen in a cartoon movie.

Confession: we both sound a bit manic, but second confession? It feels amazing.

We're having fun.

"Free hair ties are brilliant, I tell you! Honestly, it's perfect."

I love bantering like this with him. It fuels my soul.

It's the reason I've been up before my alarm clock each morning and out the door for work before I have to be at the office, the reason I've been bringing Dale and the rest of the team coffee and donuts.

I'm happy.

Brooks makes me happy. "I can't believe we're even talking

about blow jobs like it's no big deal." And I can't believe I can make jokes about it without dying of embarrassment.

"It's hilarious. I'm telling you, Abbott, we should quit our day jobs…"

I think at this moment, Brooks Bennett could talk me into just about anything, including quitting my job to begin a sex toy hair tie company.

12

DESDEMONA

What are those two idiots blathering about?

I crack an eye, two obnoxiously high-pitched screeches rousing me from a lovely slumber. Ugh, it's those two again—my human and that other…*thing*…being noisy and doing whatever it is people do when they're happy.

Do shut up, I moan, another eyelid opening.

Girl and her new friend are sitting a bit too closely for my liking, hogging my couch—the big, long sofa I'm able to perch on the back of, putting me near the window. I do most of my lounging when Girl leaves in the morning, watching the birds fly by, dogs being walked, people jogging in the big, green park below.

It's warm during the day in my spot, when the sun is beating down through the window—the window that prevents me from catching birds or killing mice in the park.

My human laughs again.

Mine.

My eyes are open but they narrow at Boy.

At least I think it's a boy.

I've seen versions of him on that square box Girl watches when she's on the other end of my couch. And now?

Boy is sitting in my spot.

Screeching like an owl.

They both are. The sound has me covering my ears with a furry paw, and I bury my head in the soft, white blanket Girl lays on her bed for me. At least, I think it's her bed?

It's also *my* bed, so it's really hard to say just who it belongs to. Most of the things in the house are mine, but she uses most of them, too.

I need something, and it appears.

Wait…what's that smell?

My nose hits the air, face tilted up, searching for a waft of…

Food.

They're eating, and my gorgeous nose twitches.

True, I have kibble or whatever that brown bullshit is, but I've barely touched it today, not in the mood for anything but shrimp, the fragrant aroma wafting out of the white container in Girl's hands.

She hands it to Boy with a smile.

A gurgle erupts from her throat and it sounds like she's choking on a hairball—except she's making the same face at Boy she makes at me when she's scratching behind my ears or under my chin, so maybe she isn't dying.

I groan, rolling to my back, mouth opening in an exaggerated yawn, pink tongue licking the air.

Blink at the ceiling.

No one comes to scratch my belly.

An irritated ear twitches, and I crane my neck to peer over at Girl, who still has those loud noises coming out of her mouth.

I dig deep into my belly and push out a loud purr, glance over at Girl.

No one comes to scratch my belly.

Fucking A, how hard is this going to be? Am I going to have to get up and walk over? It's cold in this godforsaken room and the sun isn't shining anymore. It's dark and chilly and Boy is sitting on my blanket.

Bastard.

Except.

There is that shrimp…

Clearly no one is going to hand-deliver it, more's the pity, so a trip across the room seems to be the only way I'll get my furry paws on a single morsel.

Screw the kibble.

Rolling to my feet, I manage to rise. Shake out my luscious mane like a white tiger on the Serengeti before stretching. Yawn.

Shake again.

Lick my paw.

Strut forward gracefully, amber eyes—the ones that have Girl spellbound—fixated on the white container in Boy's large hand.

Give it up, pretty boy.

I lick my chops.

"Ouoiutoiua kitty, kitty." Girl's mouth is moving and sound is coming out; she finally gives me the attention I deserve, but I have no interest in her just yet.

I jump onto the couch, into Boy's lap.

Another loud screech from his mouth hole and I startle, ears pulling back.

Keep your hole closed while you're feeding me, human. The last thing I need to hear is your intolerable voice. I'm not as impressed with him as Girl is, groaning from deep inside my chest. I don't like it when he talks, but I do like it when he feeds me.

I deserve better than to be kept waiting.

"Get him off my lap," Boy whines, annoying voice more high-pitched than before. I'm surprised I can understand him; normally I can only pick up bits and pieces of what Girl is saying, unless it's *Good kitty* or *Pretty Desi* or *That's my good girl.*

All the words I've learned have been from the talking box Girl watches when she comes back to the house after leaving me to lounge all day.

I don't know where she goes, but when she comes home, she

changes her clothes, feeds me, then sits on her side of the couch and watches TV. Then when it gets dark and she begins yawning, too, we watch TV on the big bed in her room.

"It's a she." Girl corrects him for the hundredth time, but actually, Boy is right—*I am not a girl.*

I am, in fact, a male feline.

Problem is, I have so much luxurious, fluffy fur, they couldn't find my balls when they were checking me, so—I'm Duchess Desdemona McPurrs-A-Lot.

Worst fucking name on the list of kitty names.

Desdemona? I have no choice but to occasionally exhibit a bit of evil…

Oddly enough, I'm partial to the name Boy has been calling me—Pussy of Terror.

I lick my paw. "Meow."

"OIAuoiugoiug off me!" Boy cries, and I can barely understand what the fuck he's saying, he's speaking so fast. So high-pitched, so loud and panicked. His eyes are as wide as the time Girl stuck me in the bathtub and I caught sight of my reflection in the mirror before she snapped a photo of my bulging eyes and posted it on her little phone.

"IUOIUB afiougoiug gouddig precious Desi." Girl pats me on the top of my head, stroking my supple fur.

I might not understand a fucking thing she's saying, but Girl knows what's up.

She thinks I'm wonderful and pretty.

Because I am.

I paw at the box in Boy's hands and he makes another strangled sound, moving so fast I almost fall to the carpet.

Hmm.

Being coy and cute is not going to work on Boy.

He doesn't like me.

No bother. I want shrimp, and no amount of noise from his face is going to stop me from trying to get it.

I dream about seafood all day, every day. That, and snacking on a delicious songbird. The occasional squirrel, though they look like they'd take too much effort to catch.

I swipe through the air with my paw, imagining my nails like tiny swords of glory.

Swipe, swipe—that's how I'd go after my prey if I were let loose in the park…

"Shit, iouoijaoiut fjoiaug this fucking cat."

"Be nice!" I understand Girl shouting that, albeit a bit too loudly. I do love her stinky face.

She reeks like perfume and whatever is in those bottles in the bathroom. I knocked them over once to see what was inside but couldn't get the top off, then Girl came in bellowing and kicked me off the counter.

No matter. I hop up there when she leaves the apartment and the mood strikes me. Kitchen counter, too, to drink from the sink like a leopard on the African plains sipping from a watering hole before a hunt.

Trouble is, there ain't shit to hunt in this apartment.

No mice. No birds.

Just the occasional white box of food.

I purr for Boy's benefit, hoping to soften him up, and rub my face along his arm, coarse tongue licking the skin of his wrist.

"OFF!"

I lick again, knowing he's going to yell.

He does.

"BAD KITTY!"

Bad? No one has ever called me *that* before, except maybe Nan the times she was in the apartment and I ruined what she was working on for Girl, like the flowers I tipped over when she was placing them in a vase, or the package of meats I tore through with my fierce claws.

I mean nails.

I growl, a fierce tigress.

Boy yelps. "Shit, it wants to eat me."

It? How rude.

"OIUoiuoi your shrimp. Give her some."

My ears perk up and I purr louder. Yes, please.

"No."

I scowl, and growl.

"Okay, okay, okay." He hurriedly rushes to reply, the shiny metal fork in his hand sifting through whatever else is in the container.

My mouth waters.

"Just one or two," Girl tells him, and I growl again, displeased.

I want it all.

13

ABBOTT

"Does Desi look funny to you?"

"The cat always looks funny."

"If you gave her a snack every once in a while, she'd probably leave you alone," I suggest, knowing it's not true. If Brooks gives my cat enough tasty treats, he's going to become her new favorite and win her adoration, and I will become chopped liver.

Which, incidentally, Desdemona hates.

Desi is fickle like that, though that's not how I raised her.

"I refuse to feed that cat from my lap. Look at her—her eyes are small beads of lava trying to melt my soul."

"Or…she's hungry and wants food. Or…she wants attention."

Either way, she's perched on his lap, pink tongue peeping out of her adorable mouth. Aww, my pretty kitty.

"I'd love her more from afar. Does she always have to be in my face?"

"You know, you're super dramatic for someone so big." It's an odd mix. Brooks is an imposing figure, tall and fit with dark hair and a toned body, looming when he's in my living room. A giant, really.

Frightened of my ten-pound cat.

My neighbor absentmindedly checks the watch fastened around his wrist then slaps both palms down on his thighs. "I have to grab something from my place. I'll be back in a few."

"I'll come with you." I push myself off the couch, setting my food on the coffee table, curious and bored with always being at my place.

If he's not going to do it, I'll invite myself over.

"What if I'm going home so I can take a shit in my toilet?"

I feel my nose scrunching up. "Are you?"

"No, but I remembered I have clothes I need to get out of the washer and throw in the dryer. I have one thing that needs to hang."

A guy who line-dries his delicates?

I bite down on my lower lip from the mental picture of Brooks carefully shaking out a shirt or a pair of pants then hanging it over a cabinet door to dry.

"Well I'm coming. I want to hang out at your place—I'm bored with mine. Maybe I'll stare at your embarrassingly small living room windows."

He shoots me a salty glare. "Don't insult my windows."

Too late.

Why it bothers him so bad, I couldn't begin to say. Nonetheless, I trudge behind him until he's unlocking his apartment and ushering me inside.

The first time I was at his place, I didn't make the effort to discern the little things. The details. The nuances. What makes his place distinctively more male than my apartment, but in a good way. Everything about Brooks is "in a good way."

Same flooring in the entry. Same tile in the kitchen. Same kitchen countertop stone. Appliances. Same cream color on the walls. Not white, not beige—a basic color in between.

But that's where the similarities end.

There is no table next to the front door for keys. No mirror hanging to make the space look larger. My neighbor's shoes are lined up along the wall instead of inside the coat closet, like mine are, neatly displayed on a three-tier metal shelf.

I traipse along behind him toward the double doors in the hallway where the stacked washing machine and dryer are, craning my neck to peer into the living room as we pass by.

It's dark, but I glimpse the couch (dark leather) and an ottoman (also leather). A huge television on the wall above our matching gas fireplaces. It's a stark contrast to the wall color, but I guess it goes with the furniture.

When I pay special attention to the windows, my mouth tips into a satisfied grin.

It's strange how it's the same apartment with different things inside of it. No wonder he was so wigged out at the sight of mine.

He stands in front of the compact laundry room—a luxury in an apartment complex, even one as exclusive as ours—pulling open the door and flipping the light on. It's a tidy space with a suspension rod spanning the upper length, a few dress shirts already hanging on black velvet hangers to dry.

Just as we enter, the washing machine chimes, coming to a complete stop, the bin inside done spinning.

"Perfect timing," I comment, leaning against the doorjamb, crossing my ankles and arms to watch him.

A man who times his laundry so he can swap it out?

Unheard of.

Brooks gets to work, yanking open the washing machine, arm reaching in to pull out a few wet garments. Tosses them into the dryer.

Repeat.

He sticks his arm in again, rooting around.

A dark garment catches my eye as he pulls a bag from the washing machine, unzips it, then gives it a good, healthy shake. It's a heavy fabric and looks like a blazer, but I can't be sure.

Definitely a fancy jacket of some type, made out of a fancy material.

"What's this?" I lean forward, stroking it. It feels like wet velvet.

Brooks ducks his head, embarrassed. "This is my, um—it's a smoking jacket."

Why does this not surprise me?

"I can see that now." I laugh, able to make out the trimmings of rich brocade and detail work. "What's it for? Halloween?"

"This thing I have with my friends."

"A thing?"

"Yeah, we do this thing."

"What *kind* of thing?" Guys are so strange.

"Just stuff."

"And you need a velvet and brocade jacket to do it in?"

"Yeah."

"Are you trying to tell me you and your buddies have a secret club?" I joke, not realizing I've hit the nail on the head. But I have. It's right there, written all over his panicked face.

Brooks twists his mouth into a frown.

"Lordy, please do not tell me you and your buddies have a secret club."

"I won't." He won't even look me in the eye.

Dead.

Giveaway.

They totally do. I squint over at him. "How old are you?"

"Old enough to know you're making fun of me."

"Because it's a secret club?" Man, I love teasing him. It's so easy.

He fidgets, buttoning the jacket up the front and laying it flat on top of the folding table. Pressing down on it with his palms so it dries without wrinkles. "Stop pestering me about it."

If there is one thing that frustrates me, it's when guys automatically assume you're nagging them when all you're doing is trying to find out information. To learn more about him so the two of you can become closer; what's the harm in that?

Also, I'd make an amazing spy.

"Pestering you about what? The secret club you have with your friends?"

"I didn't *say* that."

"You didn't have to—it's written all over your guilty face, and you're pressing the wrinkles out of a sopping wet smoking jacket, weirdo."

"Uh, excuse me, but this jacket is fucking awesome."

It does look fucking awesome. Impressive, too.

"I never said it wasn't fucking awesome." I almost choke on the profane word but relish the expression on his face when I let the F-bomb fly. "I'm just saying it's a strange thing to own for *no* apparent reason." My blue gaze grazes up and down his torso. He's standing in the center of his tiny laundry room, next to his stiff jacket that may or may not be for some dumb boys-only club. "Unless you're a freak about Halloween and are already planning your costume—in which case, I can't for the life of me figure out what you could possibly be."

"Can we just drop the subject?"

"Your wish is my command, your highness." I dip into a debutante curtsey, as if Brooks is royalty, but my expression is far from adoring. Then again, he's the one who owns a blue velvet jacket like a complete and utter jackass.

Once he's done starting an entirely new load of laundry and ignoring me, I follow him back through the apartment and back out the door, waiting until we're in front of my door before asking, "You don't want to hang out at your place?"

"No."

"Why? I didn't think you liked my cat. Besides, your leather couch is super comfy."

"It is, but you have better pillows for snuggling on yours."

"We'd better be careful or we're going to make a habit of this. You don't want a reputation."

And you don't want me to end up liking you…

"A habit of this? Hardly," he scoffs.

"Um, honestly—we've done nothing but hang out this week."

Brooks laughs as if I've just told a joke. "No we haven't."

Is he serious? Yes, we have.

"Brooks, do you even know how many nights we've hung out this week?"

"Two." He is extremely confident for someone so wrong, butt planting itself in the center of my sofa, remote control already in his hand. He holds up the peace sign then says, "Two," again.

I make a buzzer sound. "Uh, try four." Then, for his edification, I explain so there is no question that I'm right. "Saturday we rented movies and had takeout, Sunday you came over for lazy Sunday, Monday was soup and grilled cheese, and today is reality TV Tuesday. So yeah, I'm right—it's been four nights."

Brooks sits up on the couch like a shot has been fired. "Fuck."

I throw my hands up. "Now what?"

"I have to go."

Of course he does. Because he's a weirdo.

After he's gone and I'm in bed, lying in the dark, staring at the ceiling, the last thing I wonder before drifting off to sleep is if his reaction has anything to do with this mysterious club he and his friends have...

14

BROOKS

I'm at her place again.
 And again and again.

Like a bad habit I've picked up and can't kick, I've been flocking to Abbott's apartment like it's my second home. Except I slipped up last week and stayed far too many days in a row, breaking a rule I fabricated for the BBS.

Rule 2: *No seeing the same woman more than three nights a week. Mix it up.*

At least I have half the rule locked down. But for real, why would I 'mix it up' when Abbott is across the hall? So fucking convenient not having to go to a bar to find someone to spend time with—even if we aren't hooking up and I haven't had sex in…

Since I met her.

I've already abandoned trying to piece together the timeline.

Why?

Because lounging on Abbott's couch has become my second full-time job. Head propped on a pillow facing the television is my new favorite position (right below sitting at my drafting table, creating).

I stretch and yawn, slothful fuck I find myself becoming.

Truly, it's fantastic in Abbott's place. I've known her a few short weeks and already her apartment feels like a second home, that whore-able cat excluded.

I keep telling myself being here isn't breaking any of the club rules because she and I aren't anything except friends, but the more time I spend with her, the bigger the lie that becomes.

Right now, at this moment, I'm drunk on laziness and the wine we've been slowly sipping on.

Red. Warm. Delicious.

I stroke the sofa with the back of my hand while Desdemona Terror Pussy looks on, jealousy gleaming in her black, beady eyes.

"Your couch is really comfortable."

Addicting.

Kind of like Abbott, if I'm being honest.

"I know. I'm in love with it."

"You should ask it to marry you." I laugh dumbly. Laugh a bit harder at the expression moving across her face, first surprise, then—she rolls those blue eyes. Just as I was suspecting she would.

Abbott Margolis does not disappoint, and she's not as mature as she wants me to believe. I've seen her do a happy jig in the kitchen when I agree to watch her favorite show. I've seen her Daffy Duck slippers and her Justin Bieber hoodie, sometimes worn at the same time.

I've also seen her fist-pump during previews for the new Disney cartoon releasing soon. "I'm *so* going to see that," she says, every single time it comes on.

"I should ask the couch to marry me?" she mocks. "You're so stupid sometimes."

I am.

I really, really am.

"Come on, we've already established that I'm a moron with

bad taste in jokes." Then I do something I never thought I would do: scoot closer to the backside of the sofa, pressing my body into it to create more room. Pat on the cushions, on the empty space in front of me, inviting Abbott to fill the space. I invite her to lie down beside me and—dear Lord—cuddle?

Cuddle.

Me?

"Are you saying you want me to snuggle you?"

Fuck yeah, I want to cuddle or snuggle or whatever. "That's not at all what I'm saying."

Her blue gaze gets narrow. "Then why are you patting the cushion like that? It's clearly an invitation."

I make a pfft sound. "Patting the cushion like what?"

"Like this." Abbott makes a show out of rubbing the soft, suede-like fabric like she's stroking Desi's fur, adding a few *ahhh* noises I wouldn't dream of making. "Come here, Abbott, come snuggle."

"All I'm saying is it's damn comfortable in this position and you should be comfy, too. It's Lazy Sunday." One of a few we've already shared together…like all of them since we met.

"That's true, it is Lazy Sunday." My beautiful neighbor weighs her options, slowly—though not reluctantly—joining me when I situate the fluffy cushions, pound them into submission, uncurl myself so I'm lying down, leaving plenty of room for Abbott in front of me.

I am the big spoon.

Not that we're spooning—God no.

But if we were…

Silence fills the room as we watch a comedian on television joking on a stage in New York City, the crowd cracking up when he tears his shirt off and begins spinning tales about his wife and daughters.

I chuckle, looking down my nose to see if Abbot is amused, too.

A serene smile etches her face, brows arched.

My head flops back down on the pillow, but not before catching a whiff of her hair.

Shit.

Almonds? Cherries? Both?

What is that?

It smells like I want to stick my nose in her hair and inhale.

Intoxicating.

"The last time I lay on a couch with a guy, we played a little game called Extreme Cuddles."

That has my immediate attention and I perk up. "I'm sorry, whozeewhatnow?"

"Extreme Cuddles is the best. I invented it." She reaches forward and nabs her water from the coffee table, sips from the straw, then lies back down next to me, ass nuzzled firmly into my half-hard dick. Without a care in the world and seemingly unaware of my growing erection, Abbott continues. "I was dating this guy my sophomore year of college. I lived in the sorority house and invented this one amazing game." She uses air quotes to emphasize the word game. "Anyway, I had a sofa in my room because I drew the long straw for a single that year, and the place was huge. I could do cartwheels in it if I wanted to, and this one time I actually did. I'd gotten a—"

"Abbott, get to the point," I bellow, practically in her ear since it's directly in front of my mouth.

"Sorry. As I was saying." She clears her throat and inadvertently wiggles her ass. "Extreme Cuddling is basically like…a test in self-control."

"How?"

"Because you lie next to each other, watching television or a movie—whatever—like we're doing right now."

"So?"

"With next to or no clothes on, and you try not to have any kind of sexual relations." Abbott's chuckle is low, like she's fondly remembering a time when she lay on a couch in her sorority house in college, naked with some poor sap. "There are blankets involved. You know, to preserve modesty. And because sometimes it gets cold."

"Right." My mind is wandering, has gone so far down a rabbit hole of perverse fantasies. Plaid skirts and nerdy glasses. Netflix with no chill and *alll* fuckery. Skin. Tits. "Give me all the details and don't leave anything out. No skimping."

"Okay, well…this guy I was dating—we were lying there, on my sweet, sweet couch, fully dressed, obviously."

"Obviously." *Cause you lived in a sorority house, and no one ever had sex there*, I say to myself acerbically.

My neighbor cranes her neck to look back at me. "Are you being sarcastic?"

One hundred percent. "Me? No."

Her eyes narrow. "You want to hear this story or not?"

I nod emphatically.

"Then cool it with the sass talk."

"Fine." I press my lips together so she sees how sincere I am, how desperate I am to hear this story, although I can already tell you how this fun little tale ends:

Me, with a giant boner.

Abbott presents me with her back, "unintentionally" wiggling against my cock to resettle herself.

Fuck.

"We were watching some lame horror movie that wasn't scary at all," she's saying, oblivious to my torture. "The special effects were terrible, and I knew my date was sweaty, so I told him to take his hoodie off. As he's doing that, I say, 'While you're at it, you could take off your T-shirt, too.'"

"And he did?"

"Naturally." Abbott pauses, reflecting with a smile before continuing to torment me with a lack of detail so egregious I want to groan. *Get to the extreme part of the snuggling! Who gives a shit about what was on TV? Get to the sex and nudity.*

"So he takes his shirt off, and he's just lying there in his jogging pants or whatever. I think that's what they were, some gray, baggy pants. And he had boxers on—which I only know because I had my hand halfway down his pants and kept rubbing the fabric."

The visual of Abbott with her hand down my pants, stroking the soft cotton of my boxer briefs has me swallowing the lump forming in my tight throat.

I nod behind her, fingers white-knuckling the blanket. "Uh-huh."

"But now he's the only one lying there half-dressed. So, I stand up and take off my bottoms."

"Like how?" I play dumb.

"You know, I took off my pants."

"Your pants?"

Abbott cocks her head, and I can hear the wheels turning. She isn't sure if I'm bullshitting her, or if I'm just so stupid I don't know what it means for a chick to pull her pants off.

"Maybe you should show me."

She scoffs, not falling for my trick. "Ha ha, I'm not falling for that."

"If I take off my shirt, you can take off your pants, then it will be fair. I really want to know what Extreme Cuddles is, but I need a visual." I shrug casually. "That's the architect part of me—I need to see the entire picture. Draw me a map."

A treasure map to the P and the V.

"Ugh, okay, but only because I know you won't get turned on." She huffs, climbing off the couch to stand, and slowly peels off the blue velour bottoms that have been driving me insane, tickling my thighs.

While she's taking off her pajama bottoms, I peel off my T-shirt and lie back down, watching the rest of the show.

Her ass in a hot pink thong. Slim thighs. Smooth butt cheeks.

Fuck, fuck, fuck.

Abort, my head cries.

Touch her, my dick urges.

Everyone calm the fuck down, my brain shouts, irritated.

Abbott climbs back under the covers, dragging them up her body to cover her bare lower half, then goes on with her story. "Alright, so he wasn't wearing a shirt, and I wasn't wearing bottoms. And at some point, I finally say, 'Maybe you should take off *your* bottoms, too.'"

"What did he say?"

"His eyes got real wide, and he goes, 'Just my pants?' and I said, 'How about everything? That makes the game really dicey.'" She laughs at the memory. "I've never seen a guy pull his underwear off so fast in my entire freaking life."

"Wanna make a bet?" I can't help boasting.

I've got at least sixteen years on the pissant who played grabby-grabby with college-aged Abbott, and I bet I can move ten times faster, because I'm not a fucking boy.

And just because I'm a grown-ass man doesn't mean my hormones aren't raging like a freight train.

"Pfft. No one can get their pants off faster than Billie Belmont."

Hold up—pause.

First of all, what the fuck kind of name is that, and where the hell was she meeting her friends? The Junior league? Jesus Christ, I thought our names were bad, but Billie Belmont?

"When do you get to the part where you take your shirt off?" I desperately want to know, dying of curiosity, wondering if she'll take her top off now. I mean—what's the big deal? Knowing my neighbor, she undoubtedly has four layering shirts under the pajama top she has on.

"Not for a while. We lay there watching the show, the poor kid. I swear, he was sweating before he removed his clothes, but afterward? Wow. You'd think it had been raining outside he was so moist."

"Sexy."

"Aw, thanks."

"I didn't mean you—I meant the word moist."

"He was though. Moist, that is, getting the blanket all sticky. And I told him so."

She has seriously got to stop saying the M word. It's making my ass cheeks pucker. "Jesus, that poor kid."

"Yeah." More laughing. More wiggling. More chugging from the water on the table. "So, I'm wondering when you're going to rip off all your clothes like Billie did, just to prove a point."

"What point would that be?"

"That you can keep your hands off me while we're lying here."

Her delivery is casual, as if she didn't just drop a naked bomb. As if she isn't taunting me with nudity, which leads to touching, which leads to sex and orgasms and bliss.

"The point of the game is temptation. Sexual tension." The worst kind of torture. "That's not our endgame here."

Because we're friends. And friends don't fuck.

"Just so you know, despite what you think, keeping your hands off me would be more difficult than you think." The little shit actually yawns—or, feigns a yawn. Shit, I can't tell if it's real or fake. "You don't have the balls to lie there and not touch me and not get turned on," she goads, patting her mouth, bored and gloating, like she's already won some bet between us I wasn't aware she'd made.

Little does she know, *I win everything.*

"You don't have the lady balls to lie there and not beg me to put my hands on your tits."

"Pfft, please—you're forgetting I've played this game before." Abbott stretches, uses her core muscles to rise to a sitting position, reaches for the hem of her top, and lifts it.

I was wrong; it's one shirt, and Abbott isn't wearing a bra.

Covering her breasts, she lowers herself back down and weasels her hot little body into mine.

"What was that idiot's name you dated in college?" I need her to say it again—maybe it will make my half-hard boner deflate.

"Billie Belmont."

Stupid fucking name.

"Yeah—I'm about to smoke that guy in the pants removal competition."

"Brooks." Abbott laughs, smooth expanse of back taunting me. "It's not a competiti—"

Too late. I'm shucking off my motherfuckin' pants faster than that little douche did, guaranteed, kicking them toward the foot of the sofa, my legs caught in the ankle of one. I give it a good shake until they flop limply on the floor.

"Dear Lord, drama queen." She's laughing at me, but there's an edge to it telling me she's nervous. Not as unaffected as she's pretending to be while I lie here in all my naked glory, yanking at the blanket neatly folded on the back of the couch and pulling it over my semi-boner.

"Now what?" I want to know.

"Now we lie here and watch TV." Her tone implies that I'm an idiot for asking, her eyes glued to the screen in front of us.

"That's it?"

"Yes, just lie there."

"Naked?"

"Duh. That's where the extreme part comes in."

"This is fucking stupid," I complain, not sure where to put my hands and on the verge of bitching about how cold this living room has suddenly just become. My nut sac is now the size of two walnuts, despite my growing penis.

"You can touch me if you're weak." Abbott isn't looking back, but I hear her rolling her eyes. "But the point is to hold out and have a little self-control."

"The fuck, though—I have nowhere to put my hands!" Do I actually sound like a whiney little bitch, or do I just sound like one in my head?

"Where'd you put your hands before we took off our clothes?"

"On my hip." On my own body, keeping them to myself.

"*Welll.*"

She wants me to keep my hands to myself when she's lying there in a pink thong?

What the actual fuck, Abbott…

"Did you have something to *say*? Jesus, you're breathing so hard it sounds like you just ran eighty laps around the high school track in gym class," she taunts as my dick strains to poke its way through the thin strip of fabric of her underwear and into her ass canal. "Relax."

"I am relaxed!" comes out harsher than I intend, but how does she actually expect me to behave when she smells like roses and fucking sunshine and all that bullshit?

And to think: I was dumb enough to think I could handle a dumb game she invented in college. Leave it to a sorority girl to invent a dick-tease game.

There's a man on Abbott's TV talking some gibberish that makes Abbott laugh and me scowl, because her entire body does this shake—shoulders brushing my chest, butt rubbing my nether regions. Flesh and heat and holes wanting to be filled.

The guy says something else and Abbott snorts.

Okay, maybe snorting is not so cute.

She giggles.

Cute.

Snorts again.

Not so cute.

All the while she taunts me with her naked flesh and irresistible perfume, one Nan probably bought her at a random fancy-schmancy French boutique in the Congo where they use the sweat from rare butterflies and liquid diamonds. Or, you know—Bloomingdale's.

Where do highfalutin socialite dames shop?

It's intoxicating and driving my hormones bonkers, and now

I'm fixated on it. Fixated on the tiny hairs at the back of her neck, shorter than the rest and wispy because she has it pulled off to one side, swept back to bare the long column of her neck.

I squirm.

Cough.

Clear my throat and glance around for water.

Is it hot in here? Or is it just Abbott, who seems unaware that there's a hard-on perilously close to her butthole?

No one who invents a game like this is oblivious.

I can't stop thinking about banging her now, or sucking and thrusting, or, at the very least, dry-humping her lady parts. At this point, I'd settle for her dry-fucking my thigh…

Shit, I totally misjudged my sweet neighbor. She looks so unassuming and innocent, even while almost naked. Like a virgin, touched for the very first time…

Shut the fuck up, idiot. Focus or your dick will get stiffer and you'll humiliate yourself.

Except.

Now that Brooks Junior is dialed in to the live nudity, there's no shutting him off. And yes—by "him" I mean my cock. He's feisty today, hasn't sunk himself into a pussy in days, weeks, *months*—crap, I don't even know how long it's been, but he's antsy. Social. He wants to come out to meet and play with Abbott's vagina. Or ass. Whichever hole, he wants in-sies.

Abbott chuckles; this time, it's not at the TV. She's silently laughing at me, my dick, and my plight, concealed from prying eyes by our blankets, her shoulders bare and exposed. My gaze drifts to the curve of her upper body, porcelain and perfect. Silky. Unblemished. The slope of her neck glides into a perfect arch, and I imagine my mouth there, kissing up and down the skin. Just below her ear. Down her neck. Across her shoulder.

I imagine she'd shiver if I did.

Fuck it.

Leaning down just the barest fraction, I'm able to give her light hair a decent whiff without making any sounds. Inhale.

Exhale.

Once more and my nostrils are definitely flaring, dick hardening. Body tense.

Abbott fakes another uninterested yawn. Ass squirms. "It feels to me as if you're not going to win this one. You don't have the willpower of a Billie Belmont—he was a shutout."

"Christ," I grind out, teeth clenching. "Don't say that name to me right now. It's idiotic."

"Billie Belmont Billie Belmont Billie Belmont." The name flies out of the brat's mouth and she doesn't trip over the tongue-twister once.

Why is she being such an asshole?

Abbott Margolis is the female version of myself, and I want to strangle her and stick my dick in her at the same time. Wait —that didn't come out right, which only makes my mind wander further into the gutter: what kind of kink is Abbott into? Choking? Spanking? Biting? Licking? Bent over from behind?

Fuck fuck fuck it.

Fuck it, I'm over this.

I should put my goddamn clothes on and get the hell out of here.

My hand is over it, too, the impatient motherfucker with a mind of its own, sliding from my hip to the couch cushion, across the one-inch gap separating Abbott and me. She flinches slightly from the unplanned contact of my hand on her back but remains motionless, letting me slide it up, over her spine.

Over her rib cage.

Finally, she sucks in a breath. Lets it out. Lies still, waiting.

Don't touch her tits, don't touch her tits, don't touch her—

I touch her tits.

Run my palm over her voluminous side-boob, over an areola I can only visualize since I'm bringing up the rear and can't actually see. *Speaking of rears…*

I glide my hand down the flat planes of Abbott's stomach, waiting for that sharp intake of breath I know is coming; all girls do it and *she* is no exception. Keep running that hand down, slowly creeping until I reach her ass. Her firm, perfectly round butt. Squeeze playfully, feel her smile.

"Whatcha doin' back there?" she teases, giving her buns a wiggle and ignoring the fact that two seconds ago, my giant palm was cupping her bare tit. "You're not into butt stuff, are you?"

"I'm into whatever you're into."

"Slow your roll, cowpoke—we're supposed to be watching TV. We're just friends."

Friends—we're back to that bullshit, eh?

Abbott squirms, sending a shockwave of nerves jolting from the front of my legs down to my toes.

My dick tingles. Twitches.

"Is your dick moving?" My neighbor does a half-laugh, half-moan, half-dressed but mostly not.

"Definitely. It wants to friend-zone you, too."

"Why should I make an exception for your dick? You've been very adamant about keeping this whole thing platonic."

"In fairness, I've never used the word platonic in my entire fucking life." The truth is, I've had plenty of female friends who I've boned. The problem isn't Abbott and wanting to remain friends with her—the problem is that I don't think I can stay that way. "You're just as adamant, so let's not kid ourselves."

Abbott is the kind of girl you marry, not the kind you have a one-night stand with, something casual to get your rocks off.

She's a good girl.

Not to be confused with a goody two-shoes. Don't ask me how I know she's wholesome, but the second time I laid eyes on her (the first time I just thought she was a colossal asshole), I knew her intentions would always be pure and she would never intentionally hurt anyone.

Abbott Margolis has a kind heart.

Let's not forget her amazing, accomplished family. Abbott is sexy. Funny. Cute. Smart as a whip and doesn't put up with my shit, either.

Plus, she has a fully stocked fridge and always has food being delivered. AKA I'll never go hungry with her living across the hall.

The total package.

You don't tangle yourself up with a girl like *that* unless you're serious. And I'm not.

I have a bet to win, one I can't afford to lose.

But if I were going to lose, it would be for a girl like her.

Dangerous thoughts, not made any easier by the stirring of my junk or the shaking of her ass.

* * *

The sound of Abbott's front door opening and clicking shut doesn't register as quickly as it should, my brain still letting my dick rule my thoughts.

"Abbott? Abbott dear, are you here?" The sound of expensive heels clicking on the foyer tile reaches our ears at the same time. The heels stop clicking for the briefest moment, and a delighted voice filters to the living room. "Oh, Brooks, are you here, too?" Nan calls out.

"Holy fuck!"

Where the hell are my fucking clothes, where the hell are my fucking clothes? I stumble, clambering. Falling off the couch, onto the floor.

She must have spied my shoes next to the door, my keys resting on the table.

"Kids? Where are you? Are you in the living room?" I hear the distinct sound of grocery bags being set on the kitchen counter and her heels clicking as she gets closer and closer…

The apartment might be posh, but it's smaller than a postage stamp, so realistically, in a matter of seconds, Nan is going to walk into a scene straight out of an amateur porno, probably giving the old woman a stroke.

And if we give Nan a stroke, that means I get no more treats.

But then…Nan finds me with Abbott's leopard-print throw blanket twisted around my hips. She enters the living room holding what looks like a bag of Chinese takeout in her prim and proper hands. A black purse is slung over her other arm.

She quickly turns and heads back the way she came—but not before, "For land's sake, cover your little bits, Brooks. They're dangling out the side of the blanket like cherries."

Jesus Christ, if my balls weren't already shriveled from the cold draft, they'd be buried inside my body from the humiliation of having my neighbor's grandma seeing my fucking nuts and telling me they're dangling like cherries.

My dangling bits.

Christ Almighty, will I ever live this down?

"Nan!" Abbott exclaims after gathering her own wits. "What are you doing here? It's…it's…"

"Late," I deadpan, checking my phone for the time. "It's eight o' clock."

"I know dear, but Grandpa and I were at the club and I thought I'd pop by to invite you to lunch tomorrow."

"Did you bring me groceries?" Abbott is sliding her pants on, shouting to her grandmother in the kitchen, the only one of us with any fucking common sense at the moment.

"No, dear. These are for Brooks. Men so rarely handle these matters themselves." Her head pops around the corner as I'm pulling my shirt on. "Isn't that right, young man?"

"Uh."

This is what happens when you let your guard down and forget the rules…

Rule 3: *No giving gifts.*

Not the same as receiving gifts, but is food a gift? I should have thought about all this when Nan gave me the gift cards.

Giving is not getting—I haven't done anything wrong.

Still. A nagging guilt settles in my stomach when I step into my pants, hard-on still a touch too alert for my liking.

I yank at my shirt, dragging it down to conceal my erection.

That's not shit I need Nan seeing.

Nan doesn't seem to give a shit that you were in here dry-boning her granddaughter.

The sounds of Nan bustling around Abbott's kitchen can be heard, drawers opening and closing like she's doing a home inspection. In reality, the old broad is giving us time to pull ourselves together.

"Anyhoo, are you both free tomorrow? Who is going to meet an old woman for lunch?"

My dick might be a droopy, useless piece of shit, but my ears work just fine and what they heard was *Who wants a free meal?*

I shoot Abbott a look at the same time she shoots me one.

My shoulders rise and fall, head bobbing, and I whisper, "I could eat," to my cute, half-naked neighbor.

"Yeah?" she whispers back, putting her socks back on. Fully clothed, she still wraps herself in a blanket. "Same. I could always eat."

"Cool." I throw a few pillows back onto the couch, tucking my T-shirt into my bottoms. I raise my voice, calling to the kitchen. "Nan, we could both eat."

"Excellent. I'll just get out of your hair. Grandpa is waiting in the car." A cabinet shuts. "Abbott, darling, I'll text you the details."

Text her the details. "She could have texted you in the first place!" I hiss, too embarrassed about getting caught fooling around red-handed by a girl's grandma to actually go speak to Nan face-to-face.

"You think I don't know that!?" Abbott shakes her head. "I'll go say goodbye, you tuck in your pee-pee."

I glance down.

The cock I thought had lost its erection continues to poke at the fabric of my pants, wanting to stick itself in something hot and wet, Abbott in particular—apparently no interruptions from a seventy-year-old can keep the good man down.

I glance across the room, catching the all-knowing eye of Desdemona.

Is it just me or…does the cat have one eyebrow arched?

Judgmental bitch.

15

ABBOTT

"And then," I pause for dramatic effect, "my nan walked in."

Sophia gasps, and I know she's actually covering her mouth with the back of her hand despite the fact that I can't actually see her. "Who gave her a key?"

"All you have to say is *who gave her a key?*"

I hear my best friend take a bite of her bagel through the phone, chewing thoughtfully. "Did she actually see anything?"

"She claims to have seen Brooks' wiener, but he wasn't completely naked and she never actually walked into the living room. So, no, I don't think she saw anything. Plus, she announced herself before actually coming into the living room, probably assuming we were fooling around."

Which we kind of were.

I hear her pause. I *hear* her glare. "Did you just use the word wiener? Don't do that again. Say penis."

I shake my head vigorously. "I hate the word penis. It's weird."

Penis, fart, bloated—all words I can't bring myself to say.

Eww.

I shake my head again for good measure, on the verge of making myself dizzy. "She does the same thing to my cousins and my brother—she's like the Elf on the Shelf. Just magically appears, makes magic happen in the apartment—occasionally a mess, but most of the time it's amazing." Albeit invasive.

"Sounds amazing. It also sounds like she walked in on you while you were dry-humping the shit out of your hot neighbor, and that sounds kind of terrible."

Exactly. "I don't know who was more horrified—Nan, Brooks, or the cat."

"The cat was there, too?"

"I mean, she was on her bed, so it's not like she was *there* there."

"The cat was definitely watching."

Why is Sophia being so difficult? "No, the cat was sleeping. Can we please stay on track? I have a conference call with Bambi What'sHerFace in half an hour and then I have to scoot out for lunch."

"Right—lunch with Nan, the break-in artist, and your neighbor, who most likely has himself a bad case of blue balls."

I end my call with Sophia still shaking my head; I do that a lot when she and I talk. She can be exasperating and loves to play devil's advocate.

Taking a few minutes in my office, I primp a bit before my meeting, hoping it's short-lived and quick so I can dash out the door, hail a cab, and get to our lunch reservation before Nan or Brooks arrive.

Three minutes later, I'm heading out of my office.

I give the door to Bambi's shared, communal office a rap with my knuckles, folder clenched in my other hand. A younger man named Ryan, who has the best vantage point of the door, spins in his chair and gestures for me to enter.

It's a creative space with four desks, one in each corner of the room, separated by both wooden and file cabinets, a large counter island splitting the room down the center.

A buzz of energy zings in the air; it's a fun room, a shared design and workspace.

Bambi is one of two females in this department, and I find her slumped a bit at her desk, shoulders quaking a little.

I glance over my left shoulder at Ryan.

He shrugs, pulling a face and lifting his palms helplessly.

"Bambi?"

"Hey Abbott, what's up?" Bambi clears her throat, wiping a tear from the corner of her eye.

"We have a meeting at eleven." I'm matter-of-fact and stern, lacing my statement with the disappointment I feel upon discovering she's unprepared.

I don't plan on being late for my lunch date. It's the only thing I've looked forward to in a long time, other than Brooks coming to my place and spending time with me a few times a week.

That I love and look forward to quite a bit.

This meeting with Bambi? Not so much. The girl resents my authority and has tried to thwart me since day one, and this meeting was my chance to gain an upper hand.

"Oh shit, that's right. I forgot."

She forgot? *Nice.* I make a mental note of the oversight for her manager since she's already on my shit list.

"I'm so sorry."

Oh.

Well.

That I wasn't expecting.

Bambi turns to face me, and it's then I notice her puffy red eyes and swollen nose.

"What's wrong? Is everything okay?" It's a dumb question because clearly, everything is not okay—not if she's been bawling her eyes out at work and can't manage to be professional.

Not to be a brat, but she should have canceled our meeting and taken a personal day. She's obviously not working.

"No, everything isn't okay." Her head dips again and I take a second to glance over at Ryan, who's surveying us intently. There is no doubt that if their other two officemates weren't otherwise occupied, they'd be staring, too.

Here goes one for the company rumor mill...

"What's wrong?"

"M-My..." She sucks in a breath. "My boyfriend broke up with me."

She had a boyfriend? Dang, how did I not know that? "Oh Bambi, I'm so sorry! How long were you together?"

"Not long, but long enough. It felt like we'd known each other our whole lives."

"I am so sorry," I repeat, not knowing what else to say, torn between comforting her as if she were a true friend and keeping my distance since we've never gotten along well. "What was his name?"

Her head shoots up, and she sniffles. "Blaine."

Blaine?

Figures she'd find the one guy in town with a name douchier than Brooks. Bet Blaine is a real piece of work, too.

"I know he loved me—he'd just started saying it." Bambi's eyes narrow. "His friends hated me."

Big shocker. "How do you know?"

"They've been trying to break us up since we met." Her chin tilts arrogantly. "They're intimidated by a strong female."

Oh brother. "I'm sure they didn't hate you."

"No, no—they did. He let it slip once."

"He did?" What an idiot.

"Blaine isn't the smartest—I could talk him into anything. He's very easily influenced, so if his friends hated me, we didn't stand a chance. He's known them longer than I have, so they always won."

I stand quietly next to her desk, leaning my hip against the counter as she goes on, floodgates now open.

"Honestly, they say jump and Blaine says how high. I was getting so sick of it." She inhales a shaky breath. "Ugh, and they meet all the time at this dumb bar, never invite me along, and smoke cigars."

Sounds like a real gem.

"Maybe you're better off without some guy who can't stand up to his friends."

What kind of guy is that? One with no spine. Gross, who wants that?

"He has this one friend who is such a douchebag. The freaking worst—thinks his shit doesn't stink because he has this great job and makes all this money. Bosses them all around."

Basically like every other guy I've ever met. Typical of a group—there always has to be one in the bunch who takes charge. The ringleader, as they say.

I set the green folder I've been holding on Bambi's desk, giving it a little pat. "I'll just leave these here. Take a look at them when you can. And could I offer you a little advice?"

"Sure."

"Take the day off, go get a facial—then forget about that dickhead. Anyone who chooses his friends over you doesn't deserve the tears you're wasting on him right now. Somewhere in this city is someone who will be better for you."

Her brilliant blonde hair flips. "I know. That's what all my friends keep saying."

"Because it's true."

"It sounds easy, but it's not. I've tried. I lie in bed scrolling through Instagram, and whenever I read an insightful breakup meme, I cry."

Jeez. Drama queen. "It'll get easier."

This time, I *do* reach my hand out, placing it on her back, giving her a little rub. Round and round my hand goes, comforting the woman who only a short ten minutes ago I was dreading having to sit down with.

We're not out of the woods yet; she hasn't seen the notes I wrote then tucked away in the folder on her desk…

"I'm going to leave you alone—go home, relax. Take a hot bath and have a good cry." Another one, apparently, because it looks like that's all she's been doing. "Come back tomorrow, and when you have the chance, look over these notes. I'll have my secretary set up another meeting at the beginning of next week, and we'll touch base then. In the meantime…" Pat, pat, pat on her back. I feel like I'm soothing a sleeping lion. "Pack it up and get out of here."

"Thanks boss." She sniffles, and I pause.

Whoa.

Did she just call me boss?

Holy hell. Is that an acknowledgment that I'm a higher-up? Finally?

She's delirious and feeling vulnerable, Abbott—slow your roll. Bambi won't remember on Monday, and she almost certainly isn't going to repeat the phrase.

"Okay. I'm heading to my lunch date a little early. When I get back, I expect you to be gone." I give her a mischievous grin, kissing her ass the tiniest bit, because honestly? Bambi Warner intimidates me.

No big secret there, I know.

The list of people who do isn't long: my grandfather, my father, and Nan's sister Auntie Dibs who has nine cats and is terrifying and intriguing.

And Bambi Warner, based on her palpable dislike for me.

If she's going to be sweet and simpering, I'm going to take full advantage.

There are keys in the pocket of my slacks, and I give them a jingle. "Alright. I'm headed out." I crane my head toward Ryan, making a show and pointing a finger at him, putting him in charge. "You make sure she gets out of here. Don't you dare let her linger."

Wink-wink at Bambi, who eats it all up.

I give them both a wave as I exit the office, letting out a breath and straightening my spine, running a pair of sweaty palms down the front of my pants.

They're black and pleated, chosen with care, Brooks in mind. I didn't want to wear a skirt and look like I was trying too hard for this mini date with Nan and my neighbor, but I didn't want to look like I *wasn't* trying either. If that makes sense.

My blouse is demure but sexy, high collar with a bow that ties at the neck. It shows nothing but is somehow alluring, at least in my opinion.

My hair is straight, falling in dark sheets down my back. Sleek. Glossy. Thick. Tucked behind my ears, simple diamond studs in my lobes.

Minimal makeup, but red lips.

It's a gorgeous day, so I pass on grabbing a jacket but do make the quick jaunt to Sophia's office one block over, one last time before I won't see her over the weekend, and to fill her in on my afternoon activities.

My bestie *oohs* and *aahs* at my cherry red lips when I pucker them. "Them's blow job lips," she declares.

I deflect. "There's no way I'd be any good at a blow job. I haven't given one in ages."

"Men don't care. Brooks is going to see those lips and that's all he's going to be able to think about. Those lips, his dick." Sophia clicks out a few lines into her spreadsheet. "Just watch— he won't be able to peel his eyes away."

"Blah blah," I say for lack of anything better.

Is she right? Will he stare at my lips and think about blowies?

In the car on the way to the restaurant, I give my face another look, make sure my lips are on straight and not smudged.

It's perfect, so I confidently exit the cab and step one heeled foot out onto the concrete curb, surprised when a masculine hand extends to steady me.

It's Brooks.

He's early. *Really* early.

"You're early," I say dumbly when he fails to release my hand.

"So are you." He flicks the wrist on the opposite hand so the cuff of his shirt moves, giving him a view of his watch face. "By almost twenty minutes, you weirdo."

"I had a meeting end before it began, so I thought I'd scout the place out." Although knowing Nan, when she made the reservation, she chose a specific table.

"Grab a drink?" he asks, releasing my hand and tweaking his shirt, pulling the fabric over his watch. Brooks also gives me a cursory side glance as he holds the restaurant door open, allowing me to enter first. "You, uh, look nice, by the way."

I catch a whiff of his fresh, woodsy cologne as I breeze past him. "Thank you."

I fight the urge to tell him he looks nice, too. We match—or coordinate—both of us in soft, baby blue shirts. His is a French cuff button-down with thick, silky fabric under a navy jacket. Dark trousers. Brown polished dress shoes.

He's wearing sunglasses but removes them when we step over the threshold, casing the joint. Smiling at the hostess behind the counter.

"We have a reservation. I believe it would be under—" He glances at me. "What's your grandmother's actual name? I can't call her Nan."

That makes me giggle. "Maureen."

Brooks leans against the counter. "Maureen Margolis."

The hostess schools her impressed expression, a face I've encountered a thousand times since I was old enough to recognize when someone was fascinated by my last name, then gestures toward the dining room beyond.

"Mrs. Margolis is already seated at your table. Please follow me right this way."

"Of course Nan is already here," Brooks quips. "Good old Nan."

"Yeah—good ol' breaking and entering Nan," I volley back, throwing in to remind him, "who claims to have seen all your best bits."

I feel the faint hint of Brooks' fingertips grazing the small of my back as he lets me lead the way. "No way did she see my downtown bonanza—she didn't actually walk into the room."

"To be fair, I didn't see them either, and I was there in the room when you stripped off your pants."

"How could you have missed it? It's huge. Ginormous," he boasts, causing us to both laugh.

"I'm sure it is. How do you fit into regular pants?"

"It's a challenge."

And then.

There is Nan.

My grandmother, the icon, sitting in a corner booth, silver hair coiffed to perfection, radiating joy once she lays eyes on Brooks and me. Napkin already in her lap (a rule I was taught growing up—napkin goes in your lap as soon as you sit at a dining table), my grandmother sets it aside so she can rise and greet me with a kiss on the cheek.

One cheek, then the other. *Kiss kiss.*

She does the same to Brooks, the French-style greeting always a quintessential favorite in our household. If there's one thing Nan loves, it's anything European and cultured.

"Darling," she coos into my ear when we slide back into the booth. "You look beautiful."

I could be wearing a brown paper bag and my grandma would think I looked stunning, but I take the compliment as gospel because Nan never lies.

"Thanks, Nan. So do you—that pink is spectacular." She is striking in a true pink, Elle Woods all grown up and come to life. All Nan is missing is a pet Chihuahua and bleach blonde hair. "It's nice that your table was available."

"My table is always available, dear," she remarks, placing the white linen napkin back on her lap. Brooks and I follow suit.

"They wouldn't dare put you somewhere else," I tease. In truth? This restaurant wouldn't dare put Maureen Margolis at the wrong table.

Not that Nan is difficult or catty or would throw a fit, but she likes what she likes and is a known figure in the city. Most establishments want to keep her happy so they can keep her as a patron of their establishment.

Where Maureen Margolis goes, people will follow.

Old people, but still.

Once we're settled and drinks have been ordered, Nan relaxes into the rich burgundy material of the booth, hands clasped in front of her.

"So, what exactly was it that I walked in on last night?"

I choke on my water, wishing it were vodka. "Nothing!"

"You think I don't know fooling around when I see it? You're lucky I didn't walk straight into the living room when I entered the apartment. Who knows what my poor eyes would have witnessed."

"Nothing!" I repeat, perhaps a bit too loudly. "Nothing," I say for the third time, now in a lower tone.

"I like your style, Nan. Way to go for the jugular."

"That poor cat—what has it seen?" she goes on. "Perhaps I should get little Desdemona a mask so you don't blind the creature."

"I thought you liked Desi." After all, it was Nan's idea to get a cat in the first place. *"Just one cat, dear,"* she instructed. *"We don't want you turning into a cat lady. And some men don't like cats. You don't want to acquire a passel of them and turn anyone off once you start dating."* As if dating to find a man was my single objective in life.

She is so old-school, straight out of the 1950s. Even though she met Grandpa at work, Nan became a healthy mix of housewife and business professional I don't think I could master if I tried.

It will be one or the other with me; I cannot multitask…

"I do like Desi," Nan is saying, sipping along the rim of her martini glass. "That's why I want to get the scamp a mask." She raises her professionally shaped brows. "Maybe some ear plugs?"

My cheeks flush.

Brooks shifts uncomfortably, fiddling with the links on his cuffs. I inspect them and discover the crest of our alma mater, hewn in shiny silver.

Pleased, my secret smile is hidden when I take a drink of my own beverage, an unsweet tea Nan had brought around—no alcohol for me when I'll be returning to work after lunch. No one wants to see a tipsy Abbott, except perhaps Bambi Warner, and I sent her home for a damn spa day.

Stupid, stupid, stupid.

"Abbott, sweetie, would you like a shot of tequila? You're looking a little stiff."

Good lord, Nan can be such a bad influence sometimes.

"I'm good, thanks."

"Actually, that's not a bad idea." Brooks sits up straighter in his seat. "Maybe just what we need. I'm keyed up from a shitty —oops, excuse my language—from a meeting I left at the office."

Same, same, same. "Right, but it's still the middle of the work day."

"Oh darling, don't be such a pooh." Nan lifts an elegant hand with its collection of thin gold and diamond bracelets, motioning for the server. "We'll take two shots of tequila, please."

"Two? Why only two? Aren't you going to take a shot?" After all, it was her idea. But now that I think of it, I've never seen Nan drinking anything other than champagne or a cocktail from a martini glass.

She pulls a face and picks up a menu, pretending to study it. "Don't be silly, darling—it's Wednesday."

Brooks and I exchange glances.

When the shots arrive at the table, we tip our heads back like champs, Nan looking on, a satisfied smile etched across her graceful face.

We order more food than I'll ever be able to eat, mostly

because I'm nervous and couldn't stop myself. The bread basket was a given—I always order that—shrimp cocktail as an appetizer, lobster bisque as my soup, a wedge salad with blue cheese dressing, and for my entrée, a crab salad.

Evidently, for me, it's all about seafood today.

I always hesitate to order seafood when I'm on a date (not that I go on many) because it's so much more expensive than most other entrées on the menu, and typically I date men I know cannot afford to feed me lobster at every meal.

However, since I'm with Nan and Brooks and neither of them are going to judge me, I splurge. Plus, since it's so much food, I look forward to boxing up the leftovers for takeaway and eating them for dinner.

"How is everyone at the office, dear?" Nan asks to catch up. She stopped coming in when Grandpa decided to semi-retire, she herself having quit years before that to meddle in the lives of her grandchildren.

Her interference has become a full-time job for her, and I've come to consider the ceaseless prying a comfort, oddly enough. There will come a day Nan when won't be poking her nose into everyone's business, and we will surely miss it. The thought doesn't escape me, and I refuse to take her for granted.

Even if she does drive us bonkers.

"Everything is…" I hesitate, not wanting to lie. "It's alright. I was scheduled to have a meeting before our lunch, but the girl was having a meltdown at her desk, so that was shot." I swirl the ice around my water glass. "This woman has been a thorn in my side for months."

"Oh, tell me more," Nan enthuses, as if I'm about to dish on celebrity gossip and not the dysfunctional inner-workings of her husband's company.

"Her boyfriend broke up with her and she can't stop crying. I swear, she's the type who would set fire to the building if he didn't text her back."

Brooks shakes his head. "Why should he text her back if they broke up?"

"It would make my life easier, that's why." I laugh. "She was impossible to communicate with before, and now I'm afraid all she's going to do is cry every day. I can't afford to send her for spa treatments whenever she decides she's in a funk. It's not productive."

Brooks nods. "Two things that should be outlawed in the corporate marketplace: cigarette breaks and breakups. Bad for productivity."

"I remember when I used to smoke, I'd take my break out on the rooftop for an entire hour when we were only allowed fifteen minutes." Nan looks at me and fluffs her hair. "Grandpa was none the wiser."

"Nan, you probably reeked like an ashtray—I'm sure he knew what you were up to."

"Those days were different, darling. I smoked these long, sleek menthols, and Grandpa smoked a mahogany pipe—so debonair. We played bridge and went dancing, he would cop a feel, and that's how things were back in the day."

"Cop a feel?"

"That was your grandfather's way of flirting—he was so terrible at it. Barely cracked a smile, so serious all the time when the company was in its infancy."

"By infancy, do you mean a high-rise with fewer floors? Because as long as I can remember, it's always been nutty."

From what I can recall, once Grandpa started the company, it expanded within months, his office going from the living room of his one-bedroom apartment to a rented office space on the outskirts of town. To an office in an actual office building. To an entire floor. To the entire building.

All you need is an idea, a dream, and a little drive, he always says.

"Well yes, fewer floors." She sips her cosmo, hot pink lipstick staining the rim of the glass. "You know what I mean."

I shoot a glance at Brooks, who seems amused. I give him a wan smile of apology that my grandmother is so naively high maintenance, bless her heart.

"What about the two of you?" Nan's blue gaze is directed at Brooks, pointed and unyielding.

"Ma'am, I can assure you, I don't cop any feels where Abbott is concerned. I'm a proper gentleman."

Nan's mouth contorts, disappointed. "That's a shame."

I agree, tipping my head in acknowledgment, only Nan catching the subtle motion.

She winks.

Raises her hand slightly to catch the eye of a passing server and asks, "Would you be a doll and bring us a few glasses of your best white?"

"Ma'am?" The server's hands are behind her back, a black apron tied around her narrow waist. Black shirt. Black tie. Sleek, brunette hair.

"We're celebrating," Nan tells her in a not-so-hushed whisper.

This piques my interest. "What are we celebrating?" I thought this was just lunch.

"New friends." She's beaming at us, and I'm not sure if she's referring to her meeting Brooks, or to me meeting Brooks—if we're here celebrating my new relationship with my neighbor, I might die and shrivel up from humiliation.

The subject of my humiliation raises his glass when the drinks arrive on a silver tray. *Ooh la la.*

Nan picks the napkin up from her lap and dabs at the corner of her mouth. Scoots to the end of the seat and rises. "Well, I just remembered somewhere I have to be." Her purse gets slung over her shoulder; it's expensive, beige and silver braided chain complimenting her hair. "I hate when I double-book myself."

Double-booked my ass, I cogitate, narrowing my eyes.

That double-crossing monster! She did this on purpose, and

now I'm stuck here waiting on lunch, on a date orchestrated by my grandmother, of all people.

Talk about awkward. "Let me walk you out," I begin, starting to rise.

She puts a hand out to stop me. "No time, dear. I've got to be off."

Yeah, so you can scurry out of here like a rat—because you know I'm onto your antics!

Her soft hand pats me on the cheek. "You're so pretty when your cheeks are flushed." She leans in to hug me, whispering, "Freshen up your lipstick, dear. The red rubbed off during the bread basket course."

My lips open.

Close.

Indignant.

I'd sputter if I could get words out.

Brooks is on his feet, enveloping my tiny grandmother in his arms, rubbing her back and checking to see that she has everything she came with.

"Do you need me to call you a cab?"

"Aren't you a dear."

I'm a dear, he's a dear. *She's laying it on pretty damn thick, this one.*

"No worries, the maître d' will be glad to call one for me."

There's probably been a taxi waiting around the corner the entire time we've been sitting here, I wager to myself, confident I'd win if I were a betting woman.

I'm not.

In fact, I never win anything, let alone bets—therefore, I've learned to never make them.

I have the worst luck.

"Where are you headed?" Brooks politely inquires, waiting while Nan pulls an answer out of her ass, avoiding my penetrating gaze.

She hesitates a split second. "Gardening club."

His brows go up like I knew they would. "They have gardening clubs in the city?"

Not ones she'd be a member of, I want to grumble.

"Where do you even put the flowers? Rooftops? It's all concrete!" He's genuinely perplexed, and I wish he would stop the inquisition so he doesn't expose her lie.

That would be more embarrassing.

"Did I say gardening club?" Nan doesn't even have the courtesy to look abashed. "I meant I have a meeting at the children's wing of the new hospital. I'm on the board and there's a staff meeting this afternoon. If I want to make it across town in traffic, I should leave now."

She hasn't even waited for the food to arrive before going through with her ruse, probably paid for the entire meal well in advance and gave the server instructions for Brooks and me to have carte blanche—most likely even instructed the staff to keep the alcohol flowing.

As if he and I need alcohol to enjoy each other's company. As if he needs alcohol to find me attractive.

Beer goggles in the middle of the day, Nan? Please.

"Make bad decisions!" She tosses a wave over her shoulder, not glancing back once.

"Did she just say make good decisions, or did she say…" He scratches the top of his head, confused.

I sip my wine. "Oh you heard her correctly. She most definitely told us to make bad decisions."

Typical.

"Was she always like this?"

"Pretty much—as far back as I can remember, she's been outrageous as far as grandmothers go. It used to drive my mom crazy."

"She's your dad's mom?"

"Yup." I guzzle another mouthful, the crisp wine going down sweet and smooth. "My mom resented her when I was growing up because Nan was always too involved in our raising. But who could blame Nan? My mother worked a ton and wasn't around much, so someone had to do it."

My parents met in college, and to prove she wasn't just after his family's money, my mother insisted on holding a job the entire time they were married, working long hours and climbing the corporate ladder in an entirely different industry.

It escaped no one's notice that Mom retained the Margolis last name long after their divorce—even keeping it through her second marriage.

The marriage? Lasted until I was in my teens, but by that point, Nan had completely inserted herself as a nurturing, parental constant in my life.

Dad is a workaholic.

Mom is a workaholic.

Grandpa is a workaholic.

My brother and I had Nan to keep things normal. The Margolis version of normal, that is.

"She looks super conservative in those suits of hers."

"It's a lie," I pointedly tell him as I select a piece of bread from the basket, pull it into pieces, and drag one through olive oil and balsamic vinaigrette.

"I can see that now."

"It's all a front so she can be inappropriate and obnoxious and no one suspects her of any wrongdoing." Except maybe my grandfather, who loves every bit of her nonsense.

Which is the way it should be when you love someone unconditionally, like they do.

Ride or die, till death do they part.

Nan will go down kicking and screaming in her bouclé suits and silver jewelry specifically chosen to match her hair.

"You look just like her. It's kind of freaky-deaky."

This gives me pause. No one has ever told me that before. "Really?"

"If she wasn't so much older, I'd think she was your mom. Except for the hair."

I swirl my bread in oil, toying with it. "I actually have naturally blonde hair. Had. Have—whatever, I dye it."

Brooks is shocked by this revelation. "Why?"

I shrug but don't bite the bread in my hands. "To set myself apart. To be taken more seriously at work?"

There. I said it.

Confessions of a trust fund baby: to be taken more seriously in the workplace, change your physical appearance to appear less airheaded. Platinum blonde beauties garner way too much attention of the wrong variety.

"I want people to hear me, not just see me. So, when I first got the job out of college, I dyed my hair this color, and I've kept it this way since."

A rich brown, darker at the top than at the ends, the ombre phase I went through still going strong. I love my hair.

"So you dye your eyebrows, too?"

I nod. "Yup."

Brooks' eyes betray him, almost straying to my lap.

I know what he's wondering: he wants to know if the curtains match the drapes, but he's too much of a gentleman to ask, despite the curiosity.

The answer is: they do not.

And yes, I have hair down there, because I'm not dating anyone, and really, who cares. I'm not torturing myself by waxing that shit off.

I giggle, holding a few fingers to my laughing lips. "This alcohol is going to my head."

"Eat something. The food should be here soon, but have some more bread." He gives the basket a nudge in my direction, handsome in his blue shirt that matches mine.

I almost sigh out loud.

"For what it's worth, you're a knockout as a brunette." He winks.

A knockout.

Not a single soul has called me that. No one would ever dare tell Abbott Margolis she was anything but stunning or pretty, or —choose any highbrow word you can think of other than knockout or hot.

That word is reserved for sexy women. It's something I've never considered myself to be.

Plain. Serious. Cute.

Adorable.

Those are the words I'd assign myself—never a knockout. Never sexy.

I'm classy.

Safe.

Ugh, I want to shove this entire loaf of bread in my mouth and swallow my feelings.

He called you a knockout—stop overthinking it and nod your head, sheesh.

I do jam bread in my mouth, craning my neck toward the kitchen, eyes assessing every tray being carried out, shoulders slouching when not a one is ours.

When the food does appear, two sets arrive, not the three that were ordered when my grandmother was here.

Nan, you devious fiend…

How can I be mad about it, though, when the company sitting across from me at the table is handsome and funny, hanging on my every word. Asking me questions and being attentive, refilling my water glass from the sleek carafe. Standing when I have to use the bathroom. Perhaps the atmosphere of this old establishment is making him feel like a gentleman? Because he's definitely acting like one.

It's a nice change from the casual Brooks I've gotten to know at home. The change of scene, stepping out of the familiar same ol' same ol' of our confined apartment complex.

We've eaten and are outside on the curb, glancing up and down the busy intersection, Brooks in the direction of his office, me in the direction of mine.

I teeter a bit on my black heels, and Brooks notices.

My spine stiffens as I give the illusion of complete and utter sobriety.

That doesn't escape his notice, either, and he side-eyes me. "Do you think our nan was trying to get us drunk?"

"It's definitely possible." She's shady as fuck, now that we're discussing it. "I hate to be the one to point this out, but that all seemed very methodical and planned out."

"You think?"

I cringe. "Are you being sarcastic?"

"No, I'm being serious. You know her better than I do."

"Yes, that was a well-thought-out plot to get us alone, in a romantic setting."

"Dinner would have been better. It's too bright out here."

We squint up at the sun in tandem. "Ugh." I push at it with my hands, shielding my precious retinas from the blinding rays. "Gross, it's like a lunar eclipse."

"Stop staring directly at it!" Brooks chastises, pushing at my hands so I'll drop them and stop glaring at the offensive orb in the sky.

"I *can't* now that you mentioned it being bright outside, guh!"

"Wow, you really are drunk."

So is he, and if he's not, he has an amazing tolerance for early-afternoon alcohol.

"And on a Wednesday. How embarrassing."

"Do you never cut loose and get drunk in the middle of the week?"

"Sure," he replies. "Back when I was in college, maybe, but we're adults and it's the middle of the work day."

I'm holding my phone, ready to order a car to ferry me back to the office.

"You going back to work now?" he inquires, checking his watch and tipping slightly on the curb, courtesy of the tequila shots and all the wine we tipped back at lunch.

We are in no condition to go back to our respective offices!

Is he hinting at something? Does he want to go do something with me, or was he simply being polite by inquiring into my plans? "I was planning on it? It's so nice out though."

"We *could* play hooky. Walk around the park, or see a movie. Duck into the mall and try on cologne. I have a little leeway on my deadline, and I'm ahead, so…"

"Are you attempting to corrupt me? I have an amazing work ethic, you know. I may need more convincing to break the rules."

"Rules. Right."

"I'm a stickler for them when it comes to my job."

"I can tell."

I cross my arms. "*How* can you tell?"

"You have a look of determination, and you didn't immediately fall for the bait. Someone with shitty work ethic would have agreed to go do something right away. You? You hesitated."

I don't point out that the *reason* had nothing to do with work ethic and everything to do with me feeling out if he was asking me out or not.

"I don't do anything without thinking it through first," I admit bashfully. "That's just how I was raised." To exercise caution, weigh options and consequences, measure benefits. Sounds like a fun childhood, doesn't it?

"Live a little."

"I will when I'm sober."

"You're sober enough, and so am I. What should we go do?"

I don't know, but if we keep standing here, I'm going to get hungry again. "Skip out of work, go to the park, eat a cheap hot dog for dessert, then go back to the apartments and binge the new series they released yesterday."

"New series? Which one?"

"Have you been living under a rock?" I put my arm out and whistle loudly, hitching a cab instead of calling an Uber. There are plenty circling the block—no need to wait five minutes for a cheaper ride. "It's the street gang one. Looks violent but amazing."

He perks up, interested. "Violent but amazing? Sounds like my kind of afternoon."

A yellow taxi pulls up along the curb, and Brooks grabs the door, holding it open so I can climb in first. "East Elm Park, please," I instruct the driver as my neighbor hops in beside me.

I open my purse, ransacking it for an elastic hair tie. If we're going to the park, I'll need to put my hair up. I don't need it blowing all over the place. "I don't think we need more alcohol today, so do not offer me any tonight. Period. I smell like a vineyard from that bottle we drank after Nan skipped out on us. Pure alcohol. The last thing I need in my life is more fermented grapes."

"So what you're saying is, you want a shower and a couch?" His head is resting against the headrest, tilted toward me as we chatter, block after block.

"After we bum around the park, yes. Doesn't junk food sound like the perfect dessert?"

"No, but if that's what you want to do…" His voice trails off and he gazes out the window, watching the world fly by as we zip down the city streets. The brakes being slammed on by the cabbie, pedestrians stepping in front of the car at crosswalks.

Typical.

We lurch forward after another red light, and I can see the park from here.

"Aww, what baby wants, baby gets?" I tease him like I would if I were his girlfriend and he were spoiling me by humoring my weird request though we've just had a two-hundred-dollar lunch.

"I mean, generally, that's my rule."

Point taken—we're not dating, so that's his rule with other women, just not with me.

Well, la-di-da. I can still flirt with him if I want to, big whoop. It's a free country; I can do what I want.

"It takes more than a hot dog to turn my head, trust me."
Like two hot dogs.

"Good, 'cause we're walking around the park, not walking in
the park so I can propose marriage at the concession stand."

My hand flies to my mouth. "We're both drunkish. We can't
be held responsible for anything we say in this cab, or at the
park. Deal?"

"Deal. But we're not *that* drunk." Brooks nudges me from
his side of the back seat. "You know you want me to propose."

I roll my eyes. "Dream on, pal."

Except…that's what I'll dream about later tonight, when I'm
in bed, staring at the ceiling.

Alone.

Yay me.

Fighting midday traffic, it takes us longer than usual to reach
our destination, and we arrive at a somewhat deserted park, save
for a few vendors at the entrance.

Churros. Popcorn. Soda pop and water. The usual street
vendors, hustling for the mighty dollar.

I eyeball the hot dogs on the corner, deciding I'll hold out to
see what the next cart has to offer.

"I thought you said you wanted a dog." Brooks stuffs his
hands in his pockets, slouching as we stroll past the blue and
yellow umbrella'd cart.

"Not big enough. I'll need two stuffed into one bun."

"You say that like you've done it before."

"Oh, I've absolutely done it before."

"So just get two hot dogs then stuff them in one bun."

The last thing I need is for him to see me shoving two
wieners into my face at once. "Yes, but I don't want you
watching me."

"They're small—it won't be a big deal. Two is the size of one
ballpark frank."

So true. Which is why I always get two. "Fine. But you can't
make fun of me."

"Me? Would I do that?"

"Yes."

We double back, approaching the hot dog vendor, Brooks already reaching for his wallet and pulling out a ten-dollar bill. "Can I get two hot dogs in one bun, please?"

A set of bushy brows gets raised, but no further questions are asked as he prepares a bun, sticks two meaty franks inside, and wraps it in foil sandwich paper. "Six bucks."

Brooks hands him the cash and the man hands him the hot dog, which he immediately hands to me.

The man laughs, and I watch to make sure spit doesn't fly out of his mouth and onto the food because I'm strange like that. "Your girlfriend sure has an appetite."

"This is not my girlfriend," Brooks replies swiftly, correcting the nice man who's just handed me my dessert.

"This is *not* my girlfriend," I mimic, giving him a shove in the arm as I unwrap the dogs to squeeze condiments on them. "You don't have to say it like that. Jeez, way to insult me."

"You're not."

Yes, I know. We continue to joke and tease and argue about it, the tension building as we begin along the walking path.

Brooks likes me and I like him, except neither one of us will admit it and suddenly I feel twelve years old again, not sure how to act around a cute boy I like.

Just admit you like me! I want to shout. But instead, I take an unladylike chomp out of the double dog in my hand.

"You don't have to keep saying it!" I nip a bite off the end, chewing.

"Once. I said it *once!*" he argues back, the hot dog vendor taking a step back, hands going up in a defeated salute.

"Sorry pal, didn't mean to start a fight."

I whip my head around. "We're not fighting." Force a smile, bite down on my dog, this morsel bigger, filling my mouth. "We're being playful and flippant."

"Flippant." Brooks runs his large hand through his hair. "It shouldn't turn me on when you say things like that."

I throw out some more big words. "Capricious. Fastidious. Malaise. Perfunctory." Take a huge bite of my snack as we stroll along down the sidewalk. It weaves over a bridge, situated over a man-made "lake," through plants and flowers that have already gone dormant with the cool weather. In summer, the park is gorgeous. Romantic and perfect. Tons of couples flock here for engagement and wedding photos.

"Show-off."

"Trifle. Dally. Flirt." I pause on the bridge, halfway finished with my two hot dogs in one bun. "Delicious."

Brooks stares.

"What?" I lick at my mouth but don't taste anything that could possibly be stuck to the side of my lips.

"You have a little something..." He points at the corner of my mouth with the tip of his finger, wind whipping at his hair and mine.

I shiver when he touches me.

He shivers, too. "There."

With a hot dog in one hand, I point to my face with the other. "What?"

"You have mustard on your..."

I know where he's pointing but play dumb and point to my cheekbone. "Here?"

"No. Your mouth."

"Oh, so here." I stick out my tongue like a brat, knowing darn well there are bun chunks and bits of hot dog on it.

Brooks laughs, taking me by the shoulders. "Hold still." Gets in close, swiping a thumb over my bottom lip, pressing into that little divot in the corner. The tip of my tongue sticks out. Gives his finger a playful lick.

"Delicious."

He stares and stares, hands still braced on my shoulders,

fingers pressing into the wool of my coat; I can feel his heat through the thick fabric.

"Don't."

"Don't what?"

"Flirt with me."

"I'm not." I hold up the hot dog, practically holding the bun in his face. "I meant the hot dogs—they're delicious."

"Right," he deadpans, knowing I'm full of shit. His finger is delicious. He is delicious. I want to lick more of him—and he wants me to.

"They are. Want a bite?"

"No."

But Brooks hasn't moved away. Hasn't let go of me. Hasn't stopped staring at my mouth.

What is he doing? It looks like he's going to kiss me, but since I've been awkwardly eating, this certainly isn't the moment to get romantic for the first time.

I'm not thinking straight, because Nan plied me with wine in the hopes that we would both make questionable decisions. Nan wanted us to end up in bed, shifty matchmaking grandmother that she is. She's a sneaky minx who loves romance, who would love nothing more than to see me settled down with the love of my life.

And Nan has got it in her head that the love of my life is Brooks.

The alcohol has gone to both of our heads a bit. Here we are, standing like two fools whose lips are about to touch, and suddenly there Brooks is, bending his head and leaning in for a kiss. *Wait—what?*

What is happening?

I want to jerk back to look at his face; surely he knows what he's about to do? And with whom? You don't just kiss your friend. Friends don't just plant one on the other person out of the blue. You don't take them to romantic parks and go on leisurely strolls.

Fine. Maybe you do.

But he is kissing me, warm tongue mingling with my mustard, ketchup, and hot dog mouth, and could he have chosen a worse time for this? *Really, Brooks? Just after I've eaten two hot dogs?* Kind of gross. Even I can't deny that.

He does not care.

I'm tempted to apologize, because I wouldn't kiss him if he were the one who had just scarfed down an entire hot dog, but I think better of it. Decide to enjoy the moment despite the circumstances.

Warm, warm lips. Gentle but firm, planted over mine. And if I had to describe it, I'd say more than anything, it's a nice kiss, considering the situation. Nice. Pleasant. Lovely. Words he wouldn't love hearing, but true nonetheless.

Eventually he pulls back, removes his hands from my body a short few seconds later. Steps back and regards me, breath leaving his nose in quick puffs.

I let out a sigh. "Well."

Brooks nods. "Glad we got that out of the way."

Out of the way? "Have you been thinking about doing that?"

"Kind of but not really? It seemed like a good thing to do at the time."

"At the park while I'm eating a hot dog?" I laugh, side-eyeing him before balling up the garbage in my hands and stepping toward a nearby waste bin. Toss the crumpled silver wrapper into the trash and glance at him standing there. "You coming?"

The whole thing—the kiss—was just…strange.

Strange, but typical and fitting—for us, anyway. We can't seem to do anything like normal humans.

We make our way back through to the other side of the park, one of my hands buried in the pocket of his coat, the other in my own.

I kissed Abbott.
     I kissed her.
  It was short and unexpected, but sweet. Gross and meaty, but sweet, and oddly appropriate.

What can I say? The moment felt right.

And now it's official: *I love a seventy-year-old grandma and I ain't even mad about it.* Okay, perhaps love is a tad strong a word considering Nan is more than twice my age and married to another, far more successful man, but love can be felt in different ways. What I feel for Nan is familial, not romantic. I can love her if I want to.

I felt included today, enveloped in the Margolis family fold. Nan seems to have roped me into what appears to be a not-so-subtle version of *Operation Get Abbott Married Off.*

Nan's attempts, albeit obvious to everyone, haven't gone unappreciated (except maybe by her granddaughter). Her antics are, at the very least, entertaining. They are to me, anyway. Abbott? Not sure how she feels about it, but let's assume it grates on her nerves.

I regard Abbott on the curb, wind picking up, thrashing her beautiful ponytail into a frenzy as she lurches forward toward the approaching yellow taxi cab. I lunge faster, grabbing at the handle, besting her. Goal: open the door first, forgetting that, for today, I am the gentleman.

I am taking the lead.

The last thing I need is her taking the dominant role.

I acted like one through lunch, amusing Abbott with stories, using the few manners I was taught—and the ones picked up in movies and books—to impress her.

We both know the efforts are pointless.

Traffic is on our side on our return from the park to our apartment complex; in short order we're in front of our building, laughing as we stumble out of the cab, the driver shooting us an agitated look through the dirty plexiglass partition.

I slide him a twenty and tell him to, "Keep the change."

I'm in a great mood and feeling generous.

His eyes go wide with appreciation as I slam the door behind me and join Abbott by the elevator banks, the button already glowing. When the gold doors glide open, Abbott leans on one side of the car, I lean on the other, and—is it just me, or is there sexual tension in here? Real tension, not the kind left over from sharing a chaste kiss.

Wait…is that a half-mast boner in my pants?

Shit.

I catch her eyes sliding up and down my torso, resting briefly on the crotch of my slacks before traveling up my chest, over my shoulders.

"Are you objectifying me?"

She purses her lips. "Pfft."

"Is that a yes?"

"That's a no."

What a sweet little liar. I smirk. "Right."

"You wish."

Some nights, yeah. "Hardly." That came out rough, edgy, and far too unkind.

Her brow softens, expression changing. "Don't be a jerk so soon after you kissed me."

"Sorry." Fuck, I'm losing my touch. *Relax, buddy. Chill. Abbott is your friend—she's just teasing you.*

Friends, and not the kind with any sort of benefit. Which isn't true, because she feeds me and gives me shelter, so basically I'm a stray cat, but one with a home?

"I am sorry."

She doesn't say a word, because it's not okay, simply putting a hand up to quell my talking.

"Sorry." There. Now I've said it three times like a complete schmuck.

"I get it. It's fine." Mood killed, she's watching the numbers above the door change as we ascend to the higher floors.

Twelve.

Fourteen.

Seventeen.

At twenty, it dings and the doors slide open to the lobby of our floor.

I sweep my hand out. "After you."

Her lips purse. "Thanks."

"Movies, your place in ten?"

Abbott bites down on her lower lip, which I wonder about because it's cherry red and pouty, yet no color appears on her teeth when she releases it.

Interesting.

"Bring chips or something. Don't be a slouch," is her reply, and all is forgiven. As she hikes her sleek leather purse onto her shoulder, she tosses her hair and I catch a whiff.

Damn, I always love the way she smells.

"Race you to the couch." Why am I so competitive?

"Ha ha." She throws a look over her shoulder. "You gave me back my key, remember?"

"You should probably give it back so I have one."

"Why? We're not in a relationship."

"So?"

Another once-over by Abbott as she says, "When I start dating someone, he will have the only other copy of my key."

"Other than Nan," I correct her.

Her blue eyes sparkle before she presents me with her back. I watch her work the key into the gold lock above her handle. It inserts smoothly and turns, lock clicking out of place. Her slender hand grips the handle, pushing.

When she faces me again, her smile is soft. "Other than Nan."

I bet she's soft all over.

Abbott—not her nan.

Jesus, maybe I'm tipsier than I thought.

"Ten minutes. I'll bring snacks."

"Good. I shouldn't be the only snack in the apartment," she jokes. It startles me for a second; Abbott isn't one to make innuendos, at least not of the sexual variety, and certainly not ones that are directed at me.

It's a day for firsts.

* * *

"Do you have any single friends?"

The question comes out of left field, like a grenade dropping into the living room and exploding all over the fucking furniture, scattering debris everywhere.

My body goes tense, tortilla chip paused mid-bite, salt licking my tongue.

"Why?"

Abbott makes a noncommittal sound from the bottom of her throat that sounds suspiciously like a low chuckle. "I'm single and looking for love in all the wrong places, ha ha," she jokes halfheartedly, popping open a can of Pringles and digging in with her entire hand. She chomps, which makes me glare.

Hello, I just kissed you—now you want me to set you up with my friends? Is she insane?

Crunch, crunch. "Is that a no?"

I scoff. "None I would introduce you to."

"So you do have single friends?"

That's a *fuck no* in guy speak. "One or two, but they're douchebags."

"If they're such douchebags, why are you friends with them?"

"I don't know if you've noticed this, Abbott, but I'm also a douchebag."

"You're a wannabe."

I feel butthurt about that. "What's that supposed to mean?"

"You act like a hard-ass, but you're actually a softie. All you want is to do your job and do it well, and eat good food."

She leans back on the couch, propping her feet up on the coffee table and squeezing one eye shut, studying the Pringle she's pinching between two fingers. "Why do guys always refuse to set me up with their friends?"

Because they're too busy trying to sleep with you themselves. I refuse to explain the mentality of men. She doesn't need to know the inner working of our brains, or that I refuse to hook her up with my single friends because I'm hoarding her.

The fact is: I like her.

Much to my detriment.

"What guy has ever refused your request to set you up with their friends?" Does Abbott even have any other guy friends besides me?

"My *bruh*ther."

Ah, that makes sense. "Your brother doesn't count—no dude wants his sister dating his friends."

And by date, I mean F-U-C-K.

"Then what's your excuse?" Her head tilts. "Why are you cockblocking me?"

I almost choke on my chip. "Excuse me? I just told you— my friends are douches."

She is still studying her Pringles and avoiding my intense gaze. "What exactly is it that makes them douchey?"

"For starters, they're just like me."

Abbott nudges me across the couch with her toe, an adorable smile tipping her lips. "Oh, now now, you're not so horrible."

She really has no idea how many women I've dated and ghosted in the past. How many one-night stands I've had because I was lonely. How I never take women for dinner, only for drinks, because I don't want to waste money on someone I never plan to see again before I've seen them the first time.

Poor Abbott is under the illusion that I'm a decent guy, one of the good ones. She has no idea how jealous I am of other people who are happily coupled.

Has no idea I'm a *liar*. A fake. A fraud.

A new generation of gambling men, my friends and I want to win a bet more than we want to be in relationships, barring Blaine, who had to be railroaded into breaking up with Bambi Warner.

Am I using Abbott? Or are we friends?

Real, legitimate friends?

All I know is I am not giving up those Jags season tickets for anyone. I was an absolute fucking idiot for throwing them into the bet to begin with. The four-wheeler and timeshare I give zero shits about—I work hard enough to be able to afford that stuff on my own without needing to win them. Sure, it would be cool to save a few grand, but…not necessary.

Abbott chooses that moment to stretch out beside me. She changed into a cute matching set before I came over—tight pants and even tighter tank top—and I can't help noticing she's removed her bra.

"You're right, I'm probably not horrible, but don't assume you know everything about me, either."

She sets down the can of Pringles and settles back in against the cushions, watching me intently from her side of the couch. Licks the salt off her fingers, one by one. "Is that a fact?"

"Don't believe me?"

True, I haven't been acting like my usual self since meeting her. A few weeks ago, I was asshole mixed with a whole lot of fucker and zero compassion for anyone but myself. These days?

I'm watching chick flicks and crying on the couch, sharing chips with the neighbor girl, and stroking her pussy…

Cat.

Her pussycat.

They say the right woman will do that to a man.

My eyes stray to Abbott's tits.

I can see her nipples through her shirt, and if that wasn't her intention, I'm the future king of England.

Abbott? No. No way would she do a thing so calculating.

Would she?

I shake the feathers out of my head, glancing over at her tits again, and catch her as she smiles into her cup of ice water. Blinks at the television, not meeting my gaze.

Bites down on her lower lip, licking at her thumb as if she can't quite get the mess off.

Definitely wearing a threadbare tank top on purpose…

Awesome.

Now my dick is twitching, inconvenient for early afternoon on a Wednesday with no relief in sight. Jesus, it's not even five o'clock yet—it's not like I can waltz into her bathroom to rub one out real quick while she waits in the living room on the couch.

Not to mention, the damn cat hasn't taken its eyes off me.

Desdemona McPussyPants is less trustworthy than I am.

I hiss at the cat and grimace when Abbott chastises me. "Leave the cat alone. She likes you."

Lies. It's all lies. The cat most definitely does not like me. I'm just waiting for the day Desi tears my balls off with her sharp kitty nails. Claws? What are those things called?

Abbott lifts an arm, resting her elbow on the back of the couch. "You know cats can smell when someone is a bad person.

If Desi thought you were a douchebag, she would let you know."

I stuff a tortilla chip in my pie hole and chew. "That cat wouldn't know a villain if it flew through here wearing a cape."

"She barely tolerates Nan, but she adores you. That's saying a lot."

As much as I hate admitting it, she's right about the fucking cat. It really does like me, no matter how hard I try to make it stop. I don't want or need that furball using my leg as an object of its affection. I don't need it purring at me. I don't need it meowing incessantly at the bathroom door when I'm trying to take a piss in private.

"I think you try to pretend to be a badass, but in reality you're a nice guy."

"No guy on this planet wants to be called a nice guy. Didn't you get the memo? Nice guys finish last."

Her face lets me know she doesn't agree. "You hate the idea of being vulnerable so much you're pushing me away."

Suddenly, at her words, my chips go stale in my mouth. Taste like sandpaper. Still, it's either chew and swallow or spit them out.

Spit. Or swallow.

Gulping the chips, I force them down with water, stalling.

"Vulnerable?" I scoff. "Please."

"Well," she begins, "I'm no psychologist, but you're always in my apartment when you *used* to spend all your free time with your pals. Now you hang out here. With me. Except…you're not interested in being romantic—until today, and that kiss hardly counted because you didn't really mean it."

She only pauses to eat another Pringle, and I wait while she chews, having nothing to add.

"Do you know why you don't spend as much time with your friends anymore? It's too much work to see them. Why? Because you're pretending to be someone you're not. With me, you can be yourself. You feel comfortable and it's easy here, not at that little dive bar you claim you love so much."

My mouth falls open. Closes. "I'll have you know, The Basement isn't a 'little dive bar.'" I use air quotes. "It's a one-hundred-year-old bar that serves cognac and spirits."

Abbott rolls her eyes. "Yes, yes, I know all about this fancy, dignified bar and its overpriced drinks and pedigreed atmosphere." She fakes a bored yawn. "Incidentally, when was the last time you were at The Basement?"

I study my fingernails, the same way she does when she's avoiding a direct stare. "I can't remember." One week ago? Two? Who knows—I'm an architect, not a timeline specialist.

"See?" She crosses her legs, bobbing a foot up and down, superior. "You used to go there a few times a month. And now…" She snaps her fingers, lithe body shifting on the cushions, smug smile curving her gorgeous lips.

Smug smile curving her gorgeous lips?

Shut the fuck up, Brooks. Stop waxing poetic about your neighbor. Go home, you're drunk.

Man, she's cute.

Man, she smells good.

Those tight pants…

I growl a bit.

"What's that look you're giving me?" Her stare is poignant, directed straight at me, while mine travels her torso.

Those boobs.

That stomach.

Even her fucking toes are adorable. I want to suck them, and I'm not even a toe guy. In fact, I hate feet.

"Brooks? Are you still drunk?"

"It takes more than a bottle of wine to keep me sloshed an entire afternoon, Abbott, though Nan tried her best."

"Nan is seventy-five—leave her out of this," she says defensively, inadvertently changing the subject.

A part of me wants her to question why I'm silently stripping her naked in my mind.

Maybe it will lead to something we'll regret later.

"She might be seventy-five, but *she* kept the wine flowing like a lady boss." Like a sorority girl with an unlimited bar tab.

Abbott sticks a leg out, bending it at the knee, calf flexing. "That may be true…but she got us the rest of the day off, didn't she? And you gave me that gross kiss while I was eating a hot dog."

"Yes, but you didn't have to make up a bullshit excuse to your boss."

"You didn't call your boss, you had that intern kid do it."

Taylor? He's not really a kid, but yeah—sending him that quick note and telling him I'm playing hooky just made life more difficult because the nosey fucker wanted details. Lucky for him, he grows on me every day, and if I didn't know any better, I'd say we were…

Friends.

"Let me see the text you sent him."

"What? No." No way am I showing her the exchange between Taylor and me.

"Why?"

"Uh—because it's private?" Plus, her name is all over those damn messages. She was the first thing Taylor brought up when I said I had a lunch date and wasn't coming back.

If she checked my phone, this is the shit she'd see:

Taylor: *You had lunch with your "neighbor" didn't you?*

Me: *Yeah, so?*

Taylor: *And now your taking the rest of the day off?*

Me: **You're*

Taylor: *Don't change the subject by correcting my grammar.*

Me: *Yes, I had lunch with my neighbor and now I'm taking the rest of the day off, if you really must know.*

Taylor: *To do something WITH her, or to do HER?*

Me: *Don't be a pervert.*

Taylor: Um, *CELLO, it's a valid question—the bosses are going to want to know. Honestly, if you told them you were courting a Margolis, they'd probably not only bonus you this quarter, they'd make you partner just to get their foot in the door with that family. Quite frankly, so would I.*

Me: *Why are you like this?*

Taylor: *Oh puh-leez, don't tell me you haven't thought about it helping you at work.*

Me: *No, actually, I haven't—not once. And you wouldn't be talking like this if you met the grandmother.*

Taylor: *Is she a total queen?*

Me: *One hundred percent a bigger queen than you.*

Taylor: *Not possible.*

Me: *I can hear you flipping your hair. My point is, she would eat me alive if she caught a whiff of this conversation.*

Taylor: *The queen or the granddaughter?*

Me: *The grandma.*

Taylor: *It's a grandma—how bad could she be?*

Me: *You obviously haven't googled her.*

Taylor: *Google on company time? Me? Never.*

Me: *Please, Jarod in IT sees all the stupid shit you're looking at during the day, because instead of googling, he's spying on US.*

Taylor: *Well, the shit that comes across my desk is boring. No offense, but until someone gives me an actual chance to prove myself, I have to occupy my time in other ways that don't involve math, measurements, or angles.*

Me: *Point taken.*

And on and on it goes, and no way can I show a text thread like that to Abbott. She'd skin me alive, leave my dead carcass, and then feed the rest to Nan.

No thanks.

The booze makes it easy to be flirty. "But you can come over here and try to convince me." It's a line I've used on other women a million times that always works when I want someone to make the first move.

It doesn't work on Abbott, who eyes me suspiciously.

"I don't think so, pal." Her smile is flirty, too. "If you want to show me, you can slide on over here and whisper it in my ear."

Whoa. That sounded…innocuous, but also sexy as fuck, and if she thought I was eye-fucking her before when I wasn't, I sure as hell am doing it now.

My gaze scans the room.

Desdemona is curled up on her kitty bed, snoring in a way I've never heard a cat snore, not that I come in contact with many.

Strangest feline I've ever met.

Abbott pulls her leg down from the sofa, setting her foot on the floor—first one, then the other, spreading her knees, grin on her face. Arms go behind her head, hands intertwining.

She's daring me to.

Don't do it, Brooks.

Do. Not. Do. It.

Hands to yourself, bro. She tastes like hot dog, remember?

Keep the mouse in the house—she wants to relationship you.

I breathe in.

I breathe out.

I home in on those boobs, and while I'm not a vain man, or a greedy man, or a selfish man—

I laugh at that last one: not a selfish man? I am a selfish bastard or I wouldn't be daydreaming about getting my ass off this couch, crawling on my hands and knees to Abbott's side, and slowly removing those workout pants she's wrapped up in.

What will she sound like with my mouth on her pussy?

What face will she make when she comes?

Only a selfish bastard would be asking himself that.

I clear my throat when Abbott crosses her legs again. Uncrosses them.

It's a telltale sign she's turned on, fire no doubt burning between her thighs.

Desdemona doesn't move.

Abbott holds her breath.

Aw, fuck it—I'm going for it. It'll be Christmas in a few months and this will be the gift I give myself since I haven't fucked anyone in weeks, not since befriending my neighbor.

She's ruined me.

That's the last coherent thought I have when I ease myself off the couch and fall to my knees, just like I had in my mind moments ago. Take the few paces to her side, push her legs apart with my giant hands. They look huge on her slender thighs, tan against her light-colored leggings.

"Brooks…" *What are you doing?*

"Shh." *We'll worry about it later; let me worship you now.*

Her head hits the back of the sofa, dark hair fanning against the soft cushions. Tongue darting out when I hook my fingers in the waistband of her pants, resting them there while I lean forward, mouth and nose buried in her warmth. Buried against her tummy.

I feel her fingers bury themselves in my hair, raking across my skull—fucking bliss.

I moan.

My balls tighten.

Hands move, inching those pants down. Abbott blessedly lifts her ass off the couch so I can drag them further without struggling like an asshole.

Down they come, past her thighs, over her knees, down her calves. I pull them completely off and toss them to the carpet.

One less thing…

Her panties are the same color as her leggings; is that a coincidence or did she plan it that way in hopes we'd fuck?

Nah, that doesn't seem like Abbott—she's not a schemer.

You never know with women, though. They're far too cunning to be completely harmless.

"Let me worship you."

ABBOTT

"Worship me?" The words escape my lips in barely a whisper, for I can't find my voice.

"Yes."

He wants to go down on me.

Correction: he *is* down on me, and now he wants to put his tongue inside and give me an orgasm.

Let me worship you, let me worship you...

Sexy, seductive words making my stomach reel and insides sizzle.

"W-What are we doing?" My question has his head lifting, and he stops to look me in the eye. I can't believe I'm actually stuttering.

I never stutter.

When Brooks raises his eyes, tearing his gaze from the lower half of my body, they aren't glassy, or dilated, or hazy; Brooks is *not* drunk. Which means Brooks knows exactly what he's doing and he wants to do it with me.

"Do you not want this?" His quiet question lingers, putting the proverbial ball in my court, and I bite down on my bottom lip, a habit I seemed to have developed only recently—since spending all my free time with *him*.

If he just wants to be friends and not dedicate his downtime to being with *me*, he has a piss-poor way of showing it.

Dinner. Movies. TV.

Everything but sleeping, and everything but sex, my leggings somehow no longer on my person.

In a heap on the carpet.

Legs being spread apart with two large, warm hands grazing my bare skin. Warm. So, so warm. Large thumbs plucking at the elastic of my underwear.

I'm not quivering, you're quivering…

I will my thighs to stop shaking—*stop it! Stop!*—but it's impossible since no man has had his hands on my body in months. I'd almost forgotten what it feels like, and it feels…it feels…heavenly, those slow, gentle strokes along my skin.

It might have been forever since I've had sex or fooled around, but the sensations all come back to me. The place where I want his hands? Comes right back to me. The tingles. The want. The need. The heavy breathing and heavy petting all come surging back as I watch him kneel before me, readying himself to go down on me.

If I wasn't seeing him between my thighs, with my own eyes, I would never have believed it.

Brooks Bennett is about to down on you, Abbott. Enjoy it, girl.

Me: No freaking way will that ever happen. He's going to realize what he's doing and stop it.

Oh, it's happening, just you wait and see.

Me: Wanna make a bet?

Also me: watches as Brooks Bennett's shoulders shrug, nose pressing into the apex of my spread thighs, mouth breathing heavy into my pussy.

Pussy.

God, that word. I hate thinking it, let alone saying it out loud, and I can't believe, of all things, that's what crosses my mind. But what the hell am I supposed to call it? My kitty cat? My crotch? My vajajay?

What does a woman call her V when face-to-face with the P?

"Goddamn your pussy smells fantastic," he groans.

See? I chose the right word for this occasion, resting on my elbows for a front-row seat to the action while doing my best to relax at the sight of it.

It turns me on.

It makes me wet.

It makes me squirm and moan and wiggle my ass with anticipation. He's taking fucking forever to put his lips on my vagina (vagina sounds ridiculous, doesn't it?), and I'm not sure how much more teasing I can take.

But.

Brooks going down on me is a gift, one I'm not about to squander by complaining.

So I do the only thing I can do: I sit still, waiting, trying not to boss him around by telling him how to do his job. No man wants to be told what to do in the bedroom, unless they're royally fucking it up.

Like my first boyfriend, Daniel, who couldn't have navigated his way around my holes if I'd drawn him a topographical map of the territory. Daniel was all fumbling and poking and awkward searching—he made Billie Belmont seem like a sex god.

A few more misses followed, all of them from college, none of whom I let worship at my lady temple.

Lady temple.

That makes me snicker, which makes Brooks glance up for the briefest of seconds.

Shit. Here I am thinking about all this and chuckling—woolgathering during oral is never a good thing—when his mouth makes contact with my crotch. Heat, glorious heat covers my private parts. Brooks' breath warms me from the outside in as he presses his mouth against me. Fingers sliding up and down the thin seam of my barely-there panties.

They match my outfit, which was no accident, although he couldn't possibly know that. Right?

He still hasn't used his tongue, but it feels amazing. I'm either desperate for someone to touch me, or I'm actually feeling actual things while he's teasing my nether region.

Panties get pushed aside—excruciatingly slowly—to make way for one slowly drifting finger. One. Slowly. Drifting. Finger.

Now two, pressed together and sliding up and down my wet slit. He leans forward and licks, as if he's going at a lollipop, sweet like sugar.

He moans.

I moan.

"Fuck you taste good."

"Do I?" Cocky and sassy, knowing the answer.

He barely lifts his head to reply, "Hell yes," but manages just the same, nostrils flared.

Pussy power, I'm tempted to tell him, the advertising executive in me always dreaming up slogans. *Now is not the time for one of your one-liners, Abbott!*

"What is that?"

"What's what?"

"What smells so good?"

Why the hell is he stopping to chitchat? *Now is not the time for this line of questioning, Brooks!*

"I-I...don't..." I swallow, gasping for breath, heart racing from the endorphins coursing through my body, pulsing in my lower pelvis. "Baby powder."

"Baby powder?" He sniffs, nosing the lips of my vagina. Licks again with a loud, enthusiastic groan. "Fucking delicious."

No one has ever called me delicious before, and I love it. Do I thank him? I'd hate to be rude.

Oh my God, stop—just stop. This is sex, not a dinner party. He didn't just compliment your table linens, he complimented your pussy.

"I could live down here." He's sucking on me now, sucking on my clit, spreading me apart with his fingers, desperately seeking my orgasm and my most delicate parts. "This is the prettiest pussy I've ever seen."

This time, I do preen, because there is no doubt Brooks Bennett has seen plenty of them, and he thinks mine is the prettiest?

"Oh my God, that is such a s-s-sweet thing to s-say," I stutter, thighs quaking like a rookie.

"I'm not just saying that, baby. Fuck me, it's so tight."

From lack of use, yeah. It is tight, though—how can he tell just from sticking his nose in it and rubbing it around? Guys are so weird, so easy to please. All I'm doing is sitting here and he's gushing like he's just unlocked Pandora's box. Is my pussy really that fantastic? I'd like to think so, but it's totally subjective.

I don't shave. I keep it tidy, but there is hair. These days, not many guys are into that look. Me? I think it's sexier when I'm strutting around my apartment and catch sight of myself in my closet's full-length mirror, take a gander at the patch of blonde hair hidden between my legs.

This is the reason I love sheer panties. That tease of a hair patch—sexy.

Old-school.

Make pubic hair great again!

This too makes me smile, eyes rolling back at the same time. My teeth scrape across my bottom lip, which is a far cry from me biting down, hips lifting off the couch.

Brooks holds me down by the inner thighs, tongue now pressing into my slick heat. Slick heat—my, my, aren't I poetic…

"I'm so fucking hard," Brooks murmurs from below.

"How?"

"You're so hot, baby."

Baby, baby, baby. Normally I hate endearments. From a man I'm not dating or barely know, they feel…fake. Forced.

Cheesy.

Not that I think Brooks is an exception; he is the epitome of bad behavior and cavalier attitude. I haven't necessarily seen him in action, but I know the type.

Still. I'll take it.

I like him—have grown to like him more than anyone I've let into my life in a long time. I'm a private person; I don't trust anyone, and with very good reason: my high-profile family. We have too much to lose by stepping out of line, and having one-night stands and casual affairs was never in the cards for me.

But Brooks? Him I'll let in.

It helps that Nan has given him her stamp of approval. Odd, but true.

My legs spread of their own accord, wider, letting him sink into me deeper, still on his knees before me. Sucking, licking, oh my God.

"Oh Goddd," I whine in a low, tortured tone, sounding a lot like a cat in heat, all the pussy and none of the feline drama.

"You like that, naughty girl?"

Um, why is he asking questions?

There is way too much talking and not enough sucking.

I grab his head, getting in on the action, fingers raking through his thick hair, giving him a teensy-weensy shove into my vagina.

No. More. Talking.

The endgame here is an orgasm, and since when am I a bossy bitch? Since when am I the kind of girl who shoves a guy's head down between her legs?! Since when am I demanding?

I am officially that girl.

I am!

Without thinking, I prop one foot up on the coffee table, practically begging for it like a hussy. Moaning a porn star moan, born for this role, giving in to the sensations. Brooks is clean-shaven, smooth cheeks brushing against my equally smooth inner thighs. His tongue is long, and soft, and skilled.

I mean—he seriously knows what he's doing.

I try not to let it bother me. I try to push the question out of my head: *How many women did he have to go down on to get this good at oral?*

Now is not the time…

"Mmm…ooh!" come my coos. "Oh yeah…oh…" come my sighs. "That…do that…right there," I tell him, bossy little thing I've become. "Harder."

Harder?

Yes, harder.

I want it. Need it. Anticipation building throughout my body, I tense up. Gnaw at my bottom lip, throw my head back, no longer able to look down at him; it just feels too damn good. I want to grab his head. I want to push on his shoulders. I want to spread my legs wider, but that isn't possible. I want…I want him to…I want him to…

…fuck me.

He doesn't.

He stays between my legs until everything turns to mush. Until the shockwaves course through my pelvis, stomach, pussy. Until every part of me is devastated by tremors. Overwhelmingly incredible tremors of pleasure.

Oh my God, my lips move but no sound comes out. It's too much, and when I come, I collapse. Go slack. Relaxed, sated, like a tomcat after banging a loose stray and giving zero fucks about my partner.

If I had a paw, I'd lick it.

If I had bangs, I'd flick them.

Satisfied he's gotten me off, Brooks leans back, hands resting on his haunches. Smug and arrogant—nothing new there. He's always smug and arrogant, but this is different, because what passes through his eyes as he sits there watching me, half-naked on the sofa, I cannot explain. He's assessing me, not objectifying me, mouth glistening.

Figuring me out.

Considering, I'm sure, how I'm going to behave now that we've taken this friendship to a whole other dimension. New level won't cut it—this is something entirely singular.

Now what?

How is he going to treat me tomorrow?

Better question is: *How am I going to treat him?*

DESDEMONA

God, that sound—it's like two cats in heat. And I would know, because I am one—a cat, not one in heat. Still, the last time I heard screeching and caterwauling like that, it was *me*, the one and only time I got loose in the city and prowled the block for almost an entire evening before Girl found me and hauled me home.

Ah, I remember it well.

Sweet, sweet freedom.

I found an orange tabby who was a little worse for wear (if I'm being honest) but liberal with the liberties—if you catch my drift.

She let me stick my tiny—

"Oh yeah," comes a tortured moan. It's so long and drawn out, it gives me pause, and I glance up from licking my paws.

More muffled sounds come from the couch—in the same spot where I lie every afternoon, sunning myself, and now that spot is ruined because Girl is clearly defecating on it, or loose with the liberties.

In my spot.

My sacred spot.

How. Dare. She.

There are rules in this house, and she's breaking them.

Rule 1: What's mine is mine.

Rule 2: What's hers is also mine.

Rule 3: No pissing on the furniture (I learned my lesson the hard way, as a kitten, when I defecated on the furniture and spent the night locked in the bathroom with that grotesque contraption they call a litter box—gag).

Rule 4: Don't touch my stuff.

Rule 5: It's all my stuff.

Rule 6: Don't attack the company.

I consider rule six up for interpretation; after all, what is company, really, but family who barges in unexpectedly and Boy, who bitches like a stray tom and smells twice as foul. He bathes in water way too often when his tongue would do the trick just fine.

I spit, narrowing my eyes toward my spot—the spot where I lazily bask, day after boring day.

Girl and Boy are there, except only one of them is on the couch. Girl has her bottoms off, sitting on the furniture, Boy is on the floor in front of her, and she's hissing and twitching like she might need the veterinarian, or to be fed. Maybe she's hungry; I'm never quite sure what humans want.

My keen eyes scan a scratching post—I believe Girl refers to that one as a coffee table—food and snacks no longer in sight, and maybe that's what's wrong with her? She's still hungry but he's not feeding her? Typical. It seems everyone is always begging for food from Boy.

The whole business of theirs is loud and inconvenient, and I contemplate sauntering over to break up the party, because let's face it: now that I'm awake, my stomach is telling me I could use a scrap of tuna. Or that dry shit Girl feeds me.

She's too cheap to buy the canned goods. I wasn't born yesterday; I know for a fact some cats get the good stuff. Trust me, I've seen the commercials on the talking box in the living room; I've seen the cat that looks exactly like me, eating from her crystal goblet. Where is my glass bowl? Where is my soppy, canned sustenance made with real fish and meat and juicy drippings?

I lick my chops, mood getting sour.

Real fish. Real meat. Juicy drippings.

From pet owners who actually love their animals.

I scowl.

The one and only reason I haven't attacked Boy's dangling bits is the simple fact that he's begun leaving me scraps. Sometimes Girl forces it on him, but lately, when she's not looking, he hands me food from the palm of his stinky hand, and that's why I keep him around.

Boy is disposable.

And Boy is causing Girl to make way too much fucking noise.

I mew.

Mew again, louder, because they're mewing too and couldn't possibly hear me over the squawking.

Ugh.

Get out of my spot!

They have their places to sit, I have mine, and humans should know their places.

Sullen, I march to Girl's bedroom and jump on her bed, wishing I could slam the door shut behind me and drown out the horrific sound of their screeching.

19

BROOKS

My friends are in rare form tonight.

From the minute I arrived at The Basement, I knew they were going to be a handful; it's Friday night and none of us are in the mood to go bar-hopping, yet not a single one of us wanted to go home and be alone.

Alone, Brooks? When are you ever alone? You have Abbott now, keeping you company.

I swirl the ice around my highball glass, watching the amber liquid go round and round and round, mesmerized by it. Thirsty but not for alcohol.

Thirsty for Abbott.

The thought makes me frown, and when I look up, the guys are watching me; they exchange knowing looks. Phillip goes so far as to tap Blaine in the bicep to get his attention, and they both raise their brows at one another.

"Our boy looks defeated." Phillip grins, straight teeth a blaring white from over-bleaching. Shine a black light on the guy's smile and he looks like the Cheshire cat, they're so idiotically perfect.

"Our boy looks like he's got something on his mind." Blaine agrees, nodding along. Stroking the facial hair he's been

212 | SARA NEY

unsuccessfully trying to grow for months. It's patchy, looks ridiculous, and makes him appear younger, not older. "Or should we say some*one* on his mind?"

"What are you talking about? I'm not defeated."

Have they found out about Abbott? Do they know I've been spending all my free time with her, or are they just giving me a hard time to feel out the situation?

I haven't been forthcoming with either of them in weeks, since starting the club. Haven't given them any life updates, social updates, or work updates. Barely text them back, almost never call anymore. Even when one of them calls me at work, Taylor hasn't been given permission to patch them through to my office. I just…haven't been feeling it lately. Hate lying and hate the nauseating dip in my stomach, my loss of appetite, lack of concentration—but most of all, I hate the lustful thoughts I've been having about Abbott.

I wish I didn't have to let her down and disappoint her.

So.

I've avoided my friends and being in this place for far too long. Which is why I dragged my ass out tonight.

I needed a well-placed reminder about my priorities and where my head needs to be, and I don't mean between Abbott Margolis' legs.

"Sorry bro, you look like you're going to become the first loser in the Bastard Bachelor Society." Phillip crosses his legs, taking a drag of his scotch on the rocks. Sips it so loud I can hear it from my spot a few feet away, the pompous windbag.

"You wish."

"Actually, I do wish. Jags spring training will be approaching soon enough and I, for one, am looking forward to catching a little preseason practice. Need to work on my tan."

The Jags practice facility is out west, and I try to fly out and watch a few games when the weather in the Midwest is complete shit but glorious and sunny where they train.

I loathe Phillip right now. What a jackass.

I rearrange myself in my seat, mimicking his pose, legs crossed, expression neutral. "What makes you think I look defeated?"

Seriously, why would he fucking say that?

"You haven't called or texted in days. You don't take our calls when you're at work. You're clearly not spending any time with us, so you must be spending it with someone else. Classic case of 'I'm seeing someone new.'"

It's true that we tend to disappear when we like someone, desperate to spend all our free time with them. Which is absolutely the case with my friendship with Abbott right now.

Friendship. I damn near choke on the word. "Whatever."

"Good comeback." Blaine laughs. "What are you, ten?"

Of course, they're both right. I just can't admit it or I instantly lose the entire bet, and my season tickets.

Season tickets, season tickets, season tickets...

I'm not even a baseball junkie; I like it well enough, but I'm not obsessed with it like some dudes. So what's the big fucking deal?

The big deal is, those tickets are worth a fortune and you could sell them if you weren't interested anymore. You lose your ass if you give them away in a bet.

I try to keep that in the back of my mind, too—the street value of the seats I hold.

As a kid who grew up with nothing, I'm not about to hand off what can make me a sweet chunk of change. Retirement, a house, paying down my student loans—those are all things looming over me that I could use the money for if I were ever desperate enough.

I am not.

And I'm determined that I will never be as hungry or desperate as I was as a kid.

"You don't think I'd tell you if I was seeing someone?" I scoff, staring down into my glass. "Give me some credit."

"No can do, pretty boy. As a matter of fact, I don't think you'd tell us jack shit if you were seeing someone."

"No one has called me pretty a day in my life."

"Don't try to change the subject," Blaine sneers, biting down on a giant olive. He holds it between his thumb and forefinger, boring into the pimento then sucking it into his mouth with a slurp.

"Yeah," Phillip brilliantly adds, "don't try to change the subject."

"I'm not. And I'm not dating anyone, Scout's honor."

"Let's be real here, you were never a Boy Scout."

"Right." My tone couldn't sound more bitter. "Because we couldn't afford the fees. We couldn't afford jack shit, including school clothes or supplies, and certainly not the fees for me to play sports or participate in extracurricular activities."

My friends recoil, taken aback. Speechless, for once in their fucking lives.

"Whoa, dude." Phillip's hands go up to coax me out of my tizzy. "Whoa. Not at all the path I was trying to lead you down. Relax, bro, relax."

It takes another drink for them to lift me out of my funk. Just one drink, though, because I have someplace else I'd rather be.

I want to go home.

To my apartment and home to Abbott.

After counting down the minutes until it's safe for me to rise, I take my leave, heart racing the entire trip, winded when the elevators of my building slide open and I see Abbott there, not unlike the morning we officially met in the hallway. Adorable at her door, balancing a grocery bag in her arms, purse hanging from one as she wrestles to get the key into its rightful spot.

"Hey neighbor." As I greet her, my hands get stuffed into the pockets of my glorious blue jacket.

She turns, abandoning the task of getting inside her apartment to greet me in kind.

Her teeth are pearly white, peeking out between glossy pink lips. Her eyes? Look at my absurd velvet smoking jacket. Then at my face.

Jacket.

Face.

Jacket. Face.

Her smile becomes secretive, now buried in the brown paper bag hefted in her arms. She gathers herself, reemerging, serious this time. "Whatcha doing there, buddy?"

Buddy?

And here I thought the day after oral was going to be awkward. How wrong I was—she's still a total smartass.

"I was…" I don't want to tell her I was with my friends. She'll mock me.

"With your friends?"

How did she know? "Yeah, how did you know?"

Her eyes stray once more to my navy jacket. Get wide. Brows rise. "Lucky guess." Abbott squints in my direction, shifting on her heels. "Random question: do you actually smoke when you're wearing that thing?"

I give the sleeve a whiff. "Occasionally." Mostly on patios.

"Interesting." She smirks smugly.

"How is that interesting?"

"It just is." Her back hits the wall, and she uses it for support. "I also think it's interesting that you and your little buddies have a secret club—it reminds me of the gentlemen's clubs I've read about in romance novels."

She needs to stop using the word little to describe me and my friends; it's annoying.

Her mention of a gentlemen's club piques my interest because that's exactly the angle my friends and I were going for! Of course, I can't say *that* out loud. Abbott will think I'm loco. Crazy.

A complete dipshit.

Which, of course, *we are*—however, the last thing I need to do is add fuel to Abbott's massively flaming fire. I can see in her eyes she's in a great mood, and in the mood to tease.

I cross my arms, the blueprint in my hand getting tucked snuggly under my armpit. "Oh yeah? What do they say about those clubs? I've never read one."

Abbott cocks her head, tilting it to the side, lights from the hallway creating a halo effect above her head. Her hair is straight today, and shiny, hanging in a flat sheet.

"A few I've read have centered around these clubs. The guys are single and make these bets with their friends to remain single." Abbott chuckles, unknowingly hitting the nail on the head. "Obviously that's never what happens in the end."

"What happens in the end?"

"One by one, the single gentlemen always fall in love." Another laugh. "Honestly, the whole concept is ridiculous. You'd have to be bitter and jaded to start a club like that. Or a complete *loser*." She annunciates the word loser, thoroughly repulsed.

"Now now, let's not be hasty, throwing out insults," I start, aware that I'm about to argue my viewpoint while wearing a velvet smoking jacket, a uniform for a club doing exactly what she described from her novels. Her girly, historical romance, smutty novel bullshit. "You don't know for sure those guys are losers."

Not that I have any idea what I'm talking about.

"It's fictional." She rolls her eyes in my direction. "That would never happen in real life."

"You don't think so?"

"Are you kidding? No. These days, no self-respecting guy would be a member of a club like that. He'd be laughed out of town or roasted on social media."

Once again, here I stand in this dumb fucking jacket, like a jackass, listening to her drone on and on and on, cheeks now ablaze. I haven't blushed in years, but I'm blushing now.

"It could happen. In fact, it's not the worst idea."

She gapes at me, incredulous. "Not the worst idea? It's barbaric and archaic. Are you out of your mind?"

Yes.

The word, "apparently," slips out of my mouth before I can stop it, but Abbott is too worked up to notice the blunder.

"You would defend the concept? The plot, if you will?" Her lean sags deeper as she settles in to hear me speak. "By all means, do go on."

Is she patronizing me? It's hard to tell because she's smiling that megawatt smile, eyes sparkling with mischief. Cue a flash of teeth as she saucily bites down on her bottom lip.

Anddd there it is!

"All I'm saying is that as far as the concept goes, a few men having a club where they get together for a common goal—it's not terrible."

"Right, but we're specifically talking about them making a pact to be single."

"What's wrong with that?"

She huffs. "It's not realistic."

"Why? Plenty of people don't want to get married. Or have babies. Or have relationships."

Abbott considers this. "True." She straightens herself, coming off the wall and balancing the bag in her arms, gripping it like she's holding a toddler. I wonder what's inside—dinner? Lunch for tomorrow? Snacks? Shit, will I ever find out, or is she going to torture me by not sharing?

"You know what's archaic, Miss Know-It-All? The ideology that everyone has to be in a relationship to be happy." I volley back, taken off guard and suddenly defensive. "That's what's archaic."

So there. Take *that*.

"Most people aren't like that. Most people want to meet someone."

"I don't know who you're hanging out with, but the guys I know don't."

"Who?"

"My best friends."

"Like I care about them." Abbott is quiet for a moment, letting this new information soak in. "What about you?"

"Same."

That one word lingers in the air, in the hallway, floating above our heads, a heavy weight suddenly thrust upon the light mood and clouding over.

My cute neighbor forces herself to continue to smile, a big, fat, fake smile that I find unattractive. I prefer the fun, carefree Abbott—not this one, the one suddenly sullen in response to my declared singledom.

Sure, I get it. No single young woman on the prowl for an eligible bachelor wants to hear there is one less candidate for her to sink her claws into.

Even if Abbott is way out of my league, it still must sting that she can't have me. Not that she wants me, but I can only assume...

"You don't want to be in a relationship?"

"I thought you knew that." Pause. "That whole friend-zone thing is for a reason."

"Oh. So you don't just not like me?"

"Abbott, if I were going to hand in my Bastard Bachelor card, it would be for you."

"Your what?"

Shit. What did I just say? Why are her eyes so wide?

"What's a bastard bachelor?"

Shit. Fuck. "A what?" I ask, hoping to throw her off the scent. Maybe she'll think she misheard me if I pretend not to know what she's talking about.

"A bastard bachelor. You said '*If I were going to hand in my bastard bachelor card, it would be for you.*'"

I did say that. I said those exact words, but try getting me to admit it.

Deny, deny, deny. "What I meant was, I'd date you if I were dating. But I'm not, so…yeah."

"Are you gay?"

"No." Another pause. "Would I have gone down on you if I were gay?"

"Maybe." Her petite shoulders give me a shrug, and she adjusts the groceries in her arms. "I don't know. I'm sure some guys would take one for the team, just to make their friend happy."

"No one eats someone's pussy just to make them happy."

As those words leave my mouth, I'm unexpectedly positive there are *plenty* of people out there, gay and straight—right this second—giving oral to their good friend to make them happy. I'd put money on it. Because that's what good friends do!

Sacrifice for the sake of the team.

Abbott and me? We make a great team; if only she would get it out of her head that she can take me out of the friend-zone. Granted, she's never once said those words, or hinted at it, but I know women, and she would be a damn fool not to want me as a boyfriend.

I'm a fucking catch.

But so is she.

We'd make one amazing couple…

"Earth to Brooks." She has one hand free and is waving it in front of my face. "Hello?"

"Sorry."

"We start talking about oral sex and you start daydreaming —seems legit." One blue eye shoots me a wink, her smile authentic and real. Just like her boobs probably are.

Tits.

I've given hers a lot of thought after going down on her last night, wondering what they look like. The color of her nipples and their shape. Bet they're squishy in all the best ways.

"You're doing it again," she chastises. "So, I have dinner in this bag. If you want to get settled, I can come over in a few and we can hang out?"

"Why does it have to be my place?"

"Because we never spend any time there! It's not fair. Let's just try it, okay?"

I feel a pout coming on, repressing it with a groan. "Fine."

"Are you showering? How much time do you need?"

"Meh, I can be quick. I'll just toss on sweats."

"I'll do the same. Feed the cat and come over."

A night where that hairball isn't staring me down? Perfect.

I breathe a sigh of relief. "What's in the bag?" I know she said dinner, but I want specifics. "Be specific."

Abbott lowers it so she can peer inside, checking the contents. "Um, let's see…cashew chicken, shrimp fried rice. A few spring rolls."

My stomach growls. "You got Chinese takeout?" Honestly, could she be any more perfect? Abbott Margolis is my dream girl.

Sexy. Funny—fuck, I've been down this road before, rationalizing and listing all the things I love about her despite the bet looming.

Blaine and Phillip are in no danger of losing since neither of them are seeing anyone—dating, sexing, or otherwise. I'm the only asshole who seems to have gotten himself into something of a…predicament. One not a soul besides myself knows anything about.

If they knew about Abbott, they would hand me my ass. They would take my season tickets and battle it out between them, and I cannot allow that to happen.

Those tickets mean too much.

Why the fuck did I put them on the table? What else could I stand to lose?

Cash? Airline travel vouchers?

Not much else. I don't own a condo. I don't own land. I lease my luxury SUV (paying out the wazoo for the parking every month like a fucking idiot). No vacation properties, no timeshares.

What I do have is a fuck ton of Amazon boxes being delivered to my apartment daily, which always leaves me oddly satisfied. What I do have is an unhealthy new codependency on my next-door neighbor, who does and does not want to date me. What I do have is a relationship with her fluffy fucking cat, who hates to love me, and loves to hate me, and at any moment is going to tear my balls off.

Every day I look forward to seeing Abbott. Every day I race home, earlier and earlier and earlier—Taylor has called me pussy-whipped twice this week—to beat Abbott home, excited by the prospect of spending the evening with her.

If that isn't a relationship, I don't know what is…

My friends don't know she exists. Only Taylor knows, and he isn't telling anyone, with the hopes that I'll change my mind about her. If Taylor had his way, I'd put a ring on it so he could come live with us in the Margolis family penthouse, vacation on the Margolis family yacht, and sip from Margolis family champagne flutes, living his best life as my assistant—one who does nothing but bask in bougieness.

Bastard.

Blaine and Phillip? Do not know I spend far more than three consecutive nights hanging out with her. Don't know she feeds me, I feed her, and we spend most of our free time together. They're unaware she is my friend. And I find her incredibly sexy. And she's smart and witty and talented. No one knows I went down on her and want to fuck her, over and over again until neither of us can walk a straight line…

…to the fridge, to get more food, so we can have more energy, to have all the sex.

It's a vicious cycle, one that has only played out in my head.

It's a rough life, but I'm managing.

Abbott presents me with her back, inserting her gold key into the gold lock on her door. Turns it until the lock clicks. Shoots a glance at me over her shoulder, hair swaying.

"You better not be flirting," I warn.

"Me? Flirting?" She gives her front door a push. "Please."

"Yeah, you."

"Blah blah, I'll see you in ten minutes." As she crosses the threshold, tossing her keys onto the table next to the door, she remembers something. "Oh! You take this since I'm coming over." Abbott presses the bag of food into my waiting hands. Points a finger up at me. "Don't you dare start without me."

I'd hold my hands up in surrender, but they're full of Chinese takeout. "Wouldn't dream of it."

I am such a damn liar.

20
ABBOTT

Brooks Bennett went down on me yesterday.

Brooks. Gave. Me. Oral.

And here I am, on a Friday night, standing in front of my closet, staring up at my wardrobe, deciding what to wear so we can casually hang out in his apartment.

A first.

I thought running into him "after the deed" was going to be monumentally awkward. Kind of considered it something he would regret, thought maybe he'd ghost me, which seems like a thing he would do.

He surprised me by being mischievous, practically falling out of the elevator, breathing heavy for Lord knows what reason and wanting to see me again.

Granted, the man likes to eat and I was standing in the hall, holding a bag of takeout.

The encounter wasn't awkward at all.

Thank.

God.

I mean, if it had been weird, would I be going to his apartment for dinner? The dinner I went and bought with him in mind, wishing I'd bump into him…loitering too long in the apartment lobby...then lingering by the elevators, then dawdling at my door, rummaging for my keys.

Lucky me, 'cause it worked.

Brooks Bennett went down on me yesterday.

I've mentally repeated that sentence hundreds of times throughout the day, letting the words sink in, distracting me from work, from deadlines, from new assignments and hard-to-manage co-workers.

Brooks Bennett might have gone down on me two days ago, but that doesn't mean he's going to want a relationship with me *today*.

He doesn't want a relationship? Ever?

Like, *ever*, ever?

I absorb the information, letting that sink in, too, as I pull off my work clothes. First the fitted tweed pencil skirt, then the matching blazer. White button-up blouse. White silk bra. White silk panties.

These are not Chinese-food-eating, couch-surfing undergarments.

I replace them with cotton, fastening a basic bra I bought at Costco, determined not to get fussy. It's not as if he's going to see me naked later, although a girl can dream.

My hands go to my hips as I stand in my underwear, still deciding which casual but cute *I woke up like this* outfit I want to put on. Forsake the sweatshirts that say YAWN and NOT TODAY SATAN and NAMASTE IN BED and instead pull down a white crewneck from a neatly stacked pile of shirts atop a low shelf Nan hired someone to build for me.

Bottoms, bottoms, what do I want to wear on the bottom...

I tap my chin, blue eyes roaming over piles of black cotton yoga pants. Okay, fine, I'll admit it: I've never done yoga in any of these pants a single day in my sorry life. These pants have never known sweat. These pants have never known tears.

Black bottoms or something with a pattern?

Hey—he might not want to date me, but I know this much:

I turn him on. He was rock-hard while he was going down on me, as evidenced by the giant boner when he finally stood up and headed to my bathroom to wash up.

Jeez, do people still use the word boner when they're describing an erection?

Sighing, I reach for a pair of white and gray bottoms so he can stare at my ass good and hard. Struggle to pull the damn things on, eventually squeezing into them, then my sweatshirt.

"This is as good as it's going to get, isn't it, homegirl?" I tell my reflection in the mirror before tossing my hair.

Desdemona is nowhere to be found, most likely hiding beneath my bed, her favorite spot when she's in one of her famous moods.

My cat is certifiable.

I quickly check her food and water, just to be on the safe side, then hit the lights in the apartment. Pad my way to the door, lock up, and shuffle across the hall.

Knock.

Wait, tapping my foot impatiently. For real. He knew I was coming—what's taking him so long to answer the door?

Butterflies swarm in my stomach, and I rub small circles above my belly button, three long minutes passing before Brooks flings the door open without ceremony, cracking it just enough that I can slide my way inside.

"Did you just sniff me?" I blurt out, knowing damn well that he did. I've caught him doing it several times already when he thought I wouldn't notice.

Joke's on him because I *always* notice.

"Nope."

Liar. Deny it all you want—I definitely heard your nose sniffing the air.

I navigate to the living room, bloodhounding my way to the food laid out on the stone coffee table. Brooks has it spread out like a mini buffet, having transferred the contents from takeout containers to glass bowls.

Ooh la la. Fancy.

While I'm settling in on the couch, finding my comfy spot, he disappears, returning with ice water, two wine glasses, and a bottle of white.

"Nothing goes better with cheap Chinese food than expensive white wine," I tease, pulling the cork out of the top and pouring us each a glass.

I sip.

It's cool and crisp and absolutely perfect. Goes down way too smooth, the first few dainty sips going straight to my head.

I set it on the table and recline.

I love this time with him after a long day at work, after the arguments and the negotiations and wasting my time and energy on creative flow. Arguing with creative people—like Bambi Warner—who might have incredible talent and ideas but don't quite fit what the client wants.

Being the middle man at the office is exhausting. Things with Bambi have gotten slightly better since I sent her home early to recover from her breakup, but it's still strained, the power struggle festering between us alive and well. As much as I'd love to be more assertive, that's just not who I am, and as much as I'd love for her to wake up one morning and show me more respect, that's just not happening any time soon.

I sigh contently, sagging into Brooks' couch. It's not as comfortable as mine—his is stiff and leather and not as worn in —but it's a couch, and my ass ain't complainin'.

Surprisingly enough, I like it here, in his apartment.

"Too bad you won't let me bring Desdemona over. She'd love that plant in the corner."

Translation: she'd love to climb that plant in the corner, dig out all the dirt, and destroy the pot it's in.

"Don't you dare even think about bringing that cat in here," he warns. Plops down on the end of the couch, one foot propped on the coffee table, the other up on the cushions. "Crap. Now I can't reach my plate."

He shoots me a devilish sidelong glance. Beseeching with a pouty lower lip.

It works and I fold like a stack of cards. "You want me to make you a plate, ask nice."

"Abbott, can you pretty please make me a plate and hand it to me? I had a rough day."

I'll just bet he had a rough day, looking all cute and handsome in the light lavender shirt he wore earlier with his coordinating tie and navy slacks. The dark velvet blue jacket to match.

Rawr.

I scoop some food onto a plate for his majesty, handing it to him with a smile. Flutter my lashes. I mean seriously, who can be irritated with that face?

I want to squish it in my hands.

"How rough could your day have been if you ended it with drinks?" I'm curious to know, already chewing on a vegetable.

"I had drinks with my friends *because* it was rough, and somehow that made it worse." I note with confusion that he hasn't met my gaze.

"So you wore your jacket to work?" I know it holds some kind of sentimental value—no way did he wear that out in public.

"I brought it to work and changed into it afterward."

Ah, so I was right. It's a special jacket, for special occasions.

"What did you and your friends talk about? What are they like?" The friends he will not set me up on a date with because they are douchebags.

"My friends are…" Brooks pushes broccoli across the plate before spearing it with his fork and putting it on his tongue. "Professionals. One of them just broke up with his girlfriend, but all he does is sit and whine about that."

"Whines? How? If he broke up with her, why is he bellyaching about it?" Inquiring minds want to know.

Brooks' broad shoulders shrug, and I peel my eyes away in

time to hear him say, "Dunno." *Chomp, chomp.* "He was on the fence about it. Must feel guilty about dumping her." *Chomp, chomp.* "You know how guys are."

No, actually, I don't know how guys are. You'd have to have a myriad of experience with men to know *how guys are*, and I? Do not. I'm no Bambi Warner, who is all legs and boobs and long flowing hair—she must spend an hour each morning curling it before work. Styling it. Hours on her makeup and skincare.

I bet she shaves her legs a few times a week, unlike myself.

I've been friend-zoned more times than I can count, stick to myself when I'm at bars, and rarely get hit on. I'm a veritable wallflower. Always the bridesmaid, never the bride.

The last time I had a dick inside me was…jeez. Who even knows?

"What else do y'all do besides sit around and drink?"

Brooks has the courtesy to swallow before responding. "The usual. Bars, go to the gym and play hoops. Grab coffee, smoke stogies."

"That's what you do when you're together? Go to the gym, play hoops, and grab coffee?" It all sounds so disappointingly ordinary. I ponder this information. "Huh."

"What does *huh* mean? None of that excites you?" His chuckle is good-humored and served with a smile.

"Surprises me, that's all. I thought you were going to say something like, 'We go to biker bars, car shows, and strip clubs.'"

His eyes go wide. "Right away your brain takes you to a strip club?"

It's my turn to laugh. "I don't know why that popped into my mind, it just did." Another vegetable gets eaten, giving me time to think about what I'll say next.

"Got strippers on the brain, do ya?"

"No! But let's be honest, some very beautiful women are exotic dancers." I shoot him a shy glance.

"You're beautiful, but *you* would never do a striptease."

Hold up—let me take a nanosecond to overthink this: is he imagining me doing stripteases now? As in, prancing around and getting naked in front of him?

Or…is that him saying I'm a beautiful woman? Or is he calling me a prude?

"Are we talking about stripteases or exotic dancing? They're not the same thing," I point out.

"Both."

"You don't think I'd ever do a lap dance?" I pivot my body so I'm facing him. "How stuffy do you think I am?"

"One doesn't do a lap dance—one *performs* a lap dance." He's amused by the topic, at least. "It has nothing to do with you being stuffy."

"So you admit you think I'm stuffy?"

"First of all, can we stop using the word stuffy? You're taking it out of context. Secondly, all I'm saying is that you're not the stripping, lap dance type." He takes a swallow of wine, probably needing it since I'm being such a head case. "You're classier than that."

"I'll have you know, one of my best friends was a stripper in college, and she was classy." I'm unexpectedly indignant for all those girls who dance in clubs, getting pawed at by strangers simply to pay their rent and feed their kids.

He gapes. "Seriously?"

My shoulders droop. "No."

Brooks forks some broccoli and stuffs it in his mouth, chewing. "Not that there is anything wrong with being a stripper, though I can think of a hundred better ways to spend my hard-earned cash than at a gentlemen's club."

I scratch at my scalp. "How did we get on this subject?"

"It hardly signifies."

Hardly signifies—two words strung together that shouldn't turn me on but do. Go figure. I've always been a sucker for smart men, and Brooks is not only intelligent, but clever, too, someone who uses words like 'signifies' in casual sentences.

Lay off the wine, Abbott—it's making you stupid.

"You were saying you didn't think I was the type."

One of his dark brows goes up. "Because you're not."

Which isn't the point. The point is, he thinks I'm a buttoned-up, uptight goody two-shoes.

AKA boring.

AKA a prig.

AKA prissy.

AKA I have to stop mentally saying AKA.

My chin goes up haughtily, and I defensively cup my boobs in my hands. "Fine. Maybe I'm not the type to give a tease worthy of a gentlemen's club, but I would do one for the right person."

"Incidentally, if you did do one…" He yawns, reaching forward to spoon some chicken and cashews onto his big, round, white plate. "Who would you give a lap dance to?"

I glance around the living room, at its bare walls and stark, modern furniture. It's a bit cold and sterile, lacking personality and warmth. But as far as backdrops go, it would work.

"You."

"Bullshit." He laughs, licking sauce off his thumb. "And I wouldn't expect you to."

"Maybe I want to." *Shut up, Abbott—since when have you ever wanted to do a striptease in a man's living room?* Since never, that's when.

Jealousy rears its ugly head—not jealousy of another woman or of sexier women, but jealousy for women with balls bigger than mine. Big enough to get on a stage with one single objective: make a man go wild by showing off her body. By flaunting what the good Lord gave her. Maybe by sticking her boobs in a man's face? That seems like a good place to start…

"No you don't."

He can't tell me what to do! "Yes, I do."

Brooks laughs a strangled laugh, almost choking since his mouth is filled with food. Disgusting. "Sure, sure."

He's no longer looking at me, his attention on dinner and the television, which he powered on shortly after plopping himself down beside me, remarking how great it felt not to worry about the attack cat.

Earlier tonight I joked about giving him a kitten as a Christmas gift, to which he replied, "Don't you fucking dare."

I remove the napkin on my lap, dabbing at the invisible mess in the corner of my mouth before excusing myself to use the bathroom.

Brooks barely spares me a glance, cramming chicken into his gullet as if he hasn't had a meal in weeks.

Gross. I hope he cleans that up by the time I get back.

It takes me no time at all to do my business, wash my hands, and—what's this now?

The blue velvet jacket is hanging in the laundry room, catching my eye as I walk past, hands still damp from the sink. I wipe the moisture off on my leggings, detouring into Brooks' mini laundry center.

I finger the fabric of his smoking jacket; it's cool under my touch, but soft. Rich. Quite exquisite, actually. I briefly wonder where it came from, reaching up to remove it from its velvet hanger, and hold it out, arms outstretched in front of me.

The tiny room is chilly, but I remove my leggings first, shivering as I pull my shirt up over my torso. Then my underwear. Stand in the center to unclasp my bra and *what hell are you about to do, Abbott Margolis?*

This isn't you! You are not the girl who gives lap dances or stripteases. Put your clothes back on before you make a decision you'll regret.

But I can't silence the other voice, the one telling me to take a chance—the one telling me to step out of my comfort zone and have fun, fun, fun for a change.

Therefore…

I kick the pile of clothes aside and slide into Brooks' gorgeous blue jacket.

It hangs on me, hitting just below the hips, loose. The material lining the inside is silky smooth, gliding over my skin luxuriously.

I wish I had a mirror so I could see myself, and I imagine the look of shock he's going to have on his face when he sees me in this.

I shiver again. This time, it's not from the cold.

I t takes Brooks a few seconds to notice me standing at the entry to the living room, framed by the doorway, not wearing any pants. Takes him so long to notice I actually have to clear my throat to get his attention off the television, and when he moves his neck to glance in my direction, it's in slow motion.

Takes another silent moment for him to notice I've donned the smoking jacket. My lack of pants.

His reaction is delayed. Stunned. "Wh…at a-are you doing in that jacket? T-Take it off!" he damn near shouts, panic in his eyes. Legitimate panic.

Lord, what on earth is his problem?

Why on earth would he be *panicked* that I'm wearing this dumb jacket? It's outerwear, for crying out loud, not the precious tears of a unicorn or a diamond he must protect with his life.

He needs to relaxi-taxi. "You need to calm down."

"You need to take that off."

If he notices my hands trembling, he's polite enough not to mention it. "That is part of the plan."

"Take it off."

Duh, I'm getting to that part and he's ruining it.

"You want the jacket off? Fine. I'll take the jacket off." I slide it down my arms, shrugging it off, enjoying the feel of the rich velvet on my bare skin and the dazed countenance flashing across his eyes.

"Whoa, whoa, whoa. Wait. *Abbott...*" Brooks' voice is hoarse. "Where are your clothes?"

Why is he asking where my clothes are? What does it matter? He either cares that I'm naked and wants to see my bare skin, or he doesn't. I'm naked over here and all he seems to care about is this dumb coat?

"My clothes are on the laundry room floor."

This conversation is humiliating. Brooks was right; I'm not the type of girl who can pull off a lap dance—I can't even get the approach nailed down, standing in front of him now like a defeated puppy dog.

Maybe this wasn't a good idea. Maybe I should get dressed. Maybe I shouldn't give him a lap dance. It seemed like a good idea at the time, moments ago when I spotted the coat hanging above his washing machine, taunting me.

Daring me to take a chance.

In my defense, Brooks never said I couldn't try it on. Then again, he didn't exactly give me permission, either.

Too late now.

The luxurious fabric lies in a heap at my bare feet and I am wearing my birthday suit. "Do you want me to cover up?" He's already seen my pussy—had his mouth on it—so what's a fantastic pair of breasts thrown into the mix to get the guy twisted up?

My boobs are quite fantastic.

I stick my chest out, posturing, letting him look his fill. "If you want me to cover all this up, say 'Abbott, go get dressed. I do not want to see you naked.'"

His Adam's apple bobs in his throat, head gives a jerky nod I can't translate.

I cup a hand around my ear. "I'm sorry, I didn't hear you." I step closer, one foot after the other, creeping slowly like a tigress stalking her prey—Desdemona would be proud. "If you're disgusted by the sight of these"—I cup my breasts—"I want you to say it."

Brooks gulps.

I reach him on the couch, nudging his legs apart. As I step between them, his hands automatically reach around my hips and grip my ass, sliding up and down the backs of my hamstrings. Forehead pressing against my belly, he runs his lips across my abs.

"I don't want to pressure you," I tell him, heart beating wildly. This isn't like me at all, but sometimes, you go for broke. Perhaps my goal is to call his bluff; maybe once he's slept with me, he'll realize he can't live without me. Maybe once he's slept with me, he'll lie in bed thinking about me, too.

Maybe, maybe, maybe.

My fingers slide through his hair, and I'm able to bend down and kiss the top of his head as he kisses my stomach.

"You, pressuring *me*?" He punctuates the statement with a low laugh. "Babe, there is no such thing as you pressuring me. I don't do anything I don't want to do."

His body is big and warm and wrapped around my naked flesh, more calming than sensual.

Ready or not, here we are…

His breathing is labored, like it was when he got out of the elevator tonight. Like it was the day he walked out of the stairwell. Like he sounds after he's been out for a run. In and out, breathing hard, breath hitting my belly as his hands stroke my spine.

Fingers pressing into my flesh, wanting but controlled. Big, strong hands, fingers calloused from utilizing technical pencils at work. Working hands. Skilled hands that create buildings and communities and jobs.

Smart men turn me on.

Clever, sarcastic men turn me on.

Sweet, considerate Brooks is turning me on...

In one motion, he's standing, sweeping me up, hoisting me by the hips, hauling me over his shoulder and starting toward the bedroom.

I gasp, startled. "Brooks, what are you doing?"

"Taking you to the bedroom."

"But I didn't get to do my striptease or my lap dance."

"Sorry, babe, but you suck at sexy seduction."

Babe, babe, babe.

This is the second time he's called me babe, and I blush, basking in it.

"I just need practice," I tell him, just as he unceremoniously dumps me in the center of his bed. I fall in a heap onto a dark down comforter.

"You don't need practice, you need to stick to being sweet and sassy—you don't have to get naked to turn me on."

He's pulling at the hem of his hooded sweatshirt, yanking it up over his head and tossing it to the ground. His chest is broad and smooth, sculpted from hours of working out at the gym with his buddies.

I lean back on the mattress, admiring his pecs and wide shoulders—two of my favorite male body parts besides the pleasure trail leading down to the dick.

"You think having sex is a good idea?" I raise a brow, making room for him on the bed as he strips out of his low-slung pants.

"No, I think it's a horrible idea." Naked Brooks is a sight, lean and fit but not perfect. A surgery scar cuts across his abdomen, marring his skin. "If you want me to go down on you, I will—we don't have to have sex."

"Yeah, that's not happening." I laugh. "We're having sex."

"You're the boss." Brooks is crawling up my body, trailing kisses over my calves. My knee. The tender skin of my inner thigh, making me shiver. "Cold?"

Yes. "Warm me up."

With two hands, he spreads my legs, elbowing them apart. Settles himself in, blowing puffs of air at the apex before planting a kiss on my pussy. Thumbs the folds apart before licking, tongue tentative.

I prop myself up on my elbows, no intention of missing the show.

There's something about seeing a man's head between your legs that's as seductive as the act itself. An aphrodisiac. Sexy.

Erotic.

Brooks licks. Sucks. Runs the scruff from his unshaved beard stubble against my clit until I throw my head back, letting my body relax against the pillows.

I spread my legs wider, propping a foot on his shoulder, ass lifting off the mattress.

Squirm.

Moan.

"F…fuck me." I want him inside me.

He sucks harder, ignoring me.

"Brooks." I run my fingers through his dark hair, tugging. "I need you inside me." Pause. "Please."

I'm nothing if not polite; that's the way I was raised.

Sucks and sucks and sucks some more until I whimper. The sound of my groan has his head pulling back, and I see him lick his lips. He bends again, this time kissing my pelvis with a soaking-wet mouth.

"You taste so good." He kisses my belly. Sternum. "I could live down there."

And I'd let him, forever and ever, amen.

"Slide in slow," I demand when he's braced above me, one arm on each side of my head. It's going to be easy for him to penetrate me; I'm soaked. Giddy and excited.

"I don't know if I'll last ninety seconds," he jokes, voice hoarse when the tip of his cock brushes against my pussy. I reach up and run my palms down his arms, clasping his firm forearms.

They're quivering, slightly unsteady.

I can't see his eyes; he has them squeezed shut, brows furrowed into a deep line of concentration. He looks serious and stern—not the cavalier Brooks I'm used to.

And then…

…he slips in.

Slowly, a little bit at a time, killing us both.

We moan in tandem, tortured. His dick is gloriously snug as it stretches me; I feel full.

"Jesus. Christ." He's panting now, pausing for a break. "I'm never going to last—you're so fucking tight."

"Are you going to start dripping sweat all over me?"

Brooks laughs, head bowing so I can kiss his forehead.

"Fuck, Abbott," he curses again. "I've fucking dreamt about this."

He has? When?

I don't ask, can't get the words out, suffocated by the sensation of his body against mine. By my breasts brushing against his chest, our pelvises connecting, his thrusting in and out.

I want to remember this moment forever. Not sure if I'll have it with him again.

When I imagined myself having sex with Brooks, it was fast and hot and heated, not the slow and methodical reality—the kind of sex you have when you're not just having sex. It's the kind of sex you have when you're making love.

He's watching my face as he moves in and out. He's kissing my lips. Kissing the sensitive skin in the corner of my eye.

Burying his nose in my neck as if memorizing the way I smell. Stroking my hip with his palm as he strokes me on the inside. Saying my name, repeating it like a prayer.

"Abbott…Jesus, Abbott…" Low and gravelly. Hoarse.

My hands caress his back while he moves above me, grazing his skin, and I marvel at how smooth and soft it is. If I could touch him like this all night, I would.

My eyes trail down the length of his torso, the sight of our bodies connected fueling me on. I flex my Kegels. Flex my ass. Run my hands down his backside and squeeze his rear-end, pulling him up and in so he's deeper.

His body is beautiful. The perfect balance between fit and normal, Brooks is no superhero. He's not too hard and not too soft.

I come before he does, moaning out his name when the quivers rack my ovaries, lifting my head so I can kiss the center of his chest. Turning my head so I can press my mouth against his bicep as I whimper.

I'm not a screamer. Not a loud moaner. Not the theatrical type of girl in bed. I'm silent, with just enough noise to let the person I'm with know I'm climaxing so he knows he can come, too.

"I'm gonna come too, baby." He pumps in and pushes, circling his pelvis round and round, and I grip his ass tighter.

"Yes, come," I tell him, giving him the permission he needs.

"Where do you want it?" he asks frantically. "Where do you want me to come?"

Uh. Well, ideally? Inside me.

But we didn't put on a condom, just started having sex without the conversation—which I just now realized.

"On my stomach," I reply, speaking as if I'm asking him to pass me the salt at the supper table.

Brooks' groan is primal, his face contorted. In fact, I would never recognize him if he were making this face on the street—his sex face looks nothing like him at all, and I stifle a giggle, watching his orgasm build.

"I'm coming, I'm coming," he grunts, hips pumping. Pumping and pumping, hands gripping the headboard as he thrusts once. Twice. Three more times.

When he pulls out to spill on my abs, I'm empty inside, literally and figuratively. Wet, sticky cum coats my skin.

He flops down beside me.

Lies with his arm over his brow, breathing hard and staring up at the ceiling while I do the same.

I just had sex with Brooks Bennett and I will never be the same.

22

BROOKS

"I think we would make a great couple." Abbott rolls over on the bed, yawning and pressing her face into my pillow, laughing.

"You know I don't date." I feel like the biggest asshole pointing that fact out post-coitus, while we're still naked in my bed.

She rolls over to face me, tucking a hand under her chin, watching me with those big, blue doe eyes. They're now a bit sad. "I know. I was just saying—I wasn't saying I wanted to date you. I said we'd make a great couple. It was a simple observation."

"Well I couldn't even if I wanted to."

"That's a weird way of putting it. You can't, or you won't?"

There is no way for me to explain without sounding like a complete fucker. "Can't. Both."

"Won't? You liar—you'd love dating me. I'm awesome." She yawns again, tired and sleepy but not allowed to spend the night, though I haven't actually said that yet. "Why do you keep saying you can't date? It makes no sense. Are you the beneficiary to some fortune and the will stipulates you must remain single until your thirtieth birthday?" Abbott jokes, doing her best to make light of an awkward situation.

Her, in my bed as I try talking her out of it.

"I just can't date anyone right now."

"Why? There has to be a reason."

There is, but it's an embarrassing one, one that would get me in serious trouble with her and change the way she looks at me forever. And while I can't date her now, I don't want to risk our friendship by destroying that, too.

So I shrug. Feed her the smallest crumb of information. "I have this thing with my friends. If I started seeing someone, I would lose out on a few...opportunities."

"What opportunities? A job? A promotion?"

"Not like that." She has it all wrong, but I can't tell her about the Bastard Bachelor Society. The guys and I swore we wouldn't discuss it with women.

Abbott studies me, eyes raking over my face. "Like how, then? Just tell me—it's not a big deal. I won't judge you, if that's what you're worried about."

"It's going to sound stupid."

Abbott studies the hem of my cotton sheets, rubbing the fabric between her thumb and forefinger. "I'm sure it will. Half the shit you do is stupid."

"Gee, tell me how you really feel."

Her narrow shoulders shrug as if to say, 'I just did.'

"A few months ago, we started this society, and dating breaks some of the rules."

Obviously she's already given me shit about being in a club, so she ignores that little factoid and wants to know, "Which rules?"

"All of them."

She's propped up on an elbow now, intently watching me from across the short expanse of mattress. If I reached out, I'd be able to touch her or pull her back into my arms. "How many rules are there?"

"Why are you asking so many questions?"

She sits up, affronted. "Because, Brooks—we just slept together. Because, *Brooks*..." My name doesn't roll off her lips in the loving, adorable way she was saying it earlier today. This tone is sarcastic and unpleasant. "I care about you. So forgive me for asking a simple question about the guy I'm letting screw me when the mood strikes him. Apparently that's all I'm good for these days—oral and fucking." Abbott shoves back the blankets, scooting her ass to the edge of the bed, wiping my cum off her stomach with my clean sheet. "If you don't want to talk about it, that's your business, but I'm not going to lie here and put up with the stonewalling—message received, loud and clear."

"I wasn't stonewalling you—I *was* talking." Just not giving her the answers she desperately wants.

She steps into the slippers next to the bed—my slippers—glancing over her shoulder to glare down at me. "Don't be so literal."

She disappears into the hallway, throwing clothes on as she stalks back into the bedroom a few seconds later. I watch her step into underwear. Snap on her bra, locking away the memory of her perfect areolas...how they tasted...

"It's not on purpose. I just am not at liberty to say."

"No, I don't suppose you are." Abbott stands, and I can't stop my eyes from skimming her ass, clad in the cutest panties I've seen in a long time. "So cliché."

Ugh, fuck my life.

"Can you not tell Nan about this?" I beg, shoving down my blankets too, intent on following her.

Abbott scoffs. "Oh. Oh! Can we not tell Nan about this?" Now she's pissed. "We're telling Nan—oh boy are we telling Nan!" She's huffing, yanking her pants on. "Wait until she hears about this! No more treats for you, a-hole."

"Abbott! Come on!" I trail along, desperate and buck naked. "Don't!"

She spins. "You're afraid of a little old lady but not of me? What the hell, Brooks?"

"For the record, she's not little and she's not old. Nan is scary as fuck."

"Yes, I know she's terrifying because she's *my* grandmother, not *yours*! You should be scared of her—she'll eat you alive."

"Pfft. I'm not afraid of Nan!" I love Nan. She's my nan, too. She feeds me and brings me treats and actually gives a crap about me. Nan is the fucking shit, and if Abbott squeals on me and she gets mad at me too, I'll…

I don't know what I'd do if I lost them both.

Fuck.

If I lost them…

Without Nan, there would be no Abbott. Without Abbott in my life, I won't have Nan. They're like family.

Ohana and all that bullshit.

What does that mean?

"All you care about is the cat and Nan." She tosses her hands up in surrender. "I'm so flattered." Marches over and pokes me in the chest with a pink fingernail. "If we were dating, I'd dump your ass right now. But we're not, so I can't—because of some stupid club you won't tell me about, with its stupid rules you won't tell me about." Grabbing her keys from the kitchen counter, she pulls her shirt over her head before yanking the door open. "I hope your boys, and your useless rules—whatever they are—are enough to keep you warm at night, you turd."

"Abbott," I feebly call out after her.

But she's already through my door, slamming it behind her, and in the hallway, shouting, "*Bye!*"

I'm an idiot, and instead of going into the hall, I stand there in my foyer with my head tipped back. "Abbottttt," I yell, sounding suspiciously like Rocky Balboa—what the fuck?

"I said *bye!*" she yells back, still in the hallway. Her place is only feet away; she could have easily gone inside rather than lingering outside my door. "Find your own nan!"

"I never had a nan—mine *died*!" I shout the lie to be dramatic and hear her loud gasp through the door. In three strides, I yank it open again and stare at her. Abbott remains in the vestibule, immobile in front of her own apartment.

"Put some damn clothes on!" She gapes at me, actually covering her mouth with the palm of her dainty hand. "And don't you dare play off my sympathy to get your own way. You have a grandma—she's alive and well, so get your own nan!" she shouts again, so fucking loud I can hear a neighbor down the way cracking their door open to see what the fuss is. "And cover your dick."

I can't help it; I laugh.

Abbott's potty mouth, coupled with the indignant expression on her face and the fact that I'm standing here naked —the entire situation makes me laugh until a tear drips from the corner of my eye. I swipe at it.

Abbott crosses her arms and shoots daggers across the corridor. But how pissed can she actually be if she's still standing there glaring at me?

"Pfft, *I'm* going inside," she huffs again. "If you came into the hall to stop me, you're *too* late."

"I didn't come out here to stop you."

Her head tilts. "Well you can't, so…"

She hasn't budged an inch.

"Then why are you standing out here, staring at me?" This confrontational side of her is totally uncharacteristic and a total turn-on. Based on what I know about her, based on the few short months we've been hanging out, Abbott isn't one to pick arguments or even participate in them. She's kind and loving. Well, fine—not too kind, but enough that she's not a total asshole and wouldn't deliberately get into a quarrel.

"I'm staring because you're naked, duh. Plus, I wanted to see if you had the balls to follow me."

The balls to follow her—who is she right now? Jesus she's cute.

Her eyes stray to my balls and I laugh again, pointing to them. "Big balls."

"Apparently."

If I listen hard enough, the feeble mews of Desi coming from the inside of her apartment can be heard. That cat freaking loves me, bless its evil little heart.

She adds, "I just assumed my balls were bigger than yours."

That's the thing I love about Abbott—her ability to say dumb shit that makes me laugh and not care. She's not trying to impress me with her intellect, although she's wicked smart. Abbott makes me feel…

Good.

She makes me feel good.

Her family feels like the home I never had.

What the hell I'm supposed to do with that information is beyond me; I have way too much to lose by backing down from that bet, no matter what my feelings are toward her.

I cannot give up my season tickets. They are the only thing I've ever inherited, will ever inherit, and maybe someday I'll have a son or daughter to take to the game…

A son or a daughter? Down boy, you're not even in a relationship, let alone impregnating anyone. And for the sake of the Bastard Bachelor Society, you're not allowed to be in one, anyway.

I feel Abbott watching me, can see the questions in her eyes that she doesn't dare ask.

"Whatever is holding you back, I…" Her throat constricts as she swallows. "I won't push you. I'll leave it be. So." The brown hair she just had highlighted gets tucked behind her ears. "This is me telling you to go live your best life."

"Are you breaking up with me?" The words leave my lips before I can think twice about what I'm saying.

Her laugh is sardonic, despite the sad look in her blue eyes. "We're not dating, remember? You went down on me once, slept with me once, and now I doubt you were even going to let me spend the night. Probably some rule about that."

Leave it to Abbott to throw that back in my face.

"Abbott, I can't be in a relationship, but I also don't…" I pause, struggling to find words. "I don't want…*this*."

I don't want it to be weird. I want what we had yesterday and the day before and the day before that.

Why do sex and feelings complicate everything? I should have known this shit was going to happen, dammit. Should have pumped the brakes when I had the chance. Should have pushed her away once and for all before sticking my dick inside her.

But she smells so fucking great and *she* is fucking great and why do I have to like her so fucking much?

Watch the mouth, Brooks.

"Well what is it you want then? To be besties? I'm not going to sleep with you according to your whims—I deserve more respect than that. And since you won't tell me anything about your secret club, there is nothing I can do about that, either. So…" Her back hits her door and she continues watching me warily. "It is what it is."

"I mean…" My door is open behind me and I lean against it, crossing my bare arms over my bare chest, nuts and berries still dangling for all the world to see. Well, the security cameras at least. "Plenty of people sleep with each other and they're just friends."

"Friends." It's a deadpan reply, no question mark tacked onto the end. "Ah."

"I'm not going to ghost you, if that's what you're worried about. You're the one who blew up and stormed out of my apartment."

"Not *ghost* me? We're friends! What do you think this is?" She motions at the empty space between us in the hall. "I'm not going to settle for someone who only wants to be my friend in public and is someone else behind closed doors and pity-fucks me. That's total bullshit and completely unfair."

Wow. She's sworn at me *twice* now. Okay, so maybe the word

balls doesn't count as profanity, but it's not like she curses on a regular basis, so it still sounds odd.

She must be hurt.

"Can you keep your voice down and get out of the hallway? Come back to bed."

Her answer is a shocked laugh. "Come back to bed? *Ha!*" She makes a show of looking up and down the stark empty hallway with its cream paint, cream trim, and gold sconces lining the exteriors of every door. "Who's around to hear us? No one. So say what you have to say, or don't say it—no one cares. Except Desdemona, and she's pissed at you, too."

Behind her, the cat scratches on her door and meows pitifully.

"Desi isn't pissed at me."

"Yes, she is."

"How do you know?"

Abbott's chin goes up defiantly. "She does what I tell her to."

"No, she doesn't."

Abbott's nostrils flare. "It's *my* cat, and *my* nan, and that's that. Get your own, you mooch."

Lose the bet, Brooks, and the Abbott and the nan and the cat can all be yours. Lose the bet, lose the bet, lose the bet—those three words repeat in my head, over and over, and will probably haunt me for the rest of my damn life. *Tell her you love her. Be a man and say it, pussy.*

As if on cue, Desi mews.

Pitiful. Pathetic.

A feline actress sent to torment me.

"Well…I should go inside. As you can tell, the cat's going crazy."

I would hardly call a few meows going crazy, but I'm not about to argue with her when she's already crabby at me. Abbott needs to cool off. In a few days, I'll stop by her place and we can have a serious talk.

After I figure out what the fuck I'm going to do. How do I

explain that I want and need her to fit into my life but can't have her right this second—on the spot like this, conversing in the hallway of our apartment building where anyone could overhear us? Abbott might not think anyone is listening, but I know for a fact we have a few nosey fucking neighbors; we don't see them often, but they're lurking.

Which is hardly the point.

The point is…I need time to think.

I stop by her place a few days later. Then the next day. Then the next. And the next. And the fucking next, and I don't know if Abbott has been home any of the numerous times I've knocked on her door, but she isn't answering. My texts? They aren't being answered, either.

She's shutting me out, and it's crushing me.

Crushing me in a way my heart hasn't known since Stacey Kipplinger broke it in sixth grade, checking the "no" box when I passed her a note asking if she liked me and writing *I would never date someone who wore hand-me-down jeans* in the blank space at the bottom.

I wonder what that bitch is up to these days.

The Basement isn't kind to me tonight, either. I arrive to a crowded bar, a crowded dining area, and my friends, who are already three sheets to the wind and itching to joke around.

They're wearing their blue jackets while I've left mine at home, in no mood to wear the damn thing when it smells like Abbott and her baby powder.

I would know, because I checked.

Sulking, I slouch down in my chair, not thirsty, ill-humored and horrible company.

"Dude. What's your fucking problem?" Phillip is shoveling one too many free mints into his mouth, feet propped up on the coffee table, dress shoes shined to an unnatural gloss. Where the hell did he shine those up, the airport?

"Nothing is my problem, dude."

That's not true, but it's not like I can confess my girl problems to these idiots. They'd be up my ass so fast, calling forfeit and roasting me.

Lose the bet, Brooks, and the Abbott and the nan and the cat can all be yours.

Lose the damn bet and get Abbott back.

Back?

You fool, you never actually had her.

I shake my head, disturbed. These voices in my head have got to shut the fuck up—they're messing with my work, my sleep patterns, and my fun.

Life without Abbott sucks.

I stopped by her place a few nights ago after work, gave her door a few knocks.

Nothing.

This morning before leaving for the office, I tried again, early enough that I knew she was at home. Abbott isn't an early riser —the girl hates waking up, never skips breakfast. The only response to my knock?

Desdemona's pitiful mewing at the door. Fucking tore at my heartstrings.

"You're being a bitch." The tip of Phillip's dress shoe bumps the calf of my dress pants.

I throw my hands in the air. "I haven't done anything."

"It's not what you said, but how you haven't said it." Blaine is suddenly the authority on my mood swings? Like I'm not allowed to feel like shit? Or be crabby? Or have a few fucking moments of peace and quiet?

Phillip pops an olive into his mouth, adding, "I speak fluent body language."

"Is that so? What am I saying now?" I throw up my hands again, this time with two middle fingers tossed in his direction.

"You're showing us the size and girth of your dick." They both laugh, smacking each other in the arm.

It's official: they're the village idiots.

You're their ringleader, Brooks. You're responsible for their behavior just as much as they are. The club wasn't their idea, it was yours. Blaine and Phillip are like two children, taking my lead and running with it. They're not saying or doing anything I haven't done myself or told them to do.

They're simply playing by the rules we made; meanwhile, I'm questioning them.

Because you fell in love, dipshit, and refuse to admit it.

Refuse to lose.

Lose Abbott.

It's one or the other.

Phillip interrupts my thoughts. "Wow, you sure have a lot on your mind. For real, bro—do you want to talk about it?"

"Yeah dude, you actually look like you might cry." Blaine backs him up, as usual.

I look like I'm going to cry?

I run a finger along the bottom of my eye and sure enough —it's damp.

What the fuck?

"I am not going to cry."

"I didn't say you were—I said it looks like you might cry."

Too late.

I already am kind of.

Except I'd never fucking admit it to these two. It would only lead to more tears, not to mention twenty questions that I have no intention of answering.

"Guess I'm just…" I pause, searching for a plausible lie. "Stressed out."

"Work?"

"Sure." Let's go with that. "The partners are breathing down my neck about a development."

More like a *social* development.

"I thought you weren't on that development at work anymore. You said you were promoted."

Crap.

I didn't think these numbskulls listened when I spoke. "It's a new one. A new, um, development."

A development currently known as: self-destruction of my love life and ruining the best possible relationship I'll ever have for a vacation timeshare I'll never use and a beat-up ATV I have no storage for.

Awesome, Brooks.

Just. *Awesome.*

Blaine nods knowingly. "Ah."

Clearing my throat, I occupy my hands by shoveling in a handful of nuts then washing them down with bourbon. "What do you two have going on besides work?"

Phillip is all smiles. "Can't complain. Finally got the temp in human resources to give me a blow job in the supply closet."

Blaine's brows shoot up. "Dude, that is such a violation of company policy on so many levels."

"I know—before she'd blow me, she made me sign a document about not suing her for sexual harassment and confirming it was consensual."

"Hold on, hold on, hold on—*she* made *you* sign something? You didn't make *her* sign?"

Phillip considers this. "Um, no. She's the one in a position of authority, duh."

"But she was *blowing* you in the supply closet."

"Exactly."

"But…"

"And it was her idea."

We all sit back, *oohing* and *aahing*. "Oh, well that makes more sense."

"Was she on her knees?" Blaine asks.

Phillip stares. "No, she was in a desk chair." He pauses. "Yes she was kneeling, dumbass."

"I don't know! I've never been blown anywhere besides the bedroom. Give me a break—I was curious."

Phillip's hand goes up. "You've never been blown anywhere besides the bedroom?"

Blaine's cheeks turn pink. "You have to remember, I don't necessarily date women who are hellions in the sack, okay? They're all pretty…vanilla."

"Bambi is vanilla? Even girls who are vanilla get down on their knees from time to time."

Visions of Abbott fill my head, of the time I got down on my knees, in my living room, to eat her out, her hand holding on to the couch for support.

"Anything other than blow jobs?" I turn toward Blaine. "Speaking of which—have you spoken to Bambi lately?"

He averts his eyes, suddenly very curious about the menu that's been sitting in the center of our table the entire time we've been here. "No."

"You fucking liar," Phillip accuses. "Is she messaging you?"

"I mean…" He squirms in his chair, uncomfortable. "Yeah? She was pretty devastated when I dumped her—obviously she's going to message me." He hurries to say it, as though emphasizing that he's not at fault for her contacting him, passing any blame lest Phillip and I accuse him of losing the bet by reentering his relationship.

Which would make my life so much easier—both of my friends losing along with me—so I can go groveling back to Abbott and continue living my life with her in it.

"You need to block her stalker ass," Phillip says, after much consideration.

"Meh," I disagree. "He's right—she wasn't expecting to get dumped, and it's not like he gave her any closure."

I never believed closure was important until Abbott ghosted

me, all the unanswered questions driving me to distraction. If we're friends, how could she dump me like that?

I understand why she's pissed, and why she's carefully avoiding me, but fuck—it's starting to hurt the one goddamn feeling I have left inside me.

24

ABBOTT

"Does your ex-boyfriend happen to have a friend named Brooks?"

I'm standing in the doorway of the office Bambi shares with her co-workers, seizing the opportunity to have a word in private. Everyone else is at lunch.

I don't bother using Brooks' full name, because what are the odds there is more than one Brooks in this entire city? Bambi either knows him or she doesn't.

She spins in her desk chair. "Yes." Leans in, taking off her computer glasses and staring down her nose at me. "Why?"

My lips purse.

So. Brooks and Blaine.

Friends with a pact, choosing themselves over the women they love.

And love me he does—by now I know that bastard better than he knows himself.

Brooks Bennett loves me but broke it off with me, and I want to know why. What are his friends holding over him? For what reason are they all breaking up with their girlfriends?

It makes no sense.

Bambi silently watches the wheels in my head turning. "Why?" she repeats.

"'Cause, I…" I swallow. "I'm friends with him, and he…" I can't get the words out without becoming emotional. Wow, this sucks, and we weren't even in a romantic relationship, although we actually were and didn't realize it.

Didn't call it one. But a rose by any other name…

"He's the douche who broke up Blaine and me."

"I know."

"How?"

"He and I were really good friends—"

"Fuck buddies?" Bambi crudely blurts out. "Friends with benefits?"

"No." After all, we've only had sex once, so we can't be considered fuck buddies yet.

But the reality is, I allowed myself to become *that girl*, the one so desperate for attention and affection from a guy that I blinded myself to what he'd been telling me all along.

He didn't want a girlfriend. He didn't want a relationship. He just liked hanging out and occasionally having sex with me, while eating me out of house and home and squatting on my couch.

I pushed and pushed and pushed him until I drove him away.

Bambi must be watching the play of emotions running across my face, and I feel a warm hand on my forearm. "I'm sorry, Abbott."

"I'm sorry, too." Sorry your boyfriend dumped you to try to win the same bet.

Bambi hands me a tissue. "Do you think you'd take him back if he came groveling?"

My laugh is slightly cynical. "He's not going to come groveling back—we weren't a couple." I sniffle. "Would you take your ex back if he reached out?"

She hesitates, pressing a few random keys on her computer

keyboard to buy herself some time before answering. "I think so. I really miss him." Then she hurries to add, "I know he dumped me for a foolish reason, and that tells me maybe he didn't like me the way I like him? But we've been talking more lately, and I think we're closer friends now that we aren't dating."

This development surprises me. I would have thought Bambi Warner was the type of girl who plotted revenge on an ex to destroy him—not the type who texted them every day to mend and repair their relationship.

Maybe there is more to her than I originally thought, guilt assailing me for judging her.

"What started the whole thing with these guys, you think?" I gleaned no actual answers from Brooks, only vague statements about how he can't do this and he can't do that and I can't wear his smoking jacket and blah blah blah.

"I actually have no idea, but I'm sure this is a Brooks Bennett brainchild. He wasn't the same after his girlfriend broke up with him."

"He had a girlfriend?"

"Yeah, they weren't together long, but he really loved her, from what Blaine has told me. She randomly dumped him out of the blue, and, well—he's been a turd ever since."

"What was she like?"

"I've only seen pictures, didn't actually meet her, but I think she was blonde. Cute. Blaine said she was sweet most of the time but a total bitch if she didn't know you."

My nod of understanding is slow. "I can see that."

Bambi pulls open her desk drawer and retrieves a bag of cheese-flavored rice cakes. "Guys love a girl with a little bit of bite—at least they do in the beginning." She rips open the bag and sticks her hand inside. "God, I love these dumb things."

She munches down on a rice cake, chewing thoughtfully.

"I'm not sure what to do about Brooks. We're not dating so I'm in this weird place."

"But you want to be dating him, yeah?"

I only pause because I am not sure if I want to be so open with Bambi, this woman I'm not that close to. The last thing I want is her learning all this personal information about me before she and I find a place of neutrality, a place where I'm comfortable calling her a friend.

Screw it.

"Yes."

"Well, I don't know much about what those three have going on that they're not telling us, but as far as Blaine is concerned? He isn't willing to give up whatever bounty they've got on the table, so it must be good."

My stomach drops at the same time my heart sinks.

Bambi takes another bite of her rice cake, waving it around in the air as she thinks out loud. "I mean, think about it. You're incredible—smart, beautiful, rich. Any guy would be a fool not to want to date you. So what is it that's holding him back?" She squints, looking out the window for answers. "What the heck do those guys have going on?"

Wait.

Bambi thinks I'm incredible and smart?

My mind reels from this information, forgetting the fact that we're theorizing about our man troubles and focusing on Bambi's compliments.

I open my mouth to tell her they have a club and the club has rules, but then I close it.

Brooks didn't tell me that little tidbit so I could share it with anyone who will listen—he told me by accident, and it's not my secret to tell, even if Bambi does have a vested interest in knowing it.

25

BROOKS

"I forfeit." I remove my beloved smoking jacket, fold it in half, and gently lay it in the center of the table. "Here."

Both guys are looking at me like I'm a stranger who just sat down and began eating their food at the dinner table.

Like I'm nuts.

"Forfeit what?" This from Blaine. "What are you giving us your jacket for?"

"The bet."

"Hold on—back up. What do you mean, you forfeit?"

"I'm out. You guys win, I lose."

"I don't get it. How could you lose when you're not seeing anyone?"

"I'm not seeing anyone and I'm not dating anyone. Not technically." But I was, sort of, in a roundabout way; I just failed to mention it to my best friends, and now she fucking hates my guts, so it hardly matters.

"Then why are you telling us this?"

"Because I want her back." Even though I didn't actually have her, I'm not willing to let Abbott out of my life. Running into her in the lobby of our building won't be enough. Bumping into her in the hallway in front of our apartments won't be enough.

"I love her." The confession is strangled, the words the truest I've said in weeks.

"Who?" Phillip asks as Blaine says, "I'm confused," at the same time.

"Abbott."

Blank stares all around.

"My neighbor?"

More blank stares.

Then, "Phew. I thought you were going to tell me you were in love with my sister." Phillip laughs.

Blaine hits him. "Don't be an idiot—your sister is horrible. No one is in love with her."

"Shut up, asshole. My sister is awesome. She did a favor for your sorry ass—show some respect."

Whoa, whoa, whoa. Looks like everyone in the Bastard Bachelor Society is a wee bit testy tonight, not just me. I put my hands in the air so Blaine and Phillip will calm the fuck down, waiting while they simmer.

It's Phillip who finally calms us down, circling back around to the topic at hand: Abbott.

"You met your neighbor and his name is Abbott?"

"Her. She. Abbott is a female—I said I love her, not him."

Blaine winks. "No judgments."

Why does everything with my friends have to be so damn complicated? If they would just listen and focus, we wouldn't have to go round and round with the same shit over and over. Jesus Christ, it's exhausting.

I sit silently, waiting for them both to zip their lips so I can get a word in edgewise. Wait several minutes longer while they derail, wanting to know why I never invite them over when my apartment building is totally sweet. Why I never have them over when I have an awesome television and a liquor store nearby so we'd never run out of beer during a football game.

I wait. And wait. And wait.

Finally, "So you're in love? When the hell did this happen?"

"More importantly, why are we just hearing about it?"

"I didn't think it would matter. We were just supposed to be friends."

Phillip wrinkles up his nose. "Since when have you ever had friends who are girls?"

Since never.

"So you're in love with your neighbor? That's…different."

I sigh, already exhausted from having to explain. "She lives in my building and one day we met in front of the elevators." I have a moment of déjà vu, the memory of Abbott racing to the elevator car and pounding on the close button so she wouldn't have to ride up with me. "She didn't want me to ride up with her, which I thought was weird."

I never did ask her about that day and what her problem with me was.

I hope I get the chance to find out.

"Then," I go on, "one morning I was jogging and took the stairs up to my apartment, and when I blew through the door from the stairwell, she was standing in the hallway in front of her door, holding a steaming hot bag of takeout."

"At least it wasn't a steaming hot bag of shit," Phillip jokes.

Blaine smacks his arm. "Would you shut the fuck up and listen?"

I wait for them to stop bickering before continuing. "Anyway, she had this food and wound up inviting me in for breakfast—"

"Is breakfast the new word for sex?" Phillip interrupts, clearly a few drinks in.

"No." I can't not roll my eyes. "Breakfast is the word for *breakfast*. Would you be quiet?" He closes his mouth. "After that, she and I just…started hanging out a lot. Almost every day."

"She must be hot, eh?"

It comes as no surprise that they'd want to know, but it does come as a surprise that Abbott is not, in fact, hot. She's better than that.

"I wouldn't call her hot. I would say she's more..." How do I describe her without sounding like a lovesick chump? "Pretty. She's really girly and not at all fussy, except maybe for work. Abbott loves to eat and chill and she's funny in a cute kind of way. Like, not so much ha ha funny as adorable funny."

"Say funny *one* more time," Blaine deadpans.

"She's fucking funny, okay? Quit riding my nuts."

Phillip is quick to stick up for me. "Yeah bro, you're taking the wind out of his sails."

"I should be riding his nuts," Blaine argues. "Our boy here didn't even try to win this bet, and he's the one who came up with the idea in the first place. What kind of bullshit is that?"

Of course—he's right. I gave it a good effort for a solid week, tops, then warred with myself through most of the rest, putting in a half-assed attempt to keep my distance from Abbott once we got to know each other better.

Then, once we became friends...forget about it.

"Have you slept with her?" This from Blaine, who leans forward in his chair, insatiably interested in my answer.

I hesitate a hair too long.

"Oh dang! You did sleep with her!"

Silently, I stew, no one to blame for this but myself.

"Well." Phillip, the voice of reason, crosses his legs and studies me from his spot. "I hope she's worth it."

A sinking hole bears down in the pit of my stomach. "What do you mean?"

"You didn't just lose your heart—you lost your ass." Phillip smirks.

"Good one." Blaine puts his palm in the air so they can high-five.

I shift uncomfortably in my seat. "Guys, come on."

"What do you mean, 'Guys come on'?" Now Phillip crosses

his arms, prepared to be a hard-ass. "A bet is a bet, and you, sir, lost."

"I understand that, but what are we going to do about the season tickets and shit?"

Blaine speaks slowly as if I'm a child just learning how to speak English. "You. Forfeit."

Is it me, or has this room gotten unbearably hot? "Yeah, but…I was assuming you'd take pity on me since I'm sacrificing everything I have for love, not some hook-up."

"Ha!" Phillip smirks. "Nope."

"Yeah. *Wrong.*" Blaine's chuckle into his glass is equally as amused. "You know how much I love the Jags, and you know how broke I am. I now have a fighting chance to win those season tickets."

Phillip chimes in. "Don't worry though—we'll bring you to one or two games."

"No need to thank us." Blaine laughs, putting his hands up in a gesture meant to portray his humility.

"You two really are bastards."

I can't fucking believe these two. I really can't. They have no sympathy for me, and while we haven't been friends our entire lives, I love them like brothers. I would think they'd make an exception for me since I had my damn heart broken by Kayla, but no. They're going to be dicks about this whole thing.

"What if we say fuck it and dissolve the club?" I'm grasping at straws.

"It's a society, not a club," Phillip smartly corrects me.

"Are you insane?" Blaine's eyes are bugging. "No. I broke up with my *girlfriend* for this. I thought she was going to stab me in the thigh with a spork when we talked about it."

"*Was* she your girlfriend, though, or were you just datingggg?" Phillip teases.

"Shut up, asshole—I'm serious." Blaine shoots him a glare so salty, Phillip shrinks down in his seat. Then he turns that look on me. "You can't just start something because your life sucks, ruin ours, then decide you don't want to do it anymore. It's done —you forfeit, Phillip and I are the last men standing, and you can just sit back and watch me win."

"Hey, hey now, girls, let's not fight." Phillip tries to smooth Blaine's ruffled feathers. Our friend doesn't get pissed often, but when he does—watch out.

"I haven't ruined anything," I grumble, knowing that's a lie.

"I broke up with my girlfriend!" he shouts in outrage, and rightfully so, though I wouldn't dare admit it.

"You wouldn't have broken up with her if you actually loved her. You loved the idea of her, but you didn't love her. Huge difference."

Blaine considers this, shrugging. "Fair enough. No one twisted my arm to dump her, but I did, so sorry, loser. You forfeit, that's the end of the game for you. We're in, you're out."

"Fine." My nod of acceptance is jerky and slightly spastic.

"Good." Phillip smirks, having won this argument. "Now let's talk about this chick, Abbott, whom we've never heard of. You said she lives in your building?"

"Yes, across the hall." I shift in my seat. "We kind of became friends and then…you know the rest."

"You actually love this chick?"

I bristle at his use of the word chick but keep my lips sealed shut; Lord knows I've use far worse words to describe the women they've dated in the past.

"I think so."

"You must if you're willing to come to us with your tail between your legs and give up everything you have just to date her. I mean, is she even a sure thing?" Blaine shoves several olives into his mouth like he's hungry but doesn't want to order an actual meal, determined to survive on garnishes alone.

My laugh is sardonic. "Not. At. All. In fact, I'm pretty sure she hates me right now. I haven't actually seen her in a few days. She's avoiding me."

"Why?"

"Because after we had sex, she told me we'd make a great couple—which we totally would—and I told her I couldn't date her."

Phillip shudders. "Ouch."

"Yeah." Blaine cringes. "Bet that went over like a lead balloon."

That's an understatement if I've ever heard one. "Let's just say if looks could kill, I'd be a dead man. And I have no food in my fridge anymore, so I'm also a man who's been starving for the past few days."

"Oh, tell her that—I bet she'd take you back in a heartbeat if she knew you needed her as a food source." Phillip's sarcasm is barely humorous.

Blaine taps his chin with the tip of his forefinger. "Can she take him back if they aren't a couple?"

"No, but she can forgive him for being an ass."

"Correction: she can forgive him for being a *bastard*."

We raise our glasses and toast, wishing me luck as I try to win Abbott's heart, and her forgiveness.

26

ABBOTT

I have been avoiding Brooks for days. It wasn't my intention to completely stonewall him, but let's be honest—looking into a man's face after he tells you he isn't interested is a kind of torment I want no part of.

Saying the words *I think we would make a great couple* was hard enough. Having him reject them?

Awful.

Humiliating.

And so, I've been avoiding him, hoping I know his routine well enough not to bump into him.

It's childish because we're supposed to be friends, but I don't have the guts to see him.

Honestly? I've been depressed since I told him to shove off, which is the reason Sophia is sitting across from me on the sofa, cross-legged, spooning ice cream directly from the container.

"You want a bite?"

"No thanks, I've already eaten half of the cookies and cream. I feel sick." I groan, holding my stomach, pointing the remote control at the television but not really seeing what's on it. Who even cares?

"So, hypothetically…" Sophia begins for the hundredth time

(she loves hypothetical scenarios and has been blasting me with them since she walked in the door). "If Brooks were to knock on your door and ask to see you, what would you do?"

"I'd slam the door in his face."

The spoon Sophia has halfway in her mouth pauses, her throat humming out an unconvinced, "Hmm."

"Hmm, what? I would."

"Yeah, no. I don't believe you."

"I don't care what you believe. I don't want to see him."

She's doubtful. "Don't want to see him, or aren't ready to see him?"

"Is there a difference?"

Sophia is right—I do want to see him, but I'm just not ready. The stinging still hurts, my heart and my soul and my pride still hurt. I thought I was strong enough that a thing like this wouldn't affect me this way, but it does.

Because I love that jackass.

"Of course there's a difference, but I get it if you don't want to see him. Shit, if you want, I can break into his place and kill all his plants."

My chin goes up a notch. "He only has one plant." Not that I would let her kill it, or break into his place.

I don't hate the poor guy.

I'm lonely and I ache for him; plotting revenge might take a bit of the edge off temporarily, but I'd still be crying myself to sleep tonight.

"Babe, you okay over there?" Sophia softly asks, reaching over and placing her hand on mine. Giving me a pat with a hand that's very cold because it's been wrapped around the ice cream container for so long.

"Yes." Sort of.

"Okay, so hypothetically, what if…Brooks knocked on your door and begged your forgiveness—what would you do?"

"Nothing. He doesn't have to apologize for anything. It's not a crime to sleep with someone and not want to be in a relationship. It's called casual dating. Fuck buddies. Friends with benefits." Potato, potahto, it's all the same thing.

"Brooks Bennett is not your fuck buddy. You're actual buddies who just so happened to sleep together and then the bastard left you hanging."

"Stop trying to make me feel better."

I close my eyes, trying to remember what he said to me in the hallway, trying to remember the way he watched me and the expression on his face after I told him to go live his best life.

"Are you breaking up with me?"

I laughed at him. "We're not dating, remember? You went down on me once, slept with me once, and now I doubt you were even going to let me spend the night. Probably some rule about that." I threw everything he'd told me back in his face.

"Abbott, I can't be in a relationship, but I also don't…" He paused, struggling to find words. "I don't want…this."

Can't be in a relationship.

Can't be in a relationship?

Why?

What hold do his friends have on him? Is he in the mob? Does he owe someone money? Is he on the lam and bad guys are out to get him?

"I don't want…this."

This.

I sit in silence, listening to the sound of my best friend licking ice cream off a spoon then digging into the bowl for more, Desi mewing beside her, begging for a bit of a treat. Sophia pats my cat on the head, fluffs her hair, but doesn't give in to the pouting kitty.

Hard-ass. She and Desi have a love-hate-love relationship, much like everyone else has with my temperamental cat.

"I don't want…this."

He might not want things this way, but this is what he's getting. I might have been okay with being in the friend-zone at the beginning, but I'm not okay with it now.

Line drawn.

I will not be crossing it.

And I'll do that by staying on my side of the hallway. I just need him to stay on his.

"Has the bastard tried to call you?"

I haven't told Sophia that not only has Brooks tried to call, he's texted and knocked on my door in an effort to contact me. Just yesterday, I sat on the floor in my little entryway, back against the door as he knocked and knocked and knocked.

I could hear Brooks standing on the other side for fourteen minutes, fourteen long, excruciating minutes before he gave up and went back to his place. Fourteen minutes before I could open my door and steal to the elevator in an effort to run errands.

"Don't call him that," I snap, lost in thought.

"Sorry." She pats me on the hand again, Desdemona now curled in her lap, purring like a motor. "I love you. I hate seeing you hurt."

"I know." I love her, too, and I've never been afraid to tell anyone how I felt about them until Brooks rejected my sentiments.

"I think we would make a great couple…"

Far from a declaration, perhaps, but still packed with meaning, and it took a lot of courage for me to say.

Why did I say that to him? WHY? Guh, I'm such an idiot.

I mull this over, over and over again, tormenting myself by reliving each moment on a loop.

Then.

There's a loud knock at the door I wasn't expecting, and I start.

Sophia pauses, spoon mid-lick on her tongue. "Are you expecting anyone?"

"No, but you know Nan pops in from time to time."

Sophia reaches for her phone and checks the time. "I'll get that in case it's a murderer. You've already had a shitty week—we don't need anything else traumatic on your plate." She giggles at herself all the way to the door, yanking it open before I can protest. Instead of calling out my objection, I bury my head beneath the blanket, dread pooling in the depth of my belly.

"Oh." A brief silence. "Ohhh." Another pause. "I-I really don't know if she will…I'll have to ask. Give me a second—I'll be right back."

The door clicks closed and I crane my neck to watch as she walks back into the living room then begins pacing.

"What are you doing?" I frown. "Who was that?"

"Uh. That…" She points to the entryway. "Was Brooks."

Brooks? I rise, wipe my palms on my pajama bottoms. "What do I do?"

Shit, what do I do! I'm not ready to see him, especially like this.

"No." I'm shaking my head a bit too aggressively. "I don't want to see him."

"Abbott, you have to—you can't avoid him forever. Plus, he's really cute."

"Sophia! Like that matters." She is so ridiculous.

"Right, but he's not at all how I was picturing him!"

"Give me a break—you've been googling him for weeks, and don't lie and say you haven't."

"Fine, I was—but he's way better in person."

"Please go tell him to leave."

"No."

"Sophia!" She can't hold me hostage in my own apartment.

"Rip it off like a Band-Aid. The sooner you get this over with, the sooner you can get on with your life."

"I am getting on with my life."

"You're hiding."

So? So! I'm entitled to show a little fear and act like a coward every now and again—I'm human, dammit, and I get scared like everyone else.

But.

She *is* right.

I care about Brooks, and there will come a point where I will have to face the music.

Sophia walks over and puts her hands on my shoulders. "If you want me to stay, I will."

My head shakes. "It'll be fine. And…we can't leave him out in the hallway forever."

"Are you for real?" Sophia smirks. "I think he'd wait out there all night if we let him."

Part of me wants to. It would serve him right for acting like such a…dumbass. The other part? Misses him like crazy though it's only been a few short days since I've seen him.

"Let me go grab my shit and I'll go." She kisses me on the cheek. "If you don't text or call and tell me how it goes, you're a dead man."

Yeah, yeah, yeah—she's threatened me a million times before.

"Okay, I will."

I fluff my hair in the small gilded mirror on my living room wall, pinching my cheeks and pushing on my eyelashes with my forefinger to fluff those, too. Nothing can be done about my outfit; Sophia is already seeing herself out and letting Brooks in, the gentle footpads of his gait sending a thrill of anticipation down my spine.

I have no idea what he's going to say, but I'm tired of not knowing what he's been doing.

He looks…

Tired.

He looks like…

How I feel.

Worn out.

"Hey." He greets me, hands stuffed into the pockets of a pair of dress slacks. "Thanks for not having your friend tell me to piss off."

I tuck a stray strand of hair behind my ear and blush. "I couldn't avoid you forever."

Brooks forces a smile, and my eyes travel the length of him. The poor thing looks exhausted.

"Long day at work?"

He shrugs. "Yeah, I was working late."

"Oh." Lord, this is worse than I thought, my extensive vocabulary suddenly fleeing and leaving me with nothing. "Everything is good, I hope?"

"It's good. Work is work." He's staring at me with such intensity I can't look him in the eye anymore, glancing at the carpet then the windows, finally at Desdemona.

My nose twitches. "It smells like you *might* have been at the bar."

Chagrined, he runs a hand through his hair.

Hair that needs trimming.

A face that needs a shave.

"I was at The Basement, with the guys, um, talking about…you."

"Me?" This surprises me; I hadn't considered he tells his friends about me the way I've told Sophia about him, and I want to pry for details—as I would have done days ago, before things got weird between us.

"Yes, you."

"You were talking to your friends about me?"

"Yeah, I was. And I'm not drunk, if you're wondering."

I can tell he hasn't had much to drink; his eyes aren't red and he isn't acting goofy—two telltale signs he exhibits when he's imbibed far too much liquor.

I don't know what to do with myself, standing in the middle of the living room, so I sit back down on the couch, knees pressed together primly, back ramrod straight. Hands folded across my lap.

"You were at The Basement with your friends and you didn't wear that ridiculous jacket of yours?" He always has that jacket on when he's meeting with those guys, drinking and doing whatever it is they do in secret.

Secrets he won't share.

"I gave the jacket back."

My mouth gapes; I'm not sure what to say. He loves that jacket—why would he give it back? Is he going to tell me or do I have to ask?

"I, um…" He takes another step into the living room, large form dominating the feminine space, his hands still firmly jammed into his pants pockets. "I had to."

Don't ask, don't ask, don't ask…

"Why?"

Brooks' smile is one of relief and his shoulders sag, hands reappearing; I remember those big hands cupping my derriere and stroking my hair, and now? They're massaging the pressure points of his temple, frustration palpable.

I put him out of his misery. "What is it you want to say?"

Say you're sorry and you miss me and you made a mistake. Please, Brooks. Please tell me you miss me.

"I love you, Abbott."

I love you, Abbott, I love you, Abbott, I love you, Abbott.

Holy Hannah, it's a good thing I'm sitting down, because I would have tipped over if I heard those words standing up.

"I don't understand." Sure, there are a million better ways I could have responded—oh, say, for example *I love you, too!* or *I care about you, Brooks.*

But I chose to go with, "I don't understand," so we're both staring at one another confused. What is he supposed to say to that? Gee, thanks?

He takes a step closer, then another, until he's standing in front of me. Goes down on his knees so he's not towering above me and takes my hands in his big, warm ones. Grasps them and squeezes.

"I'm sorry. I'm sorry and I love you and I shouldn't have said what I fucking said, but I can't take any of the words back. All I can do is tell you how I feel and hope we can go back to being friends even though I fucked everything up."

"No," I say slowly, my head giving the barest hint of a shake.

Brooks backs up a few inches, as if I've tried to burn him. "You said we were friends. Friends don't just give up on each other."

"You gave up on me."

"No I didn't—I was confused, and scared, and I had a few things to decide before I could tell you how I feel."

"Ah, the rules."

"Yes, exactly. The rules."

I'm silent while I think. "So where is the smoking jacket?"

"It's in a better place."

"What, did you burn it?"

"No—I gave it to Blaine and Phillip because I lost the bet we had."

"The bet?" I knew there was something more to his disappearing than he was telling me, knew there were conditions he had to abide by and that by hanging out with me, he was breaking them. But I didn't care—I only wanted to spend time with him.

"I can't tell you the name of what's going on with my friends, but I can tell you I lost the game we were playing and it was worth it."

Game.

Shit, now I want to know more. These table scraps he's leaving me aren't feeding my insatiable curiosity.

"What does it have to do with the jacket, though?"

"I had to wear it when we had our meetings."

"Why?"

"Because...it was fun. No real reason. We actually only smoke in them on patios—they don't allow it at The Basement. Mostly we just put cigars in our mouths but didn't light them."

That seems about right. I don't know his buddies Blaine and

Phillip, but from what Bambi has told me, Brooks' friends are kind of immature.

"What's the bet you lost?"

"I…" He hesitates. "I'm not really supposed to tell you this either, so you have to promise not to say anything."

Bambi's face pops up in my mind, and I bite down on my bottom lip; whatever Brooks is about to tell me is his secret and his alone, not mine to tell someone else. Even Bambi. Even if she deserves to know what ridiculous nonsense she's up against if she wants to win her ex-boyfriend back (although if you want my opinion, she's better off without him).

"The bet was to be single, and *stay* single."

A boys' club. A bet. Smoking jackets. An old-school hangout. "Oh my God, you guys had a gentlemen's club and made a pact to stay single just like they do in historical romance novels."

"No—not like historical romance novels!" he argues.

"We just talked about this and you said the whole idea of it was ludicrous."

"Nooo, *you* said it was—I never said a word about it. You went on and on about men doing that being losers and I kept my mouth shut."

"Well duh, that's because the whole idea of guys doing it in this day and age just sounds stupid. No offense."

"None taken, because it is stupid, and I can't fucking believe I did it—and not only that, the whole thing was my dumb idea."

Lord almighty. Men, I swear. Some of them never learn.

"What did you lose?"

"Just season tickets to the Jags."

Yikesssss. That had to hurt.

"Oh Brooks, you didn't!" I had no idea he even had season tickets. The jackass never mentioned it when I told him about the suite we can use if we want to catch a game.

He inhales, taking a deep breath. "The point isn't that I lost.

The point is that I lost because I don't want to be single—I want to be with you."

"That's the most romantic thing anyone has ever said to me."

I hold my breath, waiting for him to repeat those three little words he said just moments ago.

"I love you."

I will never get tired of hearing them, and this time when he says it, I blush prettily and sigh, whispering, "I love you, too."

Still clutching my hands, Brooks leans forward, pressing his forehead against mine. "I missed you like crazy, Abbott."

Abbott, Abbott—never stop saying my name! "It's only been a few days, you goof."

But my voice is scratchy from emotion, and a tear slips out of the corner of my eye.

"It felt like months," he murmurs quietly. "God, I was going crazy without you."

I smile, though he can't see it with our heads pressed together. "Don't be so dramatic." Reach up and rake my fingers through his beautiful, dark hair. "I missed you, too. You know who missed you more?"

He shakes his head. "Do not say Desdemona."

"Okay, I won't."

EPILOGUE

DESDEMONA

My humans are at it again.

The pair of them are vulgar, screeching like owls from the bedroom—it's his bedroom now, too, I suppose, since he moved all his things into Girl's apartment before it started to snow and all the birds went away.

What's mine is mine.

What's hers is mine.

What's his is now mine, too.

Happy cat, happy life. It doesn't rhyme, but it's true nonetheless.

I'm curled up on one of Boy's soft shirts, the one that fell to the floor when Girl was putting clothes into the white box that pours water on everything and spins them around to clean them. The shirt smells like city and him, and I drag it from one room to the other, pulling it so it's on top of my little bed in the corner of the living room.

It's sunny today, and I wish they'd take me outside.

When Boy moved in, he bought me a leash—more like a harness, but who cares—and said if he couldn't have a damn dog, he'd at least try to walk the damn cat.

When dogs approach, Boy scoops me up and carries me, and I've never been happier in my life.

Girl is cheerier, too.

She hums when she's alone, and dances—and sings, although the notes are too off-key to be anything but a hideous warble.

The old lady with the silver hair still comes around when I'm alone and leaves things inside the apartment. Food. Flowers. Gifts.

Last week she came by and left a blanket. Then it was a new tag for me with my name and phone number on it. It's round like a quarter, and gold, and shines in the light like the sun.

I bat at it with my paw, bored.

Sigh from the center of my chest, which gets ignored, as usual.

Glare at the bedroom door that has been closed for hours; what are they doing in there? I tried scratching on it a while ago but was ignored. No one came for me then, either.

I know they're not dead because of the noises.

Those haven't stopped.

Won't stop until one of them gets hungry, and when they finally emerge, they'll be giggling and laughing and kissing like they always are, and I'll gag up a hairball in disgust.

Like I always do.

THE END

ABOUT THE AUTHOR

Sara Ney is the USA Today Bestselling Author of the How to Date a Douchebag series, and is best known for her sexy, laugh-out-loud New Adult romances. Among her favorite vices, she includes: iced latte's, historical architecture and well-placed sarcasm. She lives colorfully, collects vintage books, art, loves flea markets, and fancies herself British.

For more information about Sara Ney and her books, visit:
Facebook
Twitter
Website
Instagram
Books + Main
Subscribe to Sara's Newsletter
Facebook Reader Group: Ney's Little Liars

Made in the USA
Columbia, SC
30 January 2020